Praise

If the Moon Had Willow Trees | Detroit Eight Series | Book One

Hall excels at writing natural conversation and witty banter between and among friends and family.

—Five-Star Rating by *Story Circle Book Review*

. . . prescient of the current political situation . . . the bigotry, segregation and division that remains with us today. Maggie and Sam, (oh, so in love are they) set against the backdrop of Detroit's racial tension. . . . The dialogue rings true . . . gripping when Loretta takes up the cadence of Dr. King to calm the crowd after his assassination.

—Santa Fesina, Amazon

The Otherness Factor
IPPY Silver Medal for Non-Fiction

If answered, the writers' call to respect the otherness of those with different world views could go far to help resolve the murderous antagonism that seems to be ripping civilizations apart.

—Leo McLean, Award-Winning Journalist

LIVONIA

THE WHITEST CITY

A Novel

Book Two

8 DETROIT Series

KATHLEEN HALL

LIVONIA
The Whitest City

Published by Collaborative Options, LLC, Austin, Texas. Inquiries should be emailed to co.optionstx@gmail.com

ISBN: eBook: 978-0990390442
ISBN: Paperback: 978-0990390459

Cover Design: Kenneth C. Benson, Pegasus Type
Interior/Print Design: Kenneth C. Benson, Pegasus Type
Typography: Electra, designed by William Addison Dwiggins in 1935, and Futura, designed by Paul Renner in 1927. Either typeface might have been used in this book had it been published in the seventies.

DEDICATED TO URBAN, SUBURBAN AND COUNTRY DWELLERS
who stand up for human rights in our global community—the same people
who know otherness is truth, kindness is love.

Also by Kathleen Hall

NONFICTION

The Otherness Factor: Co-Creating and Sustaining Intentional Relationships

FICTION

If the Moon Had Willow Trees
Detroit Eight Series | Book One

The enemy is fear. We think it is hate; but, it is fear.

—Mahatma Gandhi

Author's Note

Like the truth and deceit of fiction finding its rhythm, my conscious choice of place, Livonia, is rooted in reality.

A thirty-six-square-mile suburb of Detroit—with over one-hundred-thousand people in 1970—Livonia held the distinction of being the whitest city in America. That same year, Detroit ranked fourth as the blackest city, behind Milwaukee, New York and Chicago. Before the next census, Detroit would hold the title as the blackest city.

Today, Detroiters and Livonians share geography, favorite restaurants, highways, employers, recreational venues and some of the biggest sport-fan bases in the country—while holding on to the converse distinctions of being one of the blackest (82%) and whitest (97%) cities in our nation.

A Petri dish for studying white flight or writing a novel. The cities are real, the characters are compilations, and the story . . . like many historical novels . . . is mostly fiction. Truth is so much stranger.

Contents

1

Revolutionary Acts

In times of universal deceit, telling the truth will be a revolutionary act.

—George Orwell

SEPTEMBER 1969—"Who are you? Seriously, who the fuck are you? I don't know you. The Sam I know wouldn't have screwed some skank in a conference room the night before he got married." Maggie felt ice-cold. Her green eyes steeled as her heart slammed shut. Yet, words and images spun out of control. She looked for an escape.

Sam reached for Maggie's hand. She jerked it away and kicked through one of the three stacked-book legs of their makeshift coffee table—sending the plywood top, pizza box and the other two book legs flying.

"Maggie, don't. Please. We gotta keep it together."

"What kind of sick game are we playing here? Tell me, Clyde, what's left to keep together? A house of cards? Another unsolved mystery to keep me in line? Screw you! You were my friend and you told Sam to keep this to himself. Some friend. I have no husband. I have no parents. I have no friends. I can't talk to Aunt Jo or my sister Issie. Who can I trust? Oh, god, I can't do this. I can't stay here." Head down, her mod-cut blue-black hair spilling over her face, Maggie crawled the few feet into the hallway. Sitting up on her knees, she jerked open the warped coat-closet door from the bottom and slid out a small suitcase. Clyde and Sam watched as Maggie stared at the small bag before flinging it down the hall. Then, slinking sideways on the uneven hardwood floor, Maggie wailed in a voice that echoed a primeval age—a cave dwellers' howl, bent and distorted.

Sam climbed over the books, plywood, and cardboard to stretch out next to her. "Maggie, Maggie, please. I never meant to hurt you. Oh, god, I'm so sorry. Part of me knew what I was doing, but the room was shifting, dreamlike, in slow motion. There was no start or finish." Maggie pushed away from Sam, stood up, and looked at Clyde as if confused to see him in the trashed living room.

Clyde, sitting on his knees, leaned forward. "Maggie, you have every right to be pissed off. I may be a total asshole, but I've always been your friend. Sam was set up. And you, you were so happy. Married, starting a new job, then shazam you were pregnant, excited about the future. I convinced myself, and Sam, you were better off not knowing." Clyde shook his head and and grimaced before he said, "What a schmuck! I must've thought this was some kind of big, strong black brother love to protect you. Ego bullshit. I was wrong. I should've loved you enough to know better. No excuse, but this so-called bachelor party was just the first piece of The Puzzle. Sam and I had no idea what we were dealing with."

Maggie glared at Sam, then turned to Clyde and said, "Talk."

"Add to this the gaslighting LSD trip during the auto show we think Tony Zito at Sheer Juice and Ben Kabul at Jingo Motors are tight. Both have Mafia ties. How tight? We don't know." Clyde paused and studied Maggie's face before he said, "As for your missing parents, or their *patrone* Jacques, we have no idea if there's a connection. Aunt Jo's suspicions about Jacques might mean he's hooked in, but right now, there's no one to ask. The only thing we're sure about is that a shitload of time, money and effort was spent to gaslight Sam. Other than that, we're dangling in the wind."

"Oh, god, I can't take this in. Not now." Reaching for her purse, she said, "Sam, give me the car keys. I'm picking up Tekla and . . ."

"Mag, do whatever you want. If you need to be alone, I'll go."

"He's right, Maggie. Not a good idea to wake up Maija and Tekla. It's late. You'll scare the crap outta them. Besides, you don't want to be grilled by your mother-in-law. Sam can ride home with me and bunk on a cot in our basement."

Maggie knew they were right, but she wanted to make the decisions, have control. For now, she needed time to think, to sort through, to cry unspent tears and escape to her inner world. Oh, god, Maija would interrogate her, insist on feeding her and tuck her in bed.

"Okay."

Clyde put out his arms and Maggie walked into his hug. Sam started toward Maggie, but she held up her hand. "Not now, Sam. Way the hell not now."

Before Maggie was fully awake, she ran her hands across the cool, empty sheet next to her and listened for the soft friction of Tekla's tiny feet pedaling the mattress, her morning coos. Instead, memory struck and replayed last night. She was alone with her dueling thoughts.

She couldn't shake the bees out of her head. Less than two months ago, everything seemed limitless. She and Sam were expecting their first baby. Sam, in a three-piece suit, was kicking ass as the Employment Manager at Jingo Motors. She was hot on the trail to find her missing parents; ready to get back to teaching and writing poetry after the baby was born; and, prepared to move from Detroit to Livonia—a white, protestant citadel—to jumpstart integration in the burbs.

That was before Sam told her about the scattered one-thousand-piece puzzle that threatened to cast their lives in someone else's freakish, psychedelic nightmare. Clyde, their best friend, had been Sam's only confidante. Now, she, Sam and Clyde were trying to be a team, The Triad. A bare-bones compass for negotiating the chaos—for solving the mystery of who, what, when, where and why Sam was being targeted, drugged and gaslighted.

Exhausted, Maggie stretched out on the bed, closed her eyes and let her mind drift to the strange series of events that brought them together.

This whole misadventure started in the summer of 1963 because Sam—an eighteen-year-old human rights activist, antiwar protester, platinum-haired, white guy from outer-suburbia—couldn't wait to swap John Phillip Sousa's jackboot marches for the ragtag dissonance of Detroit jazz and Motown sounds. No illusions. Sam knew tuition at Wayne State, a tenement flat, grunt work and a diet of Campbell's Pork and Beans was the price tag for a degree and student deferment from the draft—aka the Vietnam-Era American Dream.

After checking into the YMCA, Sam made his way to the makeshift office of the Detroit Freedom Riders. There, he ran into Clyde Webster—a native Detroiter, Vietnam vet, and black civil rights activist—who had just been promoted to his job as cook at Angelo's Restaurant & Pizzeria. Their wry, wicked humor clicked. When

Sam offered to give Clyde a lift to Angelo's, an unlikely, fierce brotherhood was formed.

Maggie smiled. In the summer of 1963, she was a desperately lonely, French-Canadian civil rights activist on a student visa at Wayne State. Thanks to Aunt Jo, Maggie was living on the American side of the Detroit River in the attic of her aunt's small bungalow and working on-call at Angelo's—helping Clyde in the kitchen and covering for waitresses, cashiers, dishwashers, delivery boys. Although she dated, most of the guys turned out to be just as desperate as she was. After a year of self-loathing, Clyde convinced her to join the Freedom Riders.

In spite of the near absence of degrees of separation, Maggie and Sam didn't meet until July 25, 1967—four years after they both showed up in Clyde's life and two days after the Detroit cops raided a blind pig on Twelfth Street and ignited the biggest race riot in American history. That same day, Maggie found herself on the other side of Sam's National Guard-issued revolver and lost herself in his blue eyes. She was sure it was karma.

And it was! thought Maggie. Karma showed up during the Detroit Freedom Riders' first meeting after the riots when she ran into Sam and he offered her a ride home and a kiss goodnight. Clyde mocked the whole idea of karma, but a week later he formed The Detroit Eight to move forward with MLK's plan for mixed-race groups to improve dialogue and pave the way for real integration. Clyde asked her and Sam to serve as the 'highly-esteemed token whites.' By then, karma was doing a full-throttle hully gully.

No small task. Stoked by fear, tens of thousands of whites got-outta-Dodge before the riot's last ember died. Fed by a system of Ike's commute-shortening highways, the white flight tidal wave found shores in bright new subs with modern schools, state-of-the-art manufacturing plants and the advent of indoor-shopping-centers called malls. Everyone knew Detroit's once-thriving, dignified Model City was losing its chassis. The Eights set their sights on saving the city and pushing civil rights through the invisible barbed wire surrounding these white citadels. As Willie Johnson, head Zamboni driver for the Detroit Red Wings, and one of The Eights, liked to say, "We're movin' behind enemy lines!"

Maggie sat up and moved her legs over the side of the bed and thought, *you'd think the rest would've been history for Sam and me—degrees from graduate programs, jobs, marriage, baby and a new house. But, none of us bargained for the draconian burlesque that Clyde and Sam uncovered.* Swirling chaos threatened to implode reality—spin truth into fiction and fiction into truth; flip friends and enemies; shadowbox shadows. *No more time for tilting at windmills, resting on laurels, or other hackneyed diversions. Time to get up!*

Sun was pouring through the venetian blinds; it was almost ten in the empty house. After making a cup of instant coffee, Maggie sat at the kitchen table and wondered why she tripped out last night. The first time she heard about Sam with another woman was just a few weeks ago, after her six-week, post-partum checkup. Maggie remembered having some weird sense of pride in her intellectual, almost clinical, response to Sam's story of being drugged, gaslighted and seduced by another woman at the auto show. At the time, the story seemed surreal, like someone's imagination on high octane. Maggie listened as Sam and Clyde described the scenes and possible motivations as if they were considering a screenplay. The distance felt familiar. After her parents disappeared, Maggie perfected this method of cocooning herself from disappointment, rejection and pain. Adept at pretending her stories were about someone else, adept at shutting out the world. Maggie knew she gave Sam and Clyde a false sense of security before her meltdown last night teed them up for the coming storm.

Still pissed off by Sam's betrayal—*more like treason*—Maggie found some comfort in Clyde's name for these cryptic forces and probable targets. The Puzzle. What at first seemed mind-blowing and unwieldy, was dumbed-down by this simple moniker. Because they didn't know who to trust or who not to trust, Maggie suggested they resort to a cold-war-charm strategy when talking to friends, family, employers and others. For now, The Triad was their only arsenal. Since no one was going to swoop in and save the day, Maggie decided to skip the poor-pitiful-me routine and pick up a few Puzzle pieces.

When Maggie heard three short rings for their party line, she grabbed the phone before it woke Tekla and whispered, "Hello?"

"Hello? Mrs. Tervo? Dr. Levy returning your call. My nurse said you're worried about Tekla."

"Yes, thanks for calling. When I was in last week, we put Tekla on formula because my milk stopped coming in. Now she sleeps all the time. She eats, gets burped, gets changed, then conks out. Sound asleep! I'm not sure what's wrong. I remember reading something about sleeping sickness."

Maggie heard a yelp before Dr. Levy burst out laughing—an astounding roar with hiccups and chokes to rival the best comedy soundtracks. After catching his breath Dr. Levy said, "Oh my, Mrs. Tervo, I'm sorry. In my twenty-five years in pediatrics, I've listened to thousands of new mothers complain their baby wasn't sleeping. But never, not once, has a mother called to complain her new baby was sleeping *too* much. Trust me, Tekla does not have sleeping sickness. In my world, you won the sweepstakes. Count your blessings and read a few books while you've got the time."

Maggie thought she had too much time. Her sexual fantasies used to be seduction scenes to surprise Sam when he got home from work or National Guard assignments. Now, pornographic scenes of Sam with strange women—or an image of Sam and other men taking turns with a model, secretary, waitress or hooker ransacked Maggie's imagination.

For Maggie, the most difficult thought terrain was putting her search for her parents on hold. Nineteen years ago, before Maggie turned five, her parents vanished on a sailing trip on the St. Lawrence Seaway. Soon after, British and Canadian intelligence forces raided their Toronto home and the pole barn that supported publication of her parent's independent radical newspaper *L'Empereur Est Nu*—translated, The Emperor is Nude. The headlines in the Toronto Tribune read: "Revolutionary Secessionists Subject of Manhunt," which was followed by claims Raymond and Anna Soulier were involved in "acts of international espionage and contraband." Issie insisted it was time Maggie woke up. If the MI5, Royal Canadian Mounties and CIA couldn't find their parents in almost twenty years, what made her think she could?

Maggie wasn't about to write off her plan to find her parents as a child's yearning. Instead, she re-pinned her hope to resurrect her family on Jacques Ruivivar, her parent's mysterious colleague and benefactor. Cooling her relationship with Jacques might risk her only surviving hope to find Raymond and Anna. Not papa and mama, Maggie and Issie always called their parents by their first names—an egalitarian family legacy she and Sam would pass on to Tekla. Issie thought their parents' disdain for British royalty trickled down to all titles, including papa and mama. Maggie wanted to believe it was more about their commitment to equality between all human beings, young or old, noble or peasant. After her parents went missing, a Quebec newspaper republished Issie's favorite quote by Raymond:

> The preposterousness of a king and queen holding status in the twentieth century is tantamount to turning our fortunes over to modern day pirates on the high seas and thanking the bloody bastards for preserving history.

Maggie was sure of one thing. Both she and Issie had inherited the Soulier sass.

Making it more difficult for Maggie to get family off her mind was Sam's take that Jacques' executive assistant, Catherine, had an uncanny likeness to old photos of Anna. Add to this, Issie confided she once thought Jacques was Maggie's real father because he gave her so much more attention and affection. Maggie almost discounted Issie's confession because her sister was only eleven when she concocted this romantic notion. And, everyone knows eleven is the perfect age to feel less than everyone. Yet, Maggie couldn't deny the psychic pull she felt when she and Sam met Jacques in Toronto last year; or heard his voice on the phone when he called to tell her about money set aside for her and Issie; or the last time she talked to him when Tekla was just weeks old.

> "*Bonjour ma douce*, Marguerite! Please don't keep me waiting."
>
> "*Bonjour*, Jacques! We have a beautiful baby girl, Tekla, Tekla Moonwalker Tervo. Six pounds, fifteen ounces and eighteen inches of sass!"
>
> "Let me guess. She was born the day Neil Armstrong walked on the moon?"
>
> "More precisely, she was born *as* Neil Armstrong made his first step on the moon. We had a TV in the delivery room and her entrance was perfectly timed!"
>
> "What's the English word? Hmm. Not serendipitous, in that realm."
>
> "Auspicious?"
>
> "Yes. That's it. Auspicious! Tekla will be an edge walker, someone who pushes the boundaries and helps us explore the unknown."
>
> Maggie laughed, "I'm holding this two-week-old explorer and she's incredible. Long black hair that the nurses say she'll lose. We watch her sleep and race to meet her every grunt, groan, sigh or imagined need. She already knows how to wield power. Totally insane!"

"So, my dear Marguerite, I can't wait to meet her and see you and Sam. I'm ready to set up a business meeting in Detroit in late September, early October. What works best for you?"

Maggie realized her legs were bouncing up and down like Issie's do when she's anxious. *Breathe*, she commanded herself. "Oh, Jacques. I don't know. It would be nice. It's just that . . . I don't mean to be rude, but right now we have to pass. You know how it is. Well, maybe not. It's just that we've got so much going on—possible move, job search to find something to keep my brain in the game, Sam's wicked schedule. Any chance we could postpone this for a while?"

Silence. Nothing. Maggie thought her heart was going to slip through her windpipe. "Jacques? You there?"

"Maggie, the last thing I want is to make you uneasy. Is there something else you want to say?"

Maggie took a deep breath, looked at Tekla and said, "No, nothing else. Just, um, uneasy about being a mother. Not about you. I guess I want to, what? Maybe take time to learn how to parent. Sam would say I'm selfishly hoarding my time and ignoring my friends, even him. He thinks Tekla put some kind of spell on me. He might be right!"

"Listen, Maggie, I get the sense there's something more, something you aren't comfortable telling me right now. But, like to hear you're keeping your own counsel, even if it means I'm delayed in meeting this bright new being. Do you have a camera?"

"An old Brownie. We're thinking of getting a Polaroid, but Issie says the film's expensive and the photos aren't very good."

"Issie's right. Let me see what I can dig up. I'm sure I've got a halfway decent camera collecting dust. I went through a photography phase that ended when I discovered I don't have the time or patience for a hobby."

"That would be great! We could send photos."

"Maggie, hear me say this. Photos would be lovely . . . however . . . the last thing I want is you worrying about me. I'm an old coot and know all too well that life takes us in different directions. I won't give up on you. I promise. And, I'll look forward to seeing you when you're ready for company. In the meantime, I want you to know, without exception, I'm here for you and Sam if you need me. For any reason."

Maggie couldn't hold back her tears—old tears, ancestral tears. She couldn't tell if Jacques' phone clicked before or after she whispered, "I'm so sorry."

2

White Flight

Fueling racial hysteria, wild rumors continue to spark fear in both black and white communities. In the suburbs, whites are organizing and joining gun clubs to protect their homes and families from attacks by black militants. In the city, blacks claim the police are planning to provoke an incident as an excuse to attack them. On both sides of the city limits, ordinary black and white families are preparing for rumored invasions—stocking up on food, medical supplies and ammunition.

—Detroit Weekly

OCTOBER 1969—"Hey, Maggie, what's shakin'?"

"Loretta Hood? Where in hell's half acre have you been? Tekla was asking about you this morning!"

"Sitting here in SistaHood ready to unplug the hair dryers and close shop. Stella just left her office and is headin' this way. Okay if we come by and get some baby hugs? We'll pick up a pizza and a six-pack of Stroh's. Beer's good for breast milk."

"Ah, no more breastfeeding. But, great timing! Sam's working late and I'm going stir crazy. Wait a minute. Are you on a mission for The Eights?"

"Relax. Pizza, beer and baby hugs will make this painless. We've got to talk. It's time."

After Maggie hung up, she looked around. The house cried baby—diapers, undershirts, rubber pants, sterilizer, formula, bottles, nipples, rattles and pacifiers took up every square inch of counter space. On the table, an old copy of *Life Magazine* held a wet diaper. Maggie caught a Walter Mitty wave and imagined a *Life* photographer showing up to take a snapshot of the modern-day housewife. He'd find Maggie dressed in a formula-stained, threadbare green and orange flowered moo-moo that served her sister through two pregnancies and her through one—not-so-stylishly topped by Sam's frayed and faded gray Wayne State sweatshirt. The photograph would catch her surveying the obstacle course of a second-hand baby swing, unfolded laundry and a giant panda. The article would be called "On the Brink of Bedlam."

Maggie laughed and stretched her arms over her head. *Oy vey! Time to feel human again.* Maggie decided to jump in the shower, squeeze into her still-too-tight cords, and buzz the kitchen before Tekla woke from her nap. Other mothers did it. Somehow, she'd find a way to budget life in four-hour increments and lose a few pounds.

Angelo's pizza was like manna. Maggie thought she might sell her soul for pizza, but she was not ready to move to Livonia.

"What the hell, Maggie? Really? You've got the chance to move to the burbs and see what the other side is all about. It's not like you have to hang there forever. Sam said you guys could afford a second set of wheels. I don't get it," said Stella.

"I'll move, just not now."

"Why not now? What's the holdup?" asked Loretta.

"Sanity, well-being, happiness."

Loretta threw her arms out and looked around before she said, "Girl, have you lost your mind? This train-wreck of a house is ready to collapse when the next eighteen-wheeler trundles down Grand River. I don't get the sanity, well-being or happiness angle."

"SistaHood, this *is* home. We rent it, but it's *our* home. All my friends are here. I know my neighbors; Buddy at the lunch counter at Cunningham's is like family." Maggie looked at Loretta then Stella. They weren't buying it. Maggie shook her hands like silent castanets to break the spell. With a raised and deliberate stage voice she said, "Okay, I get it. The house is decaying and the hood's about to explode in gang warfare, but this is where I feel safe. The burbs are like the other side of the friggin' moon. Another planet. They might as well speak a foreign language. I don't understand people who want to live in a place where everyone looks alike, talks alike, dresses alike, acts alike. It's death-by-sameness. Did I miss anything? What's so funny?"

Both Stella and Loretta were slapping their knees and cracking up. Loretta said, "Oh my god, Maggie. You're one crazy, mixed-up white chick. Every black sister I know is looking through that invisible barb-wired fence at the city limits and thinking they *want* to be Donna Reed. But you, you've got your nose turned up like this sorry ass little house is in high cotton. You are out of your mind!"

"Maybe. I don't know why you want to hog-tie me and throw me in the back of a moving van. If I had the will or energy to move to Livonia, I would. I just don't. I'll spend time there to pick up the vibes. Shop at their crafty little malls; go to their barebones, make-believe library; play putt-putt; study dress styles, idioms and knock-knock jokes. How about that? When Tekla's ready for school, we'll move; when I have more time. As it is, I'm lucky to take a bath or wash a load of clothes. I confess to being a mess, but I can't move. Not now."

Loretta looked at Stella and nodded her head. Stella said, "Maggie, we're here for you. No one's going to put pressure on you to move until you're ready. We'll plan our *coup d'état* after I rock Tekla to sleep. That should give you enough time to reset the clock."

Stella's decree sent Loretta into her noiseless, bending at the waist laughter, and bombshell tears to Maggie's eyes. "Holy crap, Loretta, it's not that funny."

"Hey, baby doll, what's going on? No one's gonna force you to move. You know that. The last thing we want is to make you sad. Stella was just jivin' you."

No way was Maggie going to bring up Jingo's offer to sell them a house on Six Mile Road in Livonia. This was the major reason she was dragging her feet. A few days before Tekla was born, Ben Kabul, President of Jingo, tried to convince Sam that he and Maggie should buy this company-owned house from Jingo and cover the mortgage through payroll deductions. Sam had no idea how Jingo knew about their plan to move to Livonia, or how Jingo was involved in The Puzzle. Once again, Maggie shook her head at the absurdity of using this simple label to describe the dread, demons and degradation of unseen, unknown, unimaginable forces aimed at Sam. Maggie played with the alliteration for a few minutes before she shook her head. *For crap sakes, this isn't material for a new poem.* Bottom line, she, Sam and Clyde needed time to decide if Jingo's house was a lair to avoid or a key to use to their advantage. Maggie thought time was on their side. *Teaching could wait. Civil rights could wait. The house in Livonia could wait. Or could it? Who warned us to keep enemies close? Machiavelli?*

Maggie heard Sam come in the side door. By now, Maggie knew his routine. Careful not to wake Tekla, he left his penny loafers in the kitchen, padded across the cracked kitchen linoleum, creaked across the hardwood floors in the living room and hall. From their bed, Maggie could see Sam's shadow cast across the short hallway. She watched as he and his shadow leaned into Tekla's door to listen to her breathe then disappeared into her room. Maggie pictured Sam's head resting on the crib rail, watching her sleep.

Almost three months had passed since they'd made love. Her Ob/Gyn had given her an all-clear after her six-week check-up, but Maggie's libido took a dive when Sam told her about his encounters with the dark side. According to Sam, the first time was the night before their wedding, almost two years ago. Sam said he was seduced at work by Carla, an administrative assistant. In his telling, Carla locked the conference room door and stripped off his pants before baring her gigantic knockers and pulling him down to the floor. After that, he lost all memory. Then, a year ago at the auto show, Sam described a sex scene in the hotel ballroom. A bunch of men in suits surrounded a half-naked, red-haired Cuban model, who was stretched across three bar stools. Sam said he didn't know if it was real or drug-induced, but remembered feeling agitated, excited and caught up in the action. Images Maggie clung to; edited and re-edited. Like the truth and deceit of fiction finding its rhythm.

Today, after talking trash with Loretta and Stella, she felt invigorated—strong, healthy, human and sexy. Clean hair, shaved legs, a red satin slip, Maggie nixed wearing her long string of Gatsby-era pearls that drove Sam over the moon. Maggie was no saint when it came to raw sex, but tonight she wanted something different, something she'd never experienced. Tonight Maggie found herself both thrilled and confused by a sense of wellbeing, a new kind of ecstasy. For reasons she couldn't fathom, the quiet tableau of infant, man, and woman excited her beyond any foreplay she'd ever known. Maggie waited for the shadow to move. In truth, she could barely contain the erotic anticipation of hearing Sam walk the few steps down the hall and fill the door. Lying still, Maggie watched as Sam undressed and slid into bed as if he were moving in slow motion. By the time he placed his hand on her hips, Maggie was somewhere else—as if she'd tripped out. A place where she watched herself arch her back, shudder and cry, "holy mother of god." Sam sat up and looked at Maggie as if she'd caught him in bed with another woman. Maggie smiled and whispered, "Do you by any chance live here?"

Sam started with her lips then lifted Maggie's red satin slip. Through shared murmurs, quiet laughter, sotto voce, Sam whispered, "There's nowhere else I'd rather be." Then, with deliberate slowness, they entered the timeless dance of bamboo flutes, mandolins and tambourines.

Maggie was standing in front of the kitchen counter filling sterilized bottles with Similac and boiling water. Tekla, on top of the small kitchen table in her infant seat, was exploring her hands in the sunlight. Mornings always aroused Maggie's reflection or contentment. Today, they were second-guessing each other. The moment Maggie drifted in the afterglow of Sam's lovemaking, pornographic images of Sam with slim, naked, buxom women popped into her head—*god forbid, am I trying to compete with high-priced call girls?*

Sam walked in, nuzzled Maggie's neck and said, "I've got to confess. I slept with a ravenous, otherworldly woman last night. What a wild ride!"

Maggie gave him the look, which Sam knew meant 'quit acting like a jerk,' 'back off,' or both. Usually both.

"Come on, Mag. Confess. Who were you fantasizing about before I walked in last night? A Red Wing? Delvecchio?"

No response, which Sam knew might mean anything or nothing.

"Hey, Moonwalker, whose hands? Mag, let's catch this? You figured out how to use Jacques' Leica?"

Without turning her head, Maggie said, "Samuelsan, between changing diapers, making formula, washing clothes, cooking dinner and walking Tekla, there's no way in hell I'm going to figure it out. You need a mechanical engineering degree to understand the instructions. Let's get an Instamatic or new Brownie before we miss her first ballet recital.

"Ballet? Huh, okay then." Sam poured his coffee before deciding to pull out all stops, "How about I pick up a bag of White Castle sliders for dinner tonight? Or, better yet, how about Greene's? A hamburger joint near work, five for a dollar!"

Maggie wiped her hands on a wet dishtowel, turned around, walked up to Sam, held his face in her hands and looked him in the eyes. Eyes she once described in a poem as *the color of an ocean filled with phosphorescent light*. "Sorry, babe. Last night was over the moon. I don't know who that man was, but hope I get to know him better." Then, Maggie kissed him. A French-Canadian French-Kiss. Maggie once told him it was more about tongue placement than tongue movement, a kind of reflexology between the mouth and body. Sam never quite got the placement thing, yet Maggie knew how to touch the inside of his mouth with her tongue and arouse every one of his erogenous zones. Splurging after three months of imposed celibacy was worth the risk. Work could wait.

3

First Impressions

Following new rumors of attacks by black militants, white suburban housewives are televised taking target practice with their new guns.
—Detroit Weekly

JUNE 1970—Surrounded by towering willow trees, the white cape cod sat like a dollhouse on a one-acre tract—green roof, green shutters, and green window boxes filled with freshly potted red geraniums. The neat, clean lines of the house reflected the moving shade from three enormous willows, while orange daylilies rescued the galvanized steel mailbox from the scorched blacktop road and hardscrabble driveway.

Next door, a mammoth two-story, brown-asphalt-shingled triplex rested on two one-acre lots with man-made hills, mature lilac bushes and gigantic oaks. A horseshoe drive, filled with pebble gravel, sat on the other side of the house and enclosed a park-like stretch of dark green lawn. There, two oaks held a rope hammock and a twenty-foot pole displayed a full-size American flag. Maggie had a flash of Tekla somersaulting or sledding down the sloped front yard, before she found herself, once again, both drawn to the mystery and repelled by the darkness of this foreboding house. Maggie rubbed the goosebumps forming on her arms and tried to shake off the feeling there was something menacing about the two-story shadow it cast on their new home.

By late afternoon, they backed the Corvair in front of the unattached garage to unload the last few boxes and unhitch the U-Haul trailer until it was time to lug the emptied boxes and junk from the garage to the landfill. After passing the Detroit City Limit sign at Six Mile and Five Points for the third time that day, they still hadn't seen a single person on the ground. No walkers, no bikers, no mowers, no porch sitters.

The stacks of musty, misshapen cardboard boxes in the apartment-sized kitchen and dining room looked doomed. "Sam, there's no way we're going to fit all this stuff in a few cupboards. We're going Zen."

"I can do Zen."

"Remind me again why we flung ourselves on a Norman Rockwell cover of the *Saturday Evening Post*. Right now, I'm so pissed off at myself and you and this prissy, green-shuttered house. We left our friends, everything we said was important to us."

"Mag, come on. We knew moving across the border into suburbia wouldn't be easy."

"I don't expect it to be easy. But, I had no idea it would be so deadly quiet. Not a leaf moving, not a person in sight. As much as I love solitude, I could lose my mind in this nothing burger."

Moving sideways through the maze of boxes, Sam reached Maggie in front of the sink and turned her around. "You will not lose that beautiful mind of yours."

"Don't count on it."

"Oh, I'm betting money on it."

"Sam, I don't want to give up our dreams for the sake of security. That's all. Wanting Tekla to live in a safe neighborhood sounds good, but what's safe? How do we know what we just walked into?"

"Security? Tell me you're kidding. Security is the last thing on my mind. Every day I walk through land mines. There's no safe place. Nothing's changed. We're just hanging fire in a new hood. But, if we're not worried someone will break into our house, or burn it down, we might spend less time looking over our shoulder and more time solving The Puzzle."

Maggie picked up a damp black and white checked dishtowel, folded it lengthwise into thirds then snaked it through the handle of the bread drawer. "Do you ever wish we had a mundane, white-picket-fence-kinda-life, where the biggest decision we make is dinnertime? An existence so dull we watch *Ozzie & Harriet* reruns for excitement? Days strung together when we aren't trying to solve The Puzzle or fight the establishment?

"I've gone down that rabbit hole once or twice. Not now. Kent State totally eviscerated any innocence I had. If the National Guard's willing to shoot down anti-war protesters, what's next?" Maggie looked down at her cutoff jeans and Birkenstock sandals. "And, whatever happens, DO NOT let me go suburban. If you ever see me in a blue and white checkered dress, with a crinoline and white flats, call The Eights for an emergency intervention!"

Sam reached for a hug and said, "My poor, eviscerated, city slicker, do you have any idea how much I love you?"

Maggie stood on her toes, nuzzled Sam's neck and took in his scent before she whispered, "Most of the time. When I get scared, I feel like we're trapped in someone else's LSD trip. But I can do this. We can do this."

After two weeks of cleaning, painting and decorating, the kitchen floor held the last few boxes. Tekla was spending the day with Maija so Maggie and Sam could finish unpacking, find some second-hand appliances, buy their first electric lawn mower and check out Jingo's Management Class Auto Discounts.

Sam leaned into the kitchen from the utility room to announce, "Drum roll, please! Last box in the garage inspected. How's it going in this wing of the house?"

"Very funny! With an acre of land, you'd think there'd be more living space."

"Well, between the over-sized utility room and the unattached, now very empty garage, there's some space we could connect for a breezeway."

"Sam, get a grip. There are only three feet between the two. If you unpack these last few boxes, I'll slap together bologna sandwiches chased with ice-cold Vernors ginger ale."

"Ah, life is good! We can eat on the back porch and survey our vast real estate holdings."

Compared to yesterday, the air was cool. The screened porch looked out on two willows separating the yard from a field of weeds. From their perch on new green-nylon-mesh aluminum folding chairs, with yellow Melmac plates balanced on their laps, the east offered unwieldy lilac bushes between their house and the large brown triplex. To the west, a cyclone fence drew a straight line to protect the neighbor's backyard and an old garage-sized shed from easy access.

"Do you think he's a photographer?" mused Sam.

"Who?"

"The guy next door."

"What makes you think he's a photographer?"

"Well, the windows on his shed are all blacked out."

"Hmm. Maybe. The realtor said they're Canadians; a couple with three older kids, one boy and two girls. She thought the girls might be old enough to babysit."

"Mag, I'm pretty sure I'm getting the offer tomorrow and not sure I want to accept."

"What? You're kidding."

"No, I'm not kidding. I'm barely qualified for the job I have. It makes no sense for Jingo to put me in the top personnel position. For god's sakes, this is an executive level job."

"Mr. Tervo, we all second-guess our ability. If not you then whom? You're smart, honest, attentive, resourceful."

"Mrs. Tervo, with all due respect, you're not the most objective person when it comes to me. What I'm saying is *I* would not hire *me* for this position. I don't begin to meet the qualifications."

"Then, let me be bold enough to remind you that these qualifications are at best some well-intentioned bureaucrat's calculation that more years of service equals competency. Such bullshit. You, my love, have qualities far beyond those dry, pedantic, measured words. Jingo Motors knows this. You will make a difference and you don't have a choice here."

Sam shook his head and suppressed a smile, "So, I take the job like a man who knows his worth, even if it has strings, tendrils, not to mention sharp hooks?"

Laughing, Maggie said, "Even if it's loaded with dynamite sticks. My new motto is keep our enemies close and make a lot of money for a quick getaway."

"Oh, Mag, I was afraid it would come to this. First, it's a picket-fence-kinda-life and an executive husband. Next, you'll be clamoring for an aluminum Christmas tree lit through revolutions of green and red cellophane."

"Well, looky here. How'd you guys make it over the barbed wire from Li-Vo-Nia?" jibed Willie. "I didn't know they were letting refugees back in."

"Willie Johnson, you shut your mouth. You don't know what you're talking about," said Robin.

"Robin, I don't know how you live with this sorry-ass husband of yours," laughed Sam as he air-boxed Willie.

"Sorry ass? You stupid limp-dick-honky, what gives you the right to talk like that to my wife?"

The room went silent. Willie slammed his fist on the table and said, "What a dumb-ass bunch of do-gooders. No shit, you think we're going to change the world by deputizing these two crackers as our narcs? These pale faces wouldn't know racism if it cold-cocked 'em. If you want whitey to fight our battles, I'm outta here."

Before Robin could get out of her chair, Clyde was at Willie's side, "Hey, man, I hear you. Sometimes it feels like the whole world is out to crush us. I know you're hurting. Let's take a walk, get some air."

Willie looked at Clyde then scanned the room. It was one of those moments when you knew it was a moment. Everyone seemed frozen in place. Loretta and Stella leaning into one another. Sam standing behind Willie, his neck stretched toward the front door. Blanche caught between the kitchen and dining room with a plate of pigs-in-a-blanket. Maggie at the table, poised forward, ready to push back her chair. And Robin, stopped in a mid-air-rise from her seat, mouth open and eyes wide.

The clatter of Robin's chair crashing to the floor was lost in her outburst, "Mr. Johnson, I'm going to say this once and only once. If you don't get your sorry act together, you're not going to have any friends, white, black, brown, yellow or red. You think you can do a better job running this screwed-up world? Well, you're on your own, cause no one, not me, not anyone else, is going to put up with your bullshit. I know you're hurting. We're all hurting. Those three white killer cops walked away from the Algiers Motel with blood all over their hands and no one, not one judge or jury, is going to make them pay. Moving that civil rights trial to Flint is window dressing. You ever heard of a venue where poor black boys got a fair trial? If you're so smart, tell me that. And, just who would you send to narc the burbs? You think you can find a black *Father Knows Best* family to move to Livonia and figure this out? Screw you, Willie." Robin put her hands on her hips and leaned forward at her waist, as if she'd just run the hundred-yard dash, then stood and gave Willie a long look. No one moved. Her voice softer, Robin said, "You want to feel better, go find a way to keep black boys out of whorehouses and jails. Become a cop and fight the 'brotherhood' from the inside. Or, maybe you're so brave you can do this like some black superman with no cape, no friends? Please tell us your plan. But when you attack Sam, or anyone else, because of skin color, you're no better than any other racist. You might as well put on a white robe and pointed hat. You hear me? If you're going to get racist on me, you're in the wrong damn marriage and the wrong damn place."

Head down, speaking in a half whisper Willie said, "Damn you to hell woman. Why are you always right? I swear I can't act like an asshole for five minutes without you jumping all over my sorry self." Taking a long slug of Stroh's Bohemian, he looked around the room. "Mrs. Johnson's right. I'm an asshole. And, I'm probably a racist because I hate like hell to depend on whitey for anything. I've seen too much shit go down and I've seen too many friends lose their power to white bosses, white cops, white neighbors who threaten cops. I'm one of those beaten men and I took it out on Sam. Sam, my man, where are you?"

Sam moved closer to the table so Willie could see him. "Sam, you're a damn fine honky. But, you're a billboard for everything I've always hated about myself—my life, being black and shucking around like some Uncle Tom, hoping I don't scare the heebie-jeebies outta a white boy in a blue uniform." Willie rolled the

Stroh's bottle between his two gnarled hands and pulled a slug of beer before he looked at Sam and said, "You see, your whiteness is a reminder of my blackness. You could be any white dude. My feelings are old as dirt. Robin's right. I'm racist because I think I have a right to be. That's totally messed up, but it's the truth."

Clyde shook his head and took a deep breath before he said, "We're screwed if we don't get this right. After Kent State, any question Nixon is ramping up his Gestapo police action? All the ranting about the militant left is feeding the flames and firing up the sheetless Klan. And here we sit, sucker punching each other, while Jim Crow makes a killing selling crosses as lawn art."

Loretta leaned across the chipped blonde-veneer tabletop and studied the faces of this motley group of civil rights activists. Her friends, confidants, bit players in an extraordinary battle. In a stage whisper, she said, "Listen up and listen up good. Clyde's right. MLK? Assassinated. RFK? Assassinated. JFK? Assassinated. Who else? Come on, who else? Medgar Evers, Malcolm X, Jimmie Lee Jackson, Andrew Goodman, Michael Schwerner. Three black boys at the Algiers' Motel. Does anyone even know their names? Aubrey Pollard nineteen. Carl Cooper seventeen. Fred Temple eighteen. All boys. All slaughtered. No different than Emmett Till's savage murder. Whites don't need a cause or a hunting license to kill our black boys. The least we can do is remember their names." Loretta looked around the room, stopped at Willie and pointed her finger, "And, what about J. Edgar and Nixon? What's their plan? A no-brainer. Stir the pot, scare the whites and kill the blacks. Worked for Hitler against the Jews, worked for slave owners for years. You buying into that plan, Willie Johnson? You want to quit? Anyone else?"

The room dimmed in the abyss of sound and energy, the threat of inattention.

Willie wiped his blue eyes with the back of his hand before he nodded at Loretta and turned to Sam making the peace sign. "Hey, bro, I'm an asshole. Peace?"

"Peace, Willie. I'm an asshole, but I've got your back. For the record, you pissed me off. I'm not some candy ass. Don't push it."

"You da man, Sammy. As much as I've fought the whole frigging idea of integration, I know we can't do this alone. Truth is, I'd rather throw myself off the Ambassador Bridge than move to the burbs. But, as god is my witness, I'll do whatever it takes to expose nigger codes in white hoods before they become America's new killing fields."

4

The Blender

How many times can a man turn his head and pretend that he just doesn't see?

—Bob Dylan, Lyrics from *Blowin' in the Wind*

SEPTEMBER 1970—"Hey Max, anything hanging fire?" Maxine, executive assistant extraordinaire, was Sam's saving grace. He never understood this term in either it's religious or nonsectarian forms, but he had no doubt he would not have survived the first few months of his promotion without Maxine's brash sense of irony and street smarts. On the 'who you know' side of the equation, Maxine was one of those rare birds with friends on all branches of the corporate tree.

"Not yet, but Maggie just called. Wants you to call before you get busy. Coffee? French cruller?"

"Yes, both, thanks. I could use a caffeine and sugar high." Which, Sam realized, was melodramatic and self-serving. He loved French crullers. Maxine knew this by now. And, it wasn't that he had a stressful commute. Jingo's sprawling four-story administration and design engineering center in Farmington was an easy fifteen-minute drive.

Maggie and Sam had finally bit the middle-class bullet and financed a second car, a bronze-colored 1970 Jingo Road Surfer. It looked and rode like a Mazda R100 coupe on steroids: a six-cylinder automatic with a tight turning radius. Truth be known, Sam looked forward to his drive to work. This was the first time his car was more than a mode of transportation.

Always leaning toward an anti-snob status, Sam liked to think of himself as a proletariat, a member of the working class. This new gig had begun to challenge his core values. Sometimes he had to stretch to find evidence of his old self. For instance, at General Motors, aka Generous Motors, the executives were segregated on the fourteenth floor of the GM Building in Detroit. Accessed by a private elevator from the garage, this space was well known as "Mahogany Row." At Jingo Motors, executive offices were on the fourth floor. By deliberate contrast, Jingo executives referred to this area as "Cedar Row." Not the rough-hewn cedar of cabins in northern Michigan, but cedar that had been cut in narrow strips, bleached, sanded, varnished and hung in a herringbone design. Sam took anti-smug pleasure in pointing out that cedar is grown in America, mahogany is not. Sam's office was at the backside of the building with large north-facing windows. The I-696 freeway may not be a great view, yet Sam felt like he did when he got his first full-size Wilson baseball mitt on his twelfth birthday. Every sense had sought its pleasure—touch, smell, taste, sight and sound. He remembered crouching down, slapping his fist three or four times into the pocket of the mitt, singing, "Hey batta, batta, swing!" Sam was totally over the moon with a window and a view. He hung his coat on the back of *his* door, sat down at *his* desk and called Maggie on *his* speakerphone.

"Hey, babe, what's up?"

"Aunt Jo called. She's got the day off and a friend of hers offered to drop her off here for a few hours while she house-hunts in Farmington. Sam, Aunt Jo wants to see our house, have lunch and get some baby hugs."

"Okay, and?"

"And . . . I know we agreed to our cold-war-charm strategy, but I have to find out what she knows, or thinks she knows, about Jacques and The Puzzle. We have no friggin' idea where any of us will be a month from now, or god knows, a year from now. Even if you and Clyde vetoed this, I might go rogue. Of all the bold steps we might have to take, this seems the most innocent. Help me."

"The soup. Jo referred to this chaos as being 'in the soup.' Go slow Mag and read her before you go too far. Jo's no innocent bystander. She's savvy. I'll talk to Clyde."

Maxine entered Sam's office doing a cobbled version of the stroll meets the watusi and set two mugs of black coffee, one French cruller and one chocolate covered donut on the small conference table.

"Everything okay, mastah?"

"Max, you've got to quit with the mastah thing. Besides being passé, the color of your skin heightens my discomfort. I am, after all, Jingo's Affirmative Action Officer, and it takes both of us to protect my raggedy-ass reputation."

"The discomfort and reputation argument don't make no mind, but passé I can't live with." Hanging her head down and channeling Prissy from *Gone with the Wind*, Maxine squealed, "Sorry boss man, I don't know nothin' bout being passé."

"You are incorrigible. Speaking of affirmative action, I haven't heard anything from Ryan lately. Do we have an update from the Affirmative Action Task Group?"

"Negative. Ryan said last week's meeting was cancelled based on a call from the president's office. He didn't say who called, but I'm sure it was Suha."

Sam shook his head and said, "Drop the Suha. Everyone knows it means stick-up-her-ass, including Karen. Help me out here. What would I do if you got fired?"

"For one thing you'd be forced to defend my Title VII discrimination suit."

"Ms. Jones, if you're insubordinate your discrimination suit won't be worth the gas money you spend driving to the EEOC."

"Look at you, Sam. Everyone knows the top brass are jacking you around. How do you stay so buttoned-up Mister Calm, Cool and Collected?"

"Give me a break, Max. Half the time I'm waiting for the corporate narcs to blow my cover. Even the guys on the line know I landed this job without putting in my time and service. What you're seeing is a well-honed defensive position. When I can't rely on my competence, I rely on my calm. It buys me time and keeps me from overt acts of stupidity."

"Maybe so, but you're a deep, still pond. Wish I could be more like you."

"Ah, no you don't, certain death-by-boredom. Let's get some work done before we both end up in the principal's office," Sam laughed.

Heading to Ryan's office on the fourth floor, Sam bit his bottom lip and shook his head. What strange set of circumstances led him here, to this job, this place? The rank and file called the fourth floor The Crypt because Ben was psycho about noise. Not his noise, noise by others—clicking pens, cracking knuckles, grinding teeth, chewing gum, whistling and talking while walking at headquarters—was strictly *verboten*. Sam remembered the day Ben interviewed him for his promotion at the local bar and grill. Just as Sam was accepting the offer, a new bartender-in-training made the mistake of crushing ice when Ben was at his usual table. To say Ben went ballistic would have been a gross understatement. The fourth floor was filled with quiet guys. Ryan's slide rule and white plastic pocket-protectors shouted engineer, but they also translated into silence. Yet, Sam knew that Ryan's savvy, sense of humor and attention to social cues broke all stereotypes about engineers and earned him the friendship and confidence of the executive team.

"Hey, Ryan, how goes it?" asked Sam.

"Fair to middlin' or somewhere in between."

"It's the in-between I worry about. Maxine said the affirmative action meeting was cancelled last week. What's up?"

"I thought you'd tell me. Got a call from Karen Kingsolver who said Jingo is taking a different tact on this and you'd give me the details."

"That's it?"

"Yep, that's it. You didn't know?"

"Beats me. I haven't said word one to Ben about affirmative action. I'll see what I can find out. Where are we on the plan?" asked Sam.

"We've done as much as we can. Had I known it was such bullshit work, I'd have run for the hills. Seriously, there must be a fucking warehouse full of bureaucrats in DC who get paid to dream up this kind of lunacy."

"Seems that way. Look, Ryan, bullshit or not, I know it was a lot of work and I appreciate you taking the lead. We'll have a template for annual reports that will become pro forma after this. Thanks, man! If any of the task group asks, let them know I'm going to meet with Ben to discuss next steps."

The chalky gray day slipped into twilight before Sam realized he'd forgotten to let Clyde know Maggie was going to talk with Jo.

He decided he'd call from home. Safer. In fact, he and Maggie shouldn't have talked on his work line. *Damn.*

Just as Sam was locking his files, the intercom rang. The president's office.

"Sam Tervo here."

"Sam, my man, glad you're there. Come on over; we need to talk."

"Sure, Ben. Is there anything I should bring?"

"Nope, just you and your usual fine sense of humor."

"Be there in a few."

Ben Kabul's office was on the far southeast corner of the fourth floor. He claimed he wanted to keep his eye on GM. His office was large by any measure, but the Grand Poobah's hood ornament was the attached conference room that seated twenty and was equipped with controls to close and lock doors, drop or raise projection screens or open a fully-equipped bar. Ben loved to show off his toys and booze. Sam recalled his first trip to the inner sanctum.

Less than a year ago, he was wading through dozens of applications from hourly workers for a vacant plant foreman position, when Riley, the Director of Building and Maintenance, walked into his office:

"Hey, Sam, I've been asked to escort you to the inner sanctum. Do not be afraid, kimosabe!"

"What's this about? Do I need to bring anyone's file?"

"Naw, Ben's entire staff is there, so I doubt he plans to rip you a new one. Ben likes to do those alone."

"Very funny!"

"No, not so funny when you're getting your ass ripped. If you ever make it to the fourth floor, you'll know what I mean. We call it time in The Blender."

"Sounds kinky."

The door to the conference room was open. After they entered, Ben said, "Sam, please take a seat at the end of the table." Once seated, the door closed on its own.

Ben then said, "If you don't mind, Sam, would you please point to the wall on your right. Go ahead, point your right index finger to the wall on your right." Sam knew he was being set up. Pointing to the wall on his right, a projector screen dropped from the ceiling. The look of amazement on Sam's face resulted in a round of snickers and guffaws.

"Now point your left index finger to the wall on your right." *Okay*, Sam thought, *I'll play this game*. Sam pointed his left index finger at the wall and the projector screen disappeared into the ceiling. Perplexed by how or who was operating the screen, Sam's non-verbal reaction provoked controlled laughter. He decided to be a good sport.

"Sam, we always ask the guest to pour the first drink. How about it? Will you please pour me three fingers of Johnnie Walker Black?" asked Ben.

Sam looked around. There were no counters or cabinets. As he stood to take a better look, the wall opened to a fully stocked bar and sink. A deep blush rose from Sam's chest to the top of his head. By now, the controlled laughter had pierced through polite bounds and Sam turned toward the locked door. With no escape in sight, he turned back, held up two palms and bowed from the waist to show his appreciation for this practical joke. Ben got up, slapped Sam on the back, and said, "Good show! Anyone who wants to be on my team needs to know how to take some ribbing."

Off balance as he was, Sam soon realized the purpose of the meeting was to vet him for the position of Director of Personnel. He didn't see it coming and later recalled this moment by saying, "In Maggie's most flagrant anti-hackneyed style, you could've knocked me over with a guitar pick."

Three months later, standing outside Ben's office, Sam could still feel the heat of that moment, the anticipation and dread of The Blender.

"Sam, come on in, have a seat. You've been in this job about ninety days now, and I thought it was time to take a look at what's working, what's not."

"Great! I wasn't expecting a ninety-day review but look forward to the feedback and the opportunity to see if I'm on track with company goals."

"Good. I think you're well aware that we promoted you in spite of the fact that you didn't meet the qualifications for the job. You made quite an impression when you recruited some of my staff, and as you well know, a known quantity is often a better choice."

"Yes, sir. I was very much aware of that and appreciate your confidence in me. I feel well supported by you and everyone I work with. Maxine and my staff are highly competent and do a good job keeping me out of trouble!"

"Glad to hear that. Before we get started, do you have any questions or concerns about where we are or where we're going?"

For some reason, Sam heard his heart thrum, like a sound effect in an Alfred Hitchcock film. His hands were heavy and his throat felt stretched by an old wishbone. Forgetting to stay calm and still, he forced air and words through his mouth. "Well, now that you ask, I do have a concern. Apparently, Karen called Ryan to cancel the Affirmative Action Task Group meeting without working through me. Since I'm responsible, I would prefer that Karen call me."

"Who do you think directed Karen to call Ryan?"

The thrumming seemed louder and Sam had a hard time hearing himself say, "Well, I imagine it was you."

"You're damned right it was me! Look, you little piss ant, our number one company goal is to reduce bureaucracy and streamline service. It's our job to make sure protocols don't get in the way when we have a goddamn business to run. If I want to pick up the phone and call some nimrod on the assembly line, then I will goddamn make that call. You have a problem with that?"

Sam reminded himself to breathe. "No problem. I was not in any way suggesting you don't have the absolute right to do whatever you want or need to do. I respect that, and I'm proud of the fact that Jingo isn't a lumbering, bureaucratic organization like the other auto companies." The plaintive, groveling, kiss-ass sound of his voice was repugnant. Sam worried he'd groaned out loud. "But, for an affirmative action plan to work, it has to have a company-wide commitment. To accomplish this, it makes sense to have a representative committee rather than a top-down edict. This way we get buy-in from all the line and staff managers who make the hiring decisions." Sam thought, *seriously, whose double-speak is this?*

"Sam, what kind of fucking drugs are you on?"

Sam wanted to tell Ben that he totally grokked his question. Instead, he said, "Ben, I don't do drugs."

"Then where the hell did you get the lamebrain idea you have the authority to pull my design engineers and operations managers off their jobs to construct a bullshit government mandated plan that isn't worth the paper it's written on? We're four months away from the North American International Auto Show at Cobo Center. We expect one million visitors to check out our new models. It takes some pretty serious goddamn time and attention. What the fuck, Sam? I thought you had some ivy-league smarts."

At this point, the thrumming moved into Sam's stomach and lower intestinal tract. He decided Ben's position made way more sense than his. He thought, *what kind of narcissistic idiot would initiate a company-wide plan just before the auto show?* Still forcing air and words through his troubled mouth, Sam responded, "I thought this was important to the company, and I thought if we had a broader consensus then departments would do a better job in hiring women and minority applicants. We need a plan that is much more than the paper it's written on." Sam thought, *what a dickhead I've become! Who am I?*

"Then, you put pen to paper and write the goddamn plan. I'm not going to spend my design engineer's time jumping through LBJ's yellow-dog liberal hoops. We have enough goddamn other laws to deal with. That's why we hired you. Your job, you do it!"

"Yes, sir."

"Listen up. Don't think for a goddamn minute that I don't support women and coloreds. I've got three sisters with PhDs and my Lebanese skin is not white. I know what it's like to have doors slammed in my face. I also know if we don't sell cars we don't have jobs to fill. First things first."

"Sure, that makes sense."

"How's that wife of yours. What's her name?"

"Maggie."

"Yes, Maggie. Pretty slip of a girl that one. Does she have her papers yet?"

"Papers?"

"Is she Americanized?"

"Well, she holds her Canadian citizenship."

"Here's the deal, Sam, if you want to keep your job you've got to get her papers. Our motto 'Built by Americans for Americans' is sacrosanct. We don't skimp on patriotism. That's why the name of the company is Jingo. No executive of mine is going to have a foreigner for a wife. Do I make myself understood?"

"Yes, sir. It's just that."

"Never mind 'it's just that.' There's no wiggle room. Just do it. If you can't, I'll find someone else to take your job. Understood?"

"Understood."

"Great! I know I'm being tough on you, but I don't have a choice. You're either with us or against us. I hope you're with us. I know you've got a lot of those tree-hugging values, and we chose you because we knew you'd be a good influence on our workforce.

All in due time! You know what they say, 'Rome wasn't built in a day.' Before I can help you with your agenda, you need to get on board. Now, let's go over your performance and set goals for the next ninety days."

Before Sam left, he called Maggie to let her know he was delayed and would be home in fifteen to twenty minutes, two hours after she expected him. *Maggie's pissed. Ben's pissed. I'm exhausted.* There were no surprises in the performance evaluation or goal setting and Sam finally broke through the dread of his first time in The Blender. Although he felt like he'd spent two hours being puréed, he didn't die. Sam walked across the unlit parking lot and felt the first autumn chill of the season. Tossing his near-empty briefcase on the passenger seat, he crawled into his car and thought about three years of car payments, thirty years of mortgage payments.

5

Fear Mongers

In white communities, there was talk of black 'killer squads' that would come from the inner city to murder children, and of black maids dispatched to suburbs to poison the residents of the household they served.

—Detroit Weekly

SEPTEMBER 1970—"For god's sakes, Maggie, I couldn't help it. Ben called the minute we hung up and I had to go to his office. It was my time in The Blender."

"Oh, crap. Sorry. Tell me."

"Absolutely mind-blowing. Intellectually, I knew what he was doing. Emotionally, I felt like a pimply-faced thirteen-year-old. He's good. I can see him brainwashing POWs. I walked out of his office thinking I was a total jackass and he was the second coming. Ironically, *goddamn* is his favorite word. I came completely unglued."

"What are you going to do?"

"Punt. I can't afford to walk away. In addition to the money, this job gives me, us, the best chance to work the system for women and minorities. We've got to be part of the solution. We know getting this job was no coincidence. If my ego gets trampled, oh well. I can live with that."

"You? Ego?"

"Very funny, still some microscopic egoist residue."

"No doubt. Tell me what he said."

"Can't now. Gotta run! I'll call before I head home in case you want me to stop at Greene's for a bag of sliders."

"Damn you to hell Sam; I'll be salivating all day. Do it! Sliders must be part of some essential food group."

Maggie did a double take of herself in the large mirror over the kitchen table—hair snarled, eyes puffy, a whitehead forming on her nose. *Ugh. Who in their right mind would put a large mirror in the kitchen?* Then it hit her. The utility room must have been an add-on. The mirror, with its small ledge, a window! She wondered how many other obvious clues she'd missed since becoming a *hausfrau*.

Bone tired last night Maggie feigned sleep rather than deal with Sam's late arrival and her irrational anger for being left with a one-year-old all day. Sam's Blender Report this morning completely sidelined yesterday's interrogation of Aunt Jo.

> "Maggie, it's been way too long. Before we know it, Tekla will be starting school, taking baton lessons, giggling over boys. What a beauty!"
>
> Tekla pounded her silver spoon on her metal highchair tray in response to Aunt Jo's full attention. The engraved spoon was a gift from Sam's brother Kenny and his girlfriend, Stella. Stella, a member of The Eights, met Kenny at Sam and Maggie's wedding party. An Oreo couple, after two years of dating they were still slamming themselves against convention, bigotry and ignorance from both whites and blacks. In the face of mounting evidence to the contrary, Maggie had a hard time

holding on to her belief that love conquers all. Even now, she looked at Aunt Jo with new eyes. *What turns love to fear, suspicion, mistrust?*

Maggie lived with Aunt Jo for five years, sleeping on a mattress on the floor in a converted attic while she completed her undergraduate and graduate studies at Wayne State. To say Maggie and Aunt Jo fell in love doesn't begin to capture the kind of love splurging that went on between them. From the beginning, Aunt Jo had been a generous, kind, loving surrogate mother to the daughter she never had. And Maggie, well, she'd spent most of her life looking for her mother, perhaps any mother. Now, because of The Puzzle, Maggie had sworn to suppress her exuberance and maintain her cold-war-charm front with everyone, including Aunt Jo. But today, Maggie was prepared to hijack the conversation to find out what Aunt Jo knew about The Puzzle.

After lifting Tekla out of her highchair, Maggie began to blow kisses and say, "*Au revoir*, Auntie Jo. See you later!"

"Oh, for heaven's sake, let me give her a hug before she takes a nap. Come here, sweet one." Maggie watched as Aunt Jo nuzzled Tekla's neck before lifting her up and blowing a raspberry on her tummy. Enchanted, Tekla hugged her trusted yellow blanket and followed Maggie to her crib for a nap. On days when Maggie was busy, Tekla would grab her blanket and lie down on the rug next to her crib. Although she quickly embraced Dr. Levy's advice to count her blessings, Maggie had not taken his suggestion to read while Tekla slept. Instead, she'd become a sloth, green algae growing on her olive skin from months of hibernation, mind-numbing daytime TV game shows, and most notably, the flat denial of a suburban lifestyle.

"Marguerite, I've missed you! I know my work schedule is nuts, but I'm home on weekends. You've stopped calling. What's up?"

"Mostly the move and getting used to the rhythm of not working—taking care of a house, husband and baby. Atrophy of the brain. Not very good company for myself much less anyone else. And, I'm worried about Sam."

"Sam? His job?"

"No, more than his job. He acts like someone is after him. . . ."

Aunt Jo put her fingers to her lips to shush the conversation then said, "Oh Maggie, that's just crazy. Sam's fine. I think he's just worried about his new promotion and making the cut. Men are like that. Add to that he's a new father. I know we don't give men much stock in parenthood, but men can feel overwhelmed by the responsibility of a young family, a mortgage, car payments. He's gone from zero to sixty in a flash. I think he's fine. Let it go!" Aunt Jo smiled then moved her arms as if she was conducting a symphony and pointed at Maggie.

"You're right, Aunt Jo. Totally crazy! Too many hours folding diapers. Might be time for me to write some poetry and make new friends. How about a cup of tea? I need practice," Maggie laughed.

"Thanks, none for me. Let's sit on the porch and take in the warm weather while we can," Aunt Jo said as she pointed to the French doors leading to the screened porch, then waved her hand to continue through the porch door to a lonely beat up picnic table under a willow tree.

Maggie whispered, "Seriously, Aunt Jo? You think someone might have bugged this house?"

"I don't know if the house is bugged, but you need to have your private conversations in the backyard or car. I wouldn't even risk the garage. Maggie, this is so much bigger than you know, than I know. Go on, finish what you were about to say."

Maggie took a long, hard look at Aunt Jo and thought about Sam's caution to go slow. Maybe she'd already said too much, moved too fast. *Screw it, too late now. We need Aunt Jo on our side. If she's not, we're toast. If she is, we have a toehold on getting out of this mess.* "Aunt Jo, if I can't trust you, I don't know who I can trust. What I'm about to say sounds unhinged, demented."

"Maggie, once you're in the soup, it's smart to question everyone. I call it soup because that's the only way I can deal with it. I've got information that might keep you safe or put you at risk. I have no idea how safe or explosive this will be. I won't withhold information unless I'm overwhelmed by concern it will hurt more than help. If you're willing to live with that, I'm ready to listen and talk."

Maggie fought back tears. Somehow the nightmare they were in became more real. And loved ones, like Aunt Jo, no longer represented shelter from harsh realities. Without shelter, Maggie was convinced she and Sam needed to accept the risk. Asking Aunt Jo for help wasn't a simple leap of faith; it was more like a conscious, springboard dive into Dante's Inferno.

"We call it The Puzzle. We're desperate to understand what's going on, who's involved. Without you, we're boxing shadows and making up stories that scare the crap out of us. The fact that you know we're not losing our minds or making this up is something. Anything you can tell us will, for all our sakes, be treated like plutonium. Here's the *Reader's Digest* version:

"Twice now, Sam found himself in sexually compromising positions. The first was at Sheer Juice after a bachelor party the night before we were married. The second was during Jingo's party to kick off the International Auto Show last year. Both he and Clyde are convinced someone deliberately slipped Sam a Mickey, or hallucinogenic—something that caused him to lose his grip on reality. In both cases, his boss at Sheer Juice upped the ante when he told Sam they had videotapes of him sexually battering these women and 'they own him.' We have no idea what or who we're dealing with, or why. So, we walk on eggs, look over our shoulders, close our eyes against a nameless boogeyman and hold our breath. I can't live like this anymore, Aunt Jo. We have Tekla now, a family. For the first time in my life, I feel like I have a real home and someone's trying to rip us apart. Aunt Jo, what the hell's going on? Are we safe with Clyde? Is this about Jacques? My parents?" Tears finally let loose, streaming down her face. Maggie looked at Aunt Jo and said, "Please, yes. Help us."

Maggie was brought back to the small, once-naked kitchen table she painted turquoise to match a hint of this gem in the art deco, confetti-splattered yellow linoleum. A significant color-lapse, an outburst likely filled with psychological innuendo, Maggie resisted the temptation to delve into the meaning. Instead, she called the table her *paroxysm*, a place to invite the unbidden.

On the screened porch, Tekla was pounding her heels against the bottom of the playpen as she chewed on the nipple of her now empty bottle. "Hey, little one, let's get dressed, watch Sesame Street and plan our day."

Tekla threw her plastic bottle over the wood railing and attempted to climb out. "Big Bird? Big Bird!" she giggled.

Maggie's calendar page for September was blank. She took the summer off to settle into their new house in Livonia. *Li-Vo-Nia*. Even in her thoughts, Maggie mimicked Willie's over-emphasized syllables of this Russian name. Why Russian? There were no colorful turrets on cornfields flattened by cookie-cutter subs. Like other Detroit suburbs, Livonia was slashed by the 'mile roads' to carry commerce from the inner city to the outer cities. The Eights put together a start-up plan for Maggie. She'd join women's clubs and volunteer groups to insert herself into the community and gain information important to integrating Livonia. Then, based on what Maggie found, The Eights would draft a longer-term plan. To maintain her sanity, Maggie decided she'd write poetry while Tekla napped. What a laugh. After losing her university position in December 1968 because she was pregnant, and therefore unfit to teach, Maggie wrote an "Ode to Baby Tervo" before Tekla was born. Other than that, she'd written zippo, zero—not one frigging line of poetry. Her black moleskin sat dormant.

Joining women's clubs meant getting another set of wheels and finding a sitter. For the last two months, their '62 Corvair was motionless in the garage; offers by Maija and Issie to take care of Tekla still pending.

Which, of course, begged the question of how vital poetry or civil rights was to her. Less than a year ago, Maggie relied on both to feed her soul fire. Now, other than a weekly fix of sliders, she wasn't sure what she wanted. She felt logy, like moss at the edge of a swamp. What did she expect to do all day in the burbs? Have tea with the neighbor ladies? Play Bridge? Join a bowling league? Maggie's overriding impulse was to sink to the floor and wail against this sterile strip of geography with manicured lawns and aproned women. If not seducing her, the reality of this place was turning her into someone she didn't know and didn't like. Maggie wondered if she was depressed; but, in the mind-over-matter, anti-whining Anna Soulier tradition, Maggie resisted labeling weakness or giving it power over her. *Okay,* she thought, *time to get off my sorry ass and introduce myself to the neighbors.*

After putting Tekla in her stroller and assessing the safety of the narrow gravel shoulder between speeding trucks and drainage ditches, Maggie charged across two over-watered lawns and three pebble driveways before reaching the Foxes, neighbors who shared their party line. The other night, when Maggie was waiting for Sam's call, she grabbed the phone without listening to the entire series of rings. The call was intended for Mr. Fox and she had to ask the caller to redial.

When Maggie reached the Fox's pale-yellow bungalow, the word *tidy* came to mind. Rich, black mulch circled mature evergreens on the edged lawn and fed colorful flowerbeds protected by twelve-inch white-picket fences. Maggie was relieved. Somehow the tidiness of it all made their house seem less prissy.

Of the two paved walkways, one to the front door and one to the side door, Maggie chose the side door because it seemed more casual, neighborly.

An attractive, well-coifed, silver-haired woman with perfect makeup answered the door. Maggie bit her bottom lip when she noticed the woman's clean, pressed black-eyed-susan print apron over a black pinstriped shirtwaist dress. Momentarily, she felt dirty, unpolished with her jeans, tee shirt and chipped nails. Her voice cracked.

"Hi, my name's Maggie Tervo and my husband, daughter and I just moved into the white cape cod two doors down."

No response.

"Apparently, we're on the same party line and I want to apologize for having to ask one of your callers to remake his call to you."

No response.

"You see, I was waiting for my husband to call and I picked up the phone too soon."

"Ah, I see. Mrs. Tervo, is there some reason you came to my side door?"

"Well, I thought it might be less formal and more convenient for you."

"I've always been taught that strangers should go to the front door so homeowners can screen them before they open the door."

"Mrs. Fox, I'm sorry if I bothered you. I just wanted to apologize for the mishap and introduce myself."

"Of course. You meant no harm. My husband Richard says I can be blunt. With all the violence and threats by Negroes, we have to be more vigilant. I can see you're not a Negro, but with your black hair, you might have been. Would you like to have some tea?"

Maggie got a whiff of onion-slathered, greasy hamburgers before she heard Sam in the kitchen. Sam was looking at the piece of paper Maggie left on the kitchen counter. Words and letters cut from magazines and catalogs, and pasted on a piece of construction paper, formed the following note:

> DON'T TALK ABOUT THE PUZZLE. WE'LL GO OUTSIDE TO THE PICNIC TABLE TO EAT AND TALK ABOUT TONIGHT'S MEETING. AFTER YOU READ THIS, TEAR IT UP INTO TINY PIECES AND SWALLOW IT. HA HA! JUST KIDDING ABOUT SWALLOWING IT.

Shaking his head, a smile forming on his lips, Sam turned to find Maggie in the kitchen doorway, hands on her hips, she said, "We're outta here! This is a freaking scene from some Roman Polanski movie."

"Polanski? As in *Rosemary's Baby?*" asked Sam, as he grabbed the hamburger bag and two Cokes. Nudging Maggie toward the porch door, he held his finger to his lips.

Once they were under the willow tree, Sam pulled five burgers out of the bag and pushed the remainder of the bag and one of the Cokes across the table to Maggie.

"Sam, there's something sinister as hell going on in this neighborhood. Minnie Fox is a cut-out-doll impersonating a woman. She makes Donna Reed look freaking radical! She told me three of her friends, quote, fired their Negro housekeepers because they were afraid of being poisoned, unquote."

"Maggie, we chose hell. Hell is where we create change. Neither of us is very good at patience, so we need to remind each other. Be patient."

"I know, I know. Maybe I need to spend more time in Detroit to tamp down this craziness and chill."

"Do it, Maggie. We need you in the trenches on both sides."

"Speaking of trenches. Did you get a chance to call Clyde? Can he meet with us tonight? I told Maija we had a romantic evening planned. She's keeping Tekla overnight.

"Makes sense. We've got a lot to cover. And, Mrs. Tervo, we'll also want to make good on the story you gave Ma. Should we do it on the picnic table before the snow flies?"

"Maggie got up and walked to the other side of the table, sat down on Sam's lap and opened the first few buttons of his shirt. After kissing the soft hollow of his neck, Maggie whispered, "My goodness, Mr. Tervo, whatever do you mean by 'do it?' "

Moving his fingers under the back waistband of Maggie's jeans, Sam found that sweet spot just above her tailbone, an area Maggie called her *Bermuda Triangle*. Talk about erogenous zones! Sam discovered it when he first kissed Maggie at her Aunt Jo's front door. Like striking gold when you were only spelunking.

6

Don't Think Twice, It's All Right

What we have here is a failure to communicate.

—*Cool Hand Luke,* Motion Picture

SEPTEMBER 1970—The Webster's bright yellow house had faded over the past few years of riots, white flight and blight. Dark green crabgrass invaded and invigorated the khaki-colored lawn. A world overstocked with metaphors, but still no poems thought Maggie.

Clyde climbed in the back of their car and said, "Hey guys, what's happening?"

"That's for me to know and you to find out," Sam laughed.

"Ignore him. I don't know where he comes up with these dorky old sayings; they keep popping out of that sweet little kisser. Between him and Tekla, it's hard to slip a word in sideways. Luckily, Tekla's spending the night with Maija."

Clyde took in their expectant, young faces. Ten years older, he wondered if he'd ever been that optimistic. "Maggie, we can only hope Tekla has your quicksilver mind, wicked good looks and kick-ass determination. By the way, if you keep saying 'slip a word in sideways,' does that become as hackneyed as 'get a word in edgewise?' "

"Probably. And, you might want to rethink the kick-ass piece. I'm going through an algae-on-the-pond phase, so far away from any action I'm not sure a map would help. Besides, you have no idea how much energy it takes *not* to get lost in the rush of freshly laundered clothes, chicken casseroles and cake walks."

"Come on, Mag. Gimme a break. We're not going to let you lose yourself in that wild and wacky world!" laughed Clyde.

Before Sam pulled into Big Boys, Maggie was struck by how dreary everything looked. The entire city seemed to be in active decline. Street lights out, potholes unfilled, trash and debris collecting around abandoned buildings, grand old homes. The dreariness was more than what she saw; the absence of sound, movement and energy compounded the sense of flatness and fatigue.

After settling in their favorite corner booth at the back of the near-empty restaurant, they each ordered the usual—Big Boy double cheeseburger, onion rings, side salad and Coke. Maggie looked at Clyde and said, "Before we start, I want to say I'm sorry for going rogue. I panicked. Aunt Jo was coming over and I knew I couldn't get through an afternoon of polite chitchat. I didn't give Sam much notice and he forgot to call you."

Clyde nodded his head and said, "Got it. Thanks for the apology."

Maggie knew Clyde got it, but she also knew Clyde didn't like surprises or disloyalty. His moral compass was set closer to absolute than anyone she knew.

"Okay, my CliffsNotes from Aunt Jo. Here goes:

- We have to assume our phones, offices, houses and garages are bugged.
- We can't trust anyone except each other, and I presume Aunt Jo includes herself in this circle. She said she still acts as if she's being watched and her phone and house are bugged.
- Her opinion is The Puzzle has to do with some cartel that might involve the mob and one or more governments—the States, Canada and/or Britain. She's certain the mob's involved.
- Based on Aunt Jo's take, The Puzzle relates back to my parents, Anna and Raymond, and their resistance against the British monarchy—or something they uncovered during their resistance.
- Jacques is likely aware or involved. Aunt Jo's not sure whose side he's on, or for that matter, what the sides are. In fact, Jacques may be friend, foe or government plant.
- And, get this, according to Aunt Jo, Angelo has been keeping his ear to the ground. Since he's the point person for each of us, Angelo seems an obvious choice. Yet, even though Aunt Jo is certain he pumped her for information, she couldn't, or wouldn't, come up with a single example."

Sam shook his head, "This is the second time I've heard Maggie's CliffsNotes and my reaction both times is this sounds like some wacko's wet dream about combining every mystery he'd ever seen into one blockbuster."

Clyde leaned back in his seat and thought for a few minutes, then said, "I'll give some thought to whether Angelo pumped me for information and you do the same. For now, Maggie, I want your take on Jo. Was she halting, emotional and authentic, or did it sound rehearsed?"

"We were sitting across from each other at the picnic table. She held my hands and looked me in the eyes. When she got emotional, she squeezed my hands and fought back tears. I got the sense she was afraid for herself and for us. I don't think I've ever seen her put on an act. Of all the people I know, she tells it like it is. That said, I might be fooled because I so want to trust her. And I do."

Clyde turned down the left corner of his mouth and said, "Hmm. Holding hands? Is that normal? Although friendly, I've always sensed a cool reserve. Have I misread her?"

"Good question. I don't know. I guess I don't remember a lot of affection. When she gave us our wedding gift, she was teary-eyed and nervous. But now that you mention it, she isn't someone I always hug like I do you and The Eights. I don't know if we've held hands. I can't remember . . . but this felt right. She knew I was scared."

"I'm not sure you can draw either line. There've been times when Jo hugged me. She's no ice queen," said Sam.

"Okay, we can come back to behaviors later. Did Jo say anything about your parents' work, anything you didn't know before?"

"One big surprise. Aunt Jo said that Jacques dated Anna, my mother, *before* she met and married Raymond. According to her, Raymond was not in any way freaked by Jacques' presence in their lives. More bizarro, she said Raymond was copacetic when Anna and Jacques wandered off on short trips together because they loved, get this, to go antiquing, check-out ethnic food stores—and stranger than fiction, check out restaurant, camping and military surplus warehouses. Which is nuts because nothing in our house was antique and the kitchen was never Anna's favorite place. Issie and I thought the word *dinner* was shorthand for *chicken-pot-pies*. As for Jacques, his office building is filled with artifacts, but the design is industrial modern. Nothing about him or his surroundings is antique."

"What does Jacques do for a living?"

Sam jumped in, "I'll start and let Maggie pick up from there. I must have asked Jacques a dozen times what he does for a living and each time he blew me off with some flip answer about his many attempts to find a job that doesn't interfere with his lifestyle. His best response was a Jack Kerouac quote that goes something like: 'I've got nothing to offer except my own confusion.' The guy's brilliant and comes across as a real mensch. It would be hard not to like him. Maggie?"

Maggie was thinking about Jacques. What if he was her father? This conversation felt dangerous. Part of her wanted to hold on to her childhood innocence and adult fantasies, but it was too dicey. Time for her to be the mother she always wanted.

"So, here's the skinny. I want Jacques to be the hero of this story. No, want doesn't begin to describe it. More like I'm blindsided and reckless in trying to force this heroic ending. I need both you and Sam as counterweights to this childish, romantic notion."

"You got it. Any idea where he gets his megabucks?"

"None."

"Okay, so big red flag there. We need to be clear about where we're going. That means we commit to talking to each other before anyone goes rogue. I can't imagine how stressed you two are, but we need to keep things tight. I think our next step is to meet with Jo and be prepared with every question we can think of. Let's start brainstorming. No editing, Maggie. We can do that later. First question, "How does Jacques get his scratch?"

By the time Maggie and Sam got home, the full moon was behind a sheet of clouds. After covering the slivered picnic table with a well-worn green and brown plaid picnic blanket, Sam lifted Maggie up, her feet dangling from the end of the tabletop.

"Mr. Tervo, I hope to hell the neighbors are sound asleep and won't hear us howling."

"Mrs. Tervo, I hope to hell you howl and cry. We've had so many months of quiet lovemaking that I'm ready to let loose. Besides, wolves can sound like humans."

"Seriously? You think any right-thinking wolf would choose to snuggle in this briar patch?"

Sam took Maggie's heels in his hands and placed them on his shoulders. Propped on her elbows, Maggie watched Sam unbuckle his belt. His white jockey shorts and platinum hair looked neon against the dark night. Yet, the contours of his face were masked. His breath untethered. Maggie slid to her back and felt warm hands lifting her skirt and pulling down her underpants. Without voice or sight, she felt the heightened sense of the unknown. The nubby blanket held the warmth of her body, but the furtive night and faceless lover stirred the air, then a storm. Their cries sent critters flying into thick ragweed behind the willows. A footfall and a flash of light silenced them. Behind the cyclone fence, Maggie caught a shadow of someone bending into the dark.

After spending most of the day cleaning and organizing the attic, Maggie decided on a relaxing bath. Then, she'd force herself to make a quick trip next door to talk to Heidi who lived in the smallest apartment in the triplex. Weeks ago, Heidi introduced herself when she heard Maggie trying to coax Tekla out from under the white lilac bush between their garage and Heidi's screened porch. *Other than being white, what were The Eights thinking when they decided I could infiltrate the burbs?* Heidi would be the second Livonian she approached in the last three months. Talk about a slow start. Maggie's feeble attempt to frame these two encounters as an accelerated work plan tickled her irony. She sure as hell didn't have to worry about whiplash!

Stripping off a pair of cut-offs and a tee shirt, Maggie took some pride in the graffiti of dirt and cobwebs. The house was small, but the attic caught the morning and afternoon sun through opposing windows and offered enough space to hold a writing desk. Shelves, tucked under the roof's slant, had been stocked with mottled dust-laden jars—pickled beets, tomatoes, sweet and sour pickles, green beans—meant to stave off The Great Depression. Now, empty shelves were waiting for the stacks of books littering the attic floor. Not Maggie's imagined writers-haunt of an old Victorian house on the coast of Maine—topped by a widow's walk and pummeled by earth-shattering weather and waves. But, in the scheme of things, their cape cod on a flat acre of land was beginning to feel just as dangerous.

Maggie stretched her arms from one wall to the other, the full width of their only bathroom. A multi-colored, twenty-four-inch rag rug created wall-to-wall carpeting between the pedestal sink and a four-foot-long tub/shower. Somehow, a leaded-glass, west-facing window redeemed this tiny space. It was the kind of glass you'd expect to see in a turn-of-the-century bank teller's window. Maggie's decision to paint everything white and use towels and rugs for color gave it a Zen feel. Not yet done, she fixated on getting a few river stones for the sink basin and placing a Mason jar of fresh lavender on the windowsill.

Well water gushed out of the tub's tap with startling force. No chlorine, the smell of iron provoked memories of mountain streams in Canada. Baby shampoo for a bubble bath and music on the transistor radio set the mood.

Knees to chin in the tub, Simon and Garfunkel filled the room with *Bridge Over Troubled Water.* Feeling overwhelmed by the move, The Puzzle, and the shadow of someone behind her neighbor's fence, the epistle's message hit her like a sledgehammer. Maggie felt the first ripple of laughter build in her solar plexus, then rise unbidden to infect every molecule of her body. She laughed so hard she had to stop and catch her breath, then started laughing again. Tears spilled down her face. For a nanosecond, she wondered if she was having a breakdown, but soon realized the laughter gave her perspective—the sense of relief, clarity and joy was therapeutic. She was not going to be devoured by this move. Although imperfect, she knew who she was.

Looking in the mirror, Maggie smiled. Nothing like a pair of black pedal pushers with a mint-green cardigan and tangerine lipstick on an autumn day! If timed right, she'd shoot the breeze with Heidi and start dinner before Sam showed up with Tekla, no doubt flying high on animal crackers.

Relieved to find only one entrance to the smallest triplex, Maggie knocked on the door. No response. She tried again. No response. Just as she started back to the house, Heidi opened the door wearing a pink mini-skirt with a matching cropped top. All arms and legs with a Barbie doll figure and short blonde hair, Heidi was deeply tanned and stunningly attractive.

"Hi, Heidi. I didn't have your number so came by to see if you had time to talk."

"Sure! Let's sit on the porch. Can I fix you a cocktail? Pop?"

"Thanks, I'm good."

"So, how's it goin'? Y'all unpacked?" asked Heidi.

"Except for a box or two in the attic that we'll never look into again, we're done."

"I know about that. I still have boxes taped shut."

"Since when?"

"Last year, over Labor Day. Anyhow, I had a come-apart in Detroit. My car got broken into twice; I was freaked. Back then I was working breakfast and lunch at a greasy spoon in Redford. One day, I turned right instead of left and drove down Six Mile. A small 'For Rent' sign was tacked next to this here door. I was blown away! Way cheaper than I thought and close to Redford." Maggie watched in awe as Heidi caught her first full breath and paused.

Maggie realized her knees were bouncing to defuse Heidi's hyper-charged dialogue. After her second full breath, Heidi continued, "Anyhow, in March, the diner went under, so I tried the Lone Pine Inn. Lucky for me they were fixin' to have a cocktail lounge and needed someone to host and check coats. I make way more than I did as a waitress and walk two hundred and ten steps to work. I know, queer as hell to count steps, I've done it since I was a kid. Except for the sleazebags, it's a good gig. You work?"

"Not now. Before Tekla was born, I taught a few freshman English classes at the University of Detroit. I'm not sure what I'll do when Tekla goes back to school. Although I'd like to teach poetry, those jobs are like fishing for amoeba in a shark tank."

"Knock me out. I love poetry! Do you write?"

"You're kidding? Someone who loves poetry? Yes, I write. Did write. These days I'm fighting writer's block or lack of interest. Time will tell. So, what's going on in the hood? Do you know your housemates?"

"Not really. Top-floor guy might as well be invisible. Never see him. Well, once. Anyhow, he was backing out of the little parking area and I was pulling in. He waved and smiled. Super cute late thirties, maybe older. I peeked in his car a few times and it's clean as a whip. Main house guy is a total letch. Guido. Not joking, *gwee-dough*, like a gangster in the mafia. That's his name. He undresses me with his eyes and totally creeps me out. Anyhow, he told me top floor guy's name is Dave and he's a traveling salesman. Then he did that undressing thing with his eyes and said, 'Dave sells exotic metals.' Ditz, he said it like the word *exotic* was going to turn me on. Anyhow, he looked at me like I was stupid and said, 'Exotic like airplane metal.'" Heidi looked around then whispered, "No shit, I think Guido works for the mob. Anyhow, I know he gets deliveries in the middle of the night. Not sure what. I keep seeing these guys unloading these big blue containers. The next thing I see is some other dude picking them up in a U-Haul. Freaking weird. Why drop them off here? Anyhow, the basement's full of cinderblock rooms with big-ass wood doors. All locked. I tried to open them when I snuck into the basement. Oh, where was I? Anyhow, one day the main house was being repainted and Guido's car was gone. So, I put on hot pants and a tee shirt with no bra and walked right in. Painters got an eyeful and must've thought I was one of Guido's hookers," laughed Heidi.

Maggie softened her initial reaction with a warm smile. Heidi was either nervous or high. Maybe both. Somehow, Maggie resisted the temptation to think in stereotypes and cut through her accumulated ego, shame and social mores. For the first time, Maggie felt another woman's vulnerability as a shared weight. Something they both owned in this white man's world.

At the sound of Sam pulling into their driveway, Maggie turned and looked across the over-zealous white lilac bush hideout. "Oh shoot. Sam and Tekla are home early. Let's have lunch one day. We can talk poetry."

7

You've Come a Long Way, Baby

The truth will set you free, but first it will piss you off.

—Unknown

MARCH 11, 1971 AFTERNOON—Jazzed by the cadence of animated voices and laughter in the high-ceilinged, gym-turned-banquet room at Eastern Michigan University in Ypsilanti, Maggie couldn't remember the last time she'd dressed up and had an entire day just for herself. When she joined the Women's League of Livonia, the last thing she expected was a conference on feminism—or feeling like she belonged.

Maggie watched Violet Johnson, the visiting speaker from the University of Michigan, wend her way between round tables and through sustained applause. Stopping to shake hands or hug a familiar colleague, Dr. Johnson's dark skin, big fro and colorful

African caftan stood in stark contrast to an audience of predominantly white women in mass-produced polyester pants, L. L. Bean cords, and random sightings of Pendleton plaid. An hour earlier, minutes before the carpool driver showed up, Maggie was frowning at her safe-choice reflection in the mirror—black polyester bellbottoms topped by a royal-blue, fur-blend sweater. At the sound of the horn in the driveway, Maggie grabbed her zebra-striped scarf and tied it around her forehead—a jolt of *joie de vivre* for her city-self, or she thought, a *très petit rèbellion!*

Lights dimmed as Dr. Johnson adjusted the microphone and greeted coeds and women leaguers with her trademark, "Women of the human race, put on your sneakers! Our time is NOW. No more debutante balls, starched aprons or standing on the sidelines; today we're in the race to become doctors, lawyers, pilots, scientists, college professors, producers, directors and astronauts. How do we qualify for the race? Look around. We get there on the shoulders of brave women and men who've broken open the starting gates. Feminists, dear sisters, come in both genders and all colors.

"For those of you who think we've achieved equal rights, let's back up this tape. It took one hundred and forty-four years for the United States to give women the right to vote under the Nineteenth Amendment in 1920—fifty years after black men, including freed slaves, were given the right to vote under the Fifteenth. That's another story. But, like it or not, our society is still reeling from the Victorian Age. Crazy as this sounds, Queen Victoria had nine kids in seventeen years. Do the math. That's eighty-one months or six and three-quarter years of pregnancy. Victoria loathed being pregnant, but birth control wasn't an option. Yet, rather than lift the status of women, the Queen—female leader of one of the greatest empires in the world—spent her entire sixty-seven-year reign shackling women's rights and sexuality. Let that sink it. Victoria was the Queen, she could have said no, but she was a lusty woman and she liked 'it.' The "it" no one talked about. Back then, Lady Gough's

Book of Etiquette was required reading for the British Empire. A how-to-handbook for virtue, one of Lady Gough's social commandments was—are you ready—*one must avoid the intolerable proximity of male and female authors on library shelves*. Yes! You heard me right. Books by a man and a woman could not be shelved next to each other unless the authors were married. Imagine, a conjugal shelf life!

"If you think you're against feminism think again. Seriously, think again. Feminism has been vilified as a radical and dangerous threat to civilization. Feminists have been depicted as man-hating menopausal crones, witches and lesbians with nothing better to do. Headlines made fun of women who burned their bras in effigy to push for equal rights, equal pay and fair treatment in the workplace. Did women actually burn their bras? Some did. Yet, the very idea of bra burning made headlines, and this 'smoke signal' helped spread the word. Our rights—to vote, to get credit without our father's or husband's approval, to own real estate and file for divorce—exist because our foremothers were willing to risk ridicule, censure, arrest, imprisonment, forced feeding and institutionalization. We're here today because feminists and suffragettes fought for access to birth control, higher education and decent jobs. Really, Virginia Slims we've come a slim way, not a long way.

Way back, in the second century, Roman Emperor Marcus Aurelius concluded that thoughts are reality. What is our reality? If we think we're less than men, are we? Do we enslave ourselves when we think we need a man to take care of us? I'm not talking trash. This black woman is talking bigotry and a socialized form of slavery. I want us to wake up. Birth control gives us more choices, more freedom, more power. No reason to save our hymen for a husband or think we're incomplete without a man. If being a virgin bride is what we want, let's make it a personal choice. But let's not kick women's lib back to the Victorian Age.

"The first Equal Rights Amendment bill was introduced in 1923, three years after the Suffragettes finally convinced Congress to give us the right to vote. For each of the forty-eight years since 1923, variations of the ERA were presented but failed to gain support in Congresses controlled by men. In 1970, our very own Representative Martha Griffiths finally pushed a bill before Congress for debate. This is the Twentieth Century. Why hasn't Congress supported a bill that gives women equal status to men?

"On March 22nd, the Senate will vote on yet another bill that affirms 'Equality of rights under the law shall not be denied or abridged by the United States or by any State on account of sex.' Look around. This room is filled with creative, smart, talented women who have not achieved equal rights. What are we waiting for, permission? If not, there's still time to write or call your senator and change the course of history." Dr. Johnson scanned the darkened room and took in the silent crowd before she lifted the microphone to her lips and in a slow, articulated whisper said, "Feminism and activism, my beloved sisters, will give us the right to shelve our books however we want."

The assembled roar—cheering, clapping and foot stomping—bounced off the gym's tall cinderblock walls and chicken-wired-windows, rumbling and rebounding with radical hope. Maggie had never seen so many women in one place—the possibilities of feminism, freedom and tribal power felt within their reach.

Cheryl Cummings, president of the Women's League of Livonia, was wearing an elegantly tailored black-watch-plaid Pendleton sheath with black flats. As the next speaker was being introduced, she said, "That's it! I can't take any more of this pagan hype. I've heard enough." Maggie knew Cheryl's formidable power was based on her family's legacy—inheritance, property ownership, political influence and genes that cornered the market on beauty. Local legend claimed Cheryl's long limbs, flawless skin, thick auburn hair and cover-girl face silenced rooms, parted crowds, and left dumbstruck the smartest, most powerful men. With her credentials, being the wife of a small-town mayor must have felt like costume jewelry against a Valentino dress, but her words ignited the coalition of women at 'Table 18: Livonia League.'

"Obvious dike. No lipstick, and as disgusting as this sounds, probably no girdle or bra under that tent," said the first woman who pushed away her untouched lunch.

"Total embarrassment to women. Doctor Johnson, my foot. She looks like a fullback with a ready-made helmet. Why on earth would she worry about birth control? Excuse my French, but who the hell would want her?" said the second woman who'd inhaled the pale salad and pickled beets, leaving her mashed potatoes and meatloaf congealed in gravy.

Jaw clenched, Maggie resisted the shortlist of razor-sharp barbs in her quiver. Instead, her mind's eye focused on Twiggy's emaciated boyish figure on runways, upping the ante that 'one can never be too thin or too rich.' *Maybe, just maybe,* thought Maggie, *these women are starved for something else.*

"So, the message is what? Get a job, work your fingers to the bone, hire someone to raise your kids and lose your husband to a younger woman who wants to keep a house and home? You can bet your sweet biscuit it's not me!" said the third woman who scraped her plate clean and picked through the leftovers.

"The question is what job? No matter what the law says, women with kids are a royal pain in the backside. My husband, Jerry, said, companies aren't in the blankety-blank business of running nursery schools. You know Jerry and his salty language, he can be hilarious. Last week he said, 'The last thing I need is some broad in safety glasses shaking her tail feathers. If I can't hire a white guy—and gotta choose between some darkie and a broad with kids—I'll hire the darkie.' Jerry's right. If the kid gets sick or has a snow day, she misses work. Women need to get off their high horses and make a choice, plain and simple. If women want to work, then don't get married and don't have babies," said the fourth woman whose burgundy shawl set off her pink cheeks and bloodshot eyes.

"Speaking of darkies, what's the proper word these days—Negro, nigra, colored or black? I swear if they spent more time working and less time worrying about what they want to be called, they wouldn't be so dirt poor. Oh, but then they'd have to give up food stamps. Sorry, that dog won't hunt!" said the fifth woman. *Between lips as mean and narrow as the sharp edge of a stiletto*, thought Maggie, in her ever-increasing tendency to turn harsh reality into fiction.

Wide-eyed and grinning from one button-pearl earring to the other, Cheryl said, "You southern belles have the cutest little ole sayings!"

Bile rose in Maggie's throat. Cheryl's comment tanked any effort to turn reality into fiction. And, Maggie's promise to serve as The Eight's social scientist and investigator was losing its cache. Taking a deep breath, Maggie thought about Loretta's advice to stay calm, talk slow and educate. Leaning over the coarse white, commercially laundered and patched tablecloth, Maggie said, "Sundown Towns. That's what people called towns who banned blacks before the 1917 Supreme Court ruled that racial discrimination in housing was illegal. You see, the term Sundown Town comes from old signs at a town's border. Signs like, *Nigger, Don't Let the Sun Set on YOU in Our Town*." Maggie looked up and saw confusion. Cheryl was looking at her with such intensity that she had a momentary lapse before she took a few breaths and said, "In any event, civil rights put some teeth in that old Supreme Court ruling. And, well . . . now all Americans are free to buy property and live where they want . . . including women and blacks." Maggie sat back in her chair and glanced at the women she'd carpooled with. This wasn't the first time she felt like an alien in the States, but the expression of shock, panic and confusion on their carefully powdered faces struck her as sadly comical. Maggie knew she'd gone too far and stretched whatever fragile relationships she'd built. Nodding, she said, "I know, I sometimes get carried away. That's one of the reasons I'm glad we moved to Livonia. A kind, decent, law-abiding city."

Cheryl's emerald eyes, lined and lashed in black, assessed her friends' reactions and level of threat before they turned to pierce Maggie. "My, my, my, what pray tell does that little lecture have to do with dikes telling us how to screw ourselves? Most of us don't want to be drafted or give up our right to alimony. And, in case you haven't noticed, most whites want to live with whites. But then, of course, you know that, or you wouldn't have moved to Livonia."

8

A Stone's Throw

What the mind doesn't understand, it worships or fears.
—Alice Walker

MARCH 11, 1971 EVENING—After stepping out of her black clogs on the utility room's threshold, Maggie plunked down at the kitchen table—her turquoise *paroxysm*. Instead of inviting 'unbidden thoughts or emotion,' she studied the dishes in the drainer from the night before and wondered if she was hungry enough to make a fried egg sandwich for dinner. The conversation on the drive home from the conference was guarded and polite; except for Maggie's non-verbal exchange with Cheryl who narrowed her cat eyes through the rearview mirror. From the cramped middle seat in the third row of Mayor Cumming's forest green Dodge van, Maggie met each of Cheryl's double-down eye scolds with a smile. No surprise when Maggie's house was the first stop.

Without doubt, Maggie's outing with the Women's League underscored her lack of finesse and wild-ass subject-matter transitions. *Time to clean up my act or I'll blow my cover.* Although both hackneyed phrases drove her bonkers, Maggie didn't want to spend the night editing her thoughts or figuring out ways to get on Cheryl's good side. Tonight was a rare gift of time. Tekla was having a sleepover with Maija and Sam was in a closed-door, post-mortem meeting to discuss Jingo's poor showing at the auto show and deal with grim first-quarter results. Sam was sure there'd be layoffs, what he didn't know was how wide or deep.

Temperatures were dropping and rain was turning to sleet as Maggie padded across the copper-colored shag carpet and sat cross-legged on the dining room floor. The bottom drawer of the blonde-veneer buffet cabinet they'd snagged from Clyde and Blanche's basement held The Triad's notes and a rough timeline for The Puzzle. Sam's last six months had been disturbingly tranquil. No threats, no naked women, no time in The Blender. Between the humdrum of suburban life, and the anticipation of the next Puzzle piece shattering the calm, Maggie fully grokked the pitfall of idleness. Both Sam and Clyde were active in the world. She was the idle one, with far too much time to conceive conspiracy theories and think about things that go bump in the night. Months and dozens of reads later, the file of their meeting with Aunt Jo continued to call her name. She didn't know why, but something still nagged her. Maggie pulled out Clyde's handwritten notes from the tape-recording. She started at the beginning.

Q: Where does Jacques get his scratch? Make his money?

A: Anna told me he was a trust fund baby. I don't know anything about his parents, but Jacques acts like he comes from wealth and privilege—someone who's traveled far and wide and knows about different cultures, languages, food.

Maggie remembered holding her breath, hoping Aunt Jo would prove she was on their side. There was something about this answer that put her on edge. It sounded like an ad for a charm school. Aunt Jo had many interesting character traits, but formality with family and friends would never make the list.

Running her finger down the eraser-smudged words on the yellow legal-size pad, Maggie was brought back to the banquet table in the basement of Hope Chapel, a safe and convenient place to meet Aunt Jo and the site of Maggie's second encounter with Sam in late July 1967. She could still picture him, and feel his energy from the row behind hers, during the Freedom Riders' specially called meeting to help post-riot Detroiters who needed shelter, food, income or medical care. That night, away from the conflagration of fear, fire and guns, Maggie and Sam sought each other out, kissed goodnight at Aunt Jo's door and began their story. Skipping through the next few pages, Maggie found the set of questions she was looking for.

Q: When did you first meet Jacques?

A: Not sure. As I told Maggie, Anna and Jacques were dating before she met and married Raymond. Must have been the mid-1930s. Anna seemed deeply in love, but Jacques kept things light and she seemed to take his lead.

Q: Why did you think she was deeply in love? Did she tell you?

A: Hmm. I don't think she told me. It was more how she acted when he was around, more giddy and girlish. That wasn't Anna's style and it surprised me.

Seriously, Maggie thought, *who writes 'hmm?' Did Clyde suspect Aunt Jo was hiding something?*

Q: Why was Jacques in her life? Did she tell you how they met? How often they saw one another?

A: Let me think. Why was Jacques in her life? I guess I assumed they met at some charity event. Don't ask me why I say that. I have no idea. She didn't say and I don't remember asking. It sounded like they spent a lot of time together then would go weeks or months without contact when Jacques traveled. I think she married Raymond about two years after I met Jacques.

Wait a minute, thought Maggie, *did Aunt Jo say ". . . after I met Jacques?"* Did she mean, '. . . after Anna met Jacques?' Aunt Jo didn't answer the question about how Anna met Jacques, but she raised the question of who knew Jacques first. Maggie wondered if she was nitpicking, or maybe her world was so small that everything seemed large—an *Alice In Wonderland* effect?

Q: Did Anna love Raymond?

A: I don't think so.

Q: Did she tell you?

A: No and I didn't ask. They were an odd couple. When I was with them, they seemed pretty uptight. I don't remember them kidding around or touching each other. But, based on our family's MO, uptight would not be unusual.

Q: Did you know Raymond's family?

A: Not personally. He had a huge family and they all pitched in to help their clan buy cars, go to college. Strange, I can't remember meeting anyone on his side of the family. Did you?

(By Maggie: Nope. I was too young to remember, but Issie said she never did. We somehow decided his parents died when he was a baby. Not sure.)

Okay, thought Maggie, *this parenthesis is so not Clyde. How did he come up with this style—a high school course in business writing? Or, was this something he learned in the Army?*

Q: Jo, do you recall what Anna said the last time you spoke with her?

A: Let me think. Um. It was over the phone. Huh.

Maggie was beginning to feel agitated. 'Hmm,' now 'um,' and 'huh.' Okay, maybe Clyde was a stenographer in the war. Did he record and transcribe interrogations? Maggie wondered if he watched when prisoners had their testicles wired to phone lines. What kinds of atrocities are tucked away in his subconscious, collective unconscious, or maybe unconscious memories?

Q: Did the authorities ask you this question?

A: Yes. I'm sure they did.

Q: Do you remember what you said?

A: Yes. I said I didn't remember.

Q: Did you remember then or did you not remember?

A: I think I remembered, but I didn't want to tell the authorities anything that would get them in trouble.

Q: Does that mean you had information that might get them in trouble?

A: At the time I didn't know.

(By Maggie: Aunt Jo, please try to remember.)

Maggie thought, *another parenthesis. How did I miss these before? Do we see what we think we see? What if we think we know each other when we don't really know each other at all?*

A: What I remember is Anna saying not to worry if the trip turns out to be a little longer than she thought. I asked what she meant and she said something like, 'we've got work to do on one of the islands before we head to Halifax.' I had no idea they were going to Halifax much less the name of the island they planned to stop by. It was a busy time in my life. I was unbelievably self-centered . . . young, in love, starting a career. My guess is I was only half listening.

Maggie dropped the legal pad and said, "Holy crap!"

Maggie couldn't shake the bees from her head. Not this time. Sam was the only one she trusted with this information and there was no way to reach him. Maggie thought a call to wish Tekla 'sweet dreams' would help her recalibrate. Not so. Once she hung up, she immediately flashed back to Aunt Jo's words.

After changing into her new leopard-print pajamas, Maggie thought about the night she modeled them for Sam and confessed that animal prints made her feel strong and feral. In response, he made a low growl then chased her through the house on tiptoes, his fingers curving and tongue quietly lapping the air to avoid waking Tekla. Maggie's soundless, open-mouthed laughter and waving arms added to the charm, like a long-lost clip from a Charlie Chaplin montage. *Was that the last time they'd made love?*

Giving into hunger, Maggie fixed herself a cup of Campbell's tomato soup and picked up *The Godfather* by Mario Puzo for the tenth time. Once again, she wondered why she couldn't find the hook that made this a best seller. The characters were interesting, if not lovable, but way too much testosterone, anger and violence. Maggie left the light on over the sink, so Sam could find his way, but clicked off the overheads as she headed for their bedroom.

The sound of glass breaking and a loud clunk in the kitchen brought Maggie to her knees as she crawled into the unlit bedroom and quietly closed the door. She could barely breathe and her heart was beating like a double-count run on a snare drum. Standing up on her knees, she inched the tall antique dresser on crooked wheels against the door, then flung her body across the double bed to the front window. Peering out, she saw taillights fishtailing away from the gravel shoulder on Six Mile. Maggie couldn't make out the model of the four-door sedan or its color. Maybe it was a diversion. Was there someone else in the house? Slowing her breath and willing all her senses to be on alert, Maggie listened to the furnace in the utility room pumping heat and thought she heard a faucet dripping in the bathroom. It was ten minutes after ten and she decided she'd wait and listen until ten thirty before she left the bedroom to make a call. If she heard someone in the house, Maggie's backup plan was to escape through the front bedroom window and sneak into their Canadian neighbor's yard. If there were no lights on in the house, she'd try the old garage studio in the back. *Oh, god,* she thought, *what if he is an ax murderer?*

At ten twenty-five, Maggie was getting ready to move the dresser away from the door when she heard footsteps. Scrambling across the top of the bed, Maggie unlatched the locks and began pushing up the window. Stuck. She slid down on her back and used the heel of her foot to push up on the top casing of the window. No movement. The footsteps on the shag rug were faint, but Maggie was sure they belonged to a man. The handle of the door turned and Maggie, still on her back, used both heels trying to force the impossibly stuck, now jammed window. Then, the intruder slammed his body against the blocked door. The dresser creaked. Frantic, Maggie's heels began to jackhammer the narrow wood frame.

"Maggie are you there? Are you okay? Oh, god, Maggie, someone pitched a rock through the kitchen window. Tell me you're okay." It was Sam.

Maggie's heart was beating so fast she couldn't catch her breath or find words. She crawled across the bed and crab-walked to the dresser. Maggie knocked on the door and whispered, "Wait. I'm okay. Just wait."

9

The Little Death

What the light reveals is danger, and what it demands is faith.
—James Baldwin

MARCH 12, 1971—Adrenalin shot through Maggie's veins at the speed of sound. Someone was rattling around the kitchen before sun from the half-closed venetian blind raised her lids—before the aroma of coffee slowed her racing heart, unclenched her fists and gave way to a sigh.

Last night she and Sam spent hours looking under furniture, checking the closets, garage, and attic; taking flash photos of foot and tire tracks in the driveway and footprints below the kitchen window. One of the few remaining unpacked boxes of books in the attic was dumped so they could use the cardboard to cover the broken window. Maggie had never seen Sam so angry and agitated. Although tempted to blame this on 'a nasty prank by one of the girls who'd gotten into her cups,' Maggie knew those words wouldn't make it past the first vowel. There was no way to rewrite this ugly attack into harmless fiction. They were both shaken.

Maggie grabbed her well-worn copy of Baldwin's *Nothing Personal*, slipped on her black terrycloth mules and headed into the kitchen. Sam met her with a long, quiet, cheek-to-cheek, rocking hug—the kind of embrace that signals the loss of innocence. Not the drop-to-the-knees kind of hug after Dr. King's assassination or the Kent State Massacre. More like the day the silent majority elected Nixon and chose money, war and black gold over morality, peace and social justice.

Janis Joplin was singing her previously recorded, now posthumous hit *Me and Bobby McGee* over the transistor radio. To muffle their conversations, Maggie and Sam had test-taped conversations about the weather and traffic congestion with the radio at different locations and volume settings. If the radio was between them on the kitchen table, with the volume set at the halfway point, it garbled their words and gave them some sense of privacy. As Joplin sang 'freedom's just another word for nothing left to lose,' Maggie wondered how close they were to that sweet spot.

"Mag, I've been thinking about this all night. We have to call the cops. I don't give a rip about the mayor's trust-fund wife or the women's league of the highest holiest grail. This is about our family and our home. We can't blow this off."

"No way I'm blowing this off. I was terrified! I thought I was going to die, that I'd never see you and Tekla again. But, freaked as I was, still am, I don't want us to go berserk and make things worse. Give me a minute to read you a passage from Baldwin," Maggie turned off the radio—stood up, flipped the book open to its bookmark, cleared her throat—then began to read and gesture as if she was reciting poetry at an open mic.

> *"It has always been much easier (because it has always seemed much safer) to give a name to the evil without than to locate the terror within . . . And this terror has something to do with that irreducible gap between the self one invents . . . a provisional self . . . and the undiscoverable self which always has the power to blow the provisional self to bits."*

Each syllable was read as if the beauty and thought behind each word had the power to transcend terror, real or imagined. For a few minutes they listened to the furnace hum and a small elm brush the top of the roof. At times like this, when Maggie revealed her deep, complex, French-Canadian self, Sam wanted to follow her into another dimension. But, his simple, rational Finnish self always kicked in.

Sam turned the radio back on and checked the volume setting before saying, "My bright, beautiful, esoteric Maggie, I get that you want us to come from love and strength, not fear. But, this isn't about our spiritual evolution. Our shattered window is about ignorance and hate. The note wrapped around the rock said, 'nigger lovers go home.' There's nothing mysterious about that. It's racist and carries an obvious threat of more violence. Singing *Kumbaya* is not in the cards. We've got to run a full-court press—file a report with the cops, turn this house into Fort Knox and teach you how to use my gun."

"Sam, give me a break here. I'm not asking anyone to sing *Kumbaya*. Baldwin's message is about *not* going ape shit and being smarter than a yo-yo. We're not stupid or evil enough to do this with brute force. Besides, there's no way we're keeping a gun in our house. I sure as hell won't pull the trigger."

"Tell me. What if this happens again—when I'm not here and Tekla's watching Sesame Street—how will you protect her?"

"Samuelsan, we'll do smart things; turn our house into Fort Knox, nail down a getaway and communication plan, learn judo."

Sam raised his eyebrows and shook his head. "You're kidding. Judo? For women?"

"Yep. I'll find someone."

"Okay, Mag. For now, I'll keep the gun in my office. But, we're going to act like ordinary Americans who call the cops when someone sends a rock through the window and threatens their family. We don't cower. If this *was* the mayor's call to some lackey to scare us off, and we don't file a report, we might as well turn tail and head back to Detroit right now." Sam scribbled a note on the back of a Detroit Edison bill and slid the envelope across the table:

NOT OFFICE. I'll keep the gun in my car. Let's see if anyone is listening.

Maggie couldn't help but smile. Just like Sam to downplay his compromise by turning it into a game or doing something covert. "So, Mr. Tervo, you think you can buy me off by agreeing to a few judo lessons?"

"Not even close, Mrs. Tervo. I just thank my lucky stars when you throw me a few crumbs and help me keep my dignity."

When Maggie slapped Sam's hand and said, 'gimme five,' he grabbed it and made a low growl. Maggie pulled away and went running through the house in her leopard-print pajamas. This time, she was laughing out loud and swinging her arms like a whirlygig. Sam in close pursuit, stomped his feet, curled his hands and growled with gargantuan force as he chased her into his lair.

Maggie was stripping off her pajamas when Sam reached the bedroom. She grabbed him by the front of his tee shirt, pulled him down on the bed and wrapped her legs around his waist. He tried to pull off his red and gray plaid flannel pajama bottoms, but Maggie wasn't waiting, her hands were moving. The energy was frantic, tormented, as if they'd been separated for months, or as if this was the last time they'd have to couple, connect and capture each other's image, sound, scent, touch. Maggie flashed on urban legends that claimed the death of a close family member or good friend led to this kind of crazed sex—a way to ritualize the celebration of cheating death. Ah, but for the French, orgasm itself was *la petite mort*—the little death.

The Livonia Police Department occupied a modern, one-story tan brick structure at the back of a lot that was far too big for the building's footprint and made up for it by paving an acre of land. Maggie imagined a city planner who'd spent most of his childhood frustrated because there was never enough space to sort the parts and assemble his next Erector Set crane, bridge or skyscraper.

Earlier, Maggie accused Sam of lewd and unusual duress when his lovemaking weakened her resistance to file the police report. To satisfy any anticipated arguments, Sam said he'd ask his mother to keep Tekla until he got off work, find someone to replace the window glass, and give Clyde a heads up. Although Sam knew far more than he wanted about the Women's League, Maggie hadn't said word one about Aunt Jo's interview or asked Sam about Jingo's plans for a layoff. Issie always said bad news came in threes. If so, Maggie thought the red flags in Aunt Jo's interview, Jingo's layoffs and the airborne rock and racist threat were mother lodes.

Grabbing the brown paper lunch bag off the front seat, Maggie exited the car as if a camera was recording every movement. Taking a deep breath, she stood and surveyed the near-empty parking lot. Then, pulled her shoulders back, swung her arms and walked like someone with a full calendar.

A young, ruddy-skinned, red-haired, uniformed and badged policeman, Officer Michael Murphy, was at the reception desk. Based on the somber colors in the empty lobby, Maggie was glad she wore her nondescript, still-too-tight tan cords, with a blue button-down under a navy crewneck sweater.

"May I help you?"

"Yes, please. My name's Maggie Soulier and I live on Six Mile and . . ."

"Miss or Missus Soulier?"

"Missus. I mean Mrs. Tervo. Soulier's my birth name."

"You mean your maiden name?"

"Tervo's my married name."

"You're sure?"

"Yes, just a little unnerved."

"Mrs. Tervo, before you give me any information, what's your purpose today?"

"I'd like to report an incident."

"Okay. An accident, a missing person's report, a crime?"

"Someone hurled a rock through our kitchen window last night."

"And you're reporting it to the police because?"

"Because it had a note attached to it with a threat."

"Do you have any teenagers living in your house?"

"No. Just me, my husband and our eighteen-month-old daughter."

"Any idea who tossed this stone?"

"No. But my sense is others may have had this same experience and thought, well we thought, you might be able to identify the writing or fingerprints from the note."

"I think *we've* been reading too many who-done-it mysteries. Our department doesn't have the time or workforce to chase stone throwers. Tell me about the threat. Do you have the note with you?"

Maggie held up the paper bag before she dropped it on the metal desk with a distinct thud and said, "Yes, I have the ROCK and the note."

"Let's do this, little lady. You take a seat, and I'll see if one of the detectives has time to see you."

Nailed for her passive-aggressive behavior, Maggie realized she couldn't afford to piss off anyone else. But halfway through that thought, she gave in to an irresistible urge to scan the empty lobby before she replied, "Got it."

After sitting down on one of the beige Naugahyde chairs, Maggie crossed and uncrossed her legs five times before she commanded herself to sit still. *What was Sam thinking? Of course, they're not going to investigate something like this. Worse, it will bring unwanted attention—make it harder for The Eights to show up in Livonia and short-circuit any attempts to integrate the burbs.* Taking a deep breath and clearing her head, she flagged that thought, *or would it?*

Twenty tedious, and likely disciplinary, minutes passed before Officer Murphy called her name.

"Mrs. Tervo, Detective Harris will see you now. If you hit the buzzer to the right of the door, someone will let you in." Maggie was sure Officer Murphy smirked, but she nodded her head and kept her retorts to herself.

After buzzing her in, the clerk slid open a bulletproof window and pointed his finger to a metal folding chair along a barefaced wall with a drinking fountain. Maggie had to curb a delicious impulse to throw herself against the wall as if she was in a criminal lineup. Instead, she sat on the cold, hard chair and listened to the muffled percussion of typewriters, Xerox copiers, ten-key adding machines and telephones—heightening her sense of isolation, lack of industry, and outsider status.

After ten minutes, a tall, lanky, good-looking guy, in a gray suit with well-worn elbows, walked up to Maggie and said, "Mrs. Tervo, Detective Harris. My apologies. I thought we'd have time to talk, but I just got called back to the courthouse. Time for the hot seat! I'll keep the stone and note on my desk and give you a call tomorrow."

Before Maggie could reply, he was out the door. Digging in her purse for the car keys, she heard the clerk slide the window open. "Mrs. Tervo, do you need an absence excuse for your boss?"

Maggie corked her sneer before it spread across her face. "No, but thanks for asking. I lost my job when I got pregnant. Next time,

I'll look for a boss who treats me like a man." Maggie saw the clerk's confusion but didn't try to explain herself. She smiled and thought, *he knows, men know.*

"Hey, Mag, I'm on a short leash, another closed-door session on layoffs. Just wanted to let you know I've got the window guy set up to replace the glass on Monday. He doesn't work weekends and said we could tape a garbage bag on the inside of the window to keep the cold out. Bad news is there's no way I can pick up Tekla before six. But, there's a slight chance I can still make The Eights' meeting at Clyde's. You up for bringing Tekla with you?"

"I'm up for not being home by myself. I'll pick up Tekla and head to Clyde's. We need to talk, but it can wait."

"How did the police report go?"

"On its way."

"Got it. When I know more about my schedule, I'll give Clyde a call. If I don't make it to The Eights' meeting, why don't you and Tekla spend the night with Ma."

"I'd rather stay in town, Aunt Jo's or Loretta's. I'll let Clyde know."

"Okay, babe. We good?"

"Yep. We're good."

Maggie wished The Triad had come up with another way to say life was clicking along without mind-altering, psychotropic drugs, hookers and boogiemen. The word 'good' was so banal, which is exactly why they picked it. If things weren't good, she, Sam or Clyde would use the words 'fine, see you.' The word 'fine' meant things were off kilter, menacing. 'See you' meant at Big Boys with the appointed time based on the number of letters in the next word. See you *tonight* was seven o'clock tonight; see you *tomorrow* meant eight o'clock tonight; see you *later* by either person was 'wait for me to call you again or show up at your front door.' So far, no one had used a response other than 'good.' It wasn't because things were good. It was because they were still waiting for the sky to fall, or the other shoe to drop, or like Washington Irving's *Legend of Sleepy Hollow*, watching to see if the headless horseman finds his head. *Of course, that's the problem with being targeted* thought Maggie—*always on defense, waiting for someone else to make the next move. Why couldn't they take the offense, make the next play—throw that pigskin into the end zone, slam that puck into the net? Sam's wrong; we do cower.*

Only three short blocks from Grand River Avenue, Maija's house was in the middle of Farmington, a small, bustling suburban downtown that grew up around her two-bedroom red brick bungalow. Sidewalks led to restaurants, parks, schools, churches and town fairs. No gravel shoulders or speeding eighteen-wheelers. Maggie wished they'd landed in Farmington. As she pulled into the driveway, she saw Maija holding Tekla behind the storm door. Maggie jumped out and ran up the porch steps. When she opened the door, Tekla buried her head in Maija's shoulder and began to whimper.

"Hey, pumpkin girl. What's the matter?"

Maija kissed Maggie on the cheek and moved into the living room. "Oh my, these second molars are having a hard time breaking through and she's cranky as hell. Neither of us got any sleep and you might want me to keep her if you're going to Clyde's. Those boys can get a little rough, and I'm here to tell you she's not in the mood for teasing.

"Come here Moonwalker. Let me hold you."

Maija attempted to move Tekla off her shoulder, but Tekla clung to Maija and began to wail. Maggie, surprised and a little embarrassed by tears welling up in her own eyes, headed into the kitchen. Taking a deep breath, she wiped her tears with the back of her hand and called, "How about a tea party? Just Tekla, Maija and

Maggie! I bet Maija has some cookies in this cookie jar. What kind of cookies, Moonwalker?"

Kicking wildly to execute a slide down Maija's front side, Tekla race-walked head first into the kitchen in her heavy pink-fleeced footy pajamas—dark blond hair standing on end from static electricity with drool streaking her chin. Without hesitation, Tekla hung from the edge of the counter holding the teddy bear cookie jar and attempted to find a foothold on the cupboards. Maggie lifted her up and nuzzled her before sitting her on the counter.

"Works every time!" laughed Maija. "Oh yeah, before I forget, Sam told me someone threw a rock at your kitchen window last night and you might want to stay until he gets off work."

"That would be nice, but I need to talk to Clyde, and depending on traffic, I might stop by Aunt Jo's. She'll want some Moonwalker time. As to the rock, I hope it was just some prank. I sure don't want to run scared."

"What I don't get is why anyone thinks you or Sam are nigger lovers. I mean, seriously. You like Negroes, but you aren't like Kenny who risks everything to date one. Now if Kenny got a rock through his window, I'd say he deserved it. But not you or Sam! Good grief. What's the world coming to? Look what happened at Kent State. Good thing Nixon's president. We could use a little more law and order."

As much as Maggie wanted to grab Tekla and flee to the inner city, it made no sense. Maija's friends and neighbors *are* the silent majority; she isn't interested in politics, she just wants to belong. Besides, it would be harebrained to take Tekla out when she's running a low fever and her gums are red and tender. Instead, Maggie accepted Maija's offer to keep Tekla—showed her how to rub whiskey on Tekla's gums, gave her Clyde's number, and promised she or Sam would be back by eleven to take over.

Before she left, Maggie called Angelo's to see if she could catch Clyde before he headed home.

"Angelo's Restaurant and Pizzeria. May I help you?"

"Hey, Angelo, this is Maggie. What's up?"

"Maggie? I used to know a Maggie. Good friend, but you know how that goes. Falls in love, gets married, has a baby and bingo bango, she goes missing."

"Huh. I used to work for a guy named Angelo who owned a pizzeria. He was a serial curmudgeon who sounds a lot like you. Could be you. In fact, I'm pretty sure he's you."

"Gigs up! How's my Maggie?"

"Doing good! You?"

"Not so good. Goddamn city is taking its last gasp and this pop stand is on life support. My business plan calls for two Super Bowls a year, but that ain't gonna happen. Best bet is to stir up one major riot a year to keep the ovens burning."

"I always suspected you were one of those money-grubber, anarchist, activist jocks. Is Clyde there?"

"Ha! I resemble the money-grubber anarchist, not the activist jock. These days my only exercise is pulling the arm on the La-Z-Boy. Let me take Clyde off the clock for a few minutes, then back to the coal mines. Don't be a stranger! We named a pizza after you—*Maggie*, a small pepperoni with black and green olives."

"Hey, Maggie!"

"Hey, Clyde! Angelo threatened to take you off the clock so I'll talk fast. Any chance Sam and I can grab some time after The Eights meeting?"

"Sure. How's it going?"

"Fine, Clyde. We're doing fine. See you later."

As Maggie backed out of the driveway, Tekla was flattened against the inside of the storm door—tears streaming, snot running, fists banging, mouth bellowing in wordless denouncement of being left behind. Maggie wanted to run back in. Instead, she drove a few blocks, parked along the curb and cried like a two-year-old.

10

Fire and Rain

Stop The Robberies, Enjoy Safe Streets, is better known by its acronym STRESS. The Detroit Police Department promotes it as 'an elite, clandestine, roaming, safety unit.' To the black community, STRESS is an experiment in terror, an execution squad. One of the undercover officers recently assigned to this unit has killed a number of black men in his short career, most unarmed. Vilified by blacks and renowned by fellow cops, both sides call him Mr. STRESS.

—Detroit Weekly

MARCH 12, 1971, EVENING—Cars lined the street in front of Clyde and Blanche's house, evidence of the post-war 'two cars in every garage' promise that led to increased auto sales, new highways and traffic jams. Dirty snow and mud clung to tires and wheel wells, leaving a series of Rorschach inkblots on the street, while footprints of different shapes and sizes on the sidewalk led the way to the

Webster's once shiny black door. Temperatures were dropping fast and roads were beginning to ice up. Watching her breath crystallize in the air, Maggie decided to let go of any guilt for leaving Tekla in a warm, comfy home with storybooks and a cookie jar.

Maggie was famished. Other than two stale Fig Newton's from Maija's cookie jar, she hadn't eaten all day. The adrenalin rush that kept her moving had vaporized with her tears.

"Hey, Blanche, any chance I can raid the kitchen? I'll take anything."

"Sure, baby girl. You want a PB&J? I'm not doing pigs-in-the-blanket tonight. I forgot the pigs."

"Sounds great. I'll get it."

"Nope, you sit tight and tell me what's going on. My kids say I'm the best PB&J maker in the world," Blanche laughed. "That's because I get so much practice. Give me two minutes."

Blanche pulled out a Ball canning jar filled with a swirl of purple and tan, dipped a narrow spatula in the mixture and spread it on two slices of Wonder Bread. "Voila! I decided I'd mix peanut butter and grape jelly together in one jar to make my life easier. I was thinking I should patent something like this, but who has time to patent with our wrecking crew?"

"Seriously, Blanche, you have to patent this! What about using hyphens and calling it 'Lunch-In-A-Jar' or 'Once-In-A-Jar?' You know what Plato said about necessity being the mother of invention. That's because mothers are needier and more inventive. If they've got a job, they need to cover twenty-four hours of work in less than six. I swear I had no idea how much time one mostly-sweet toddler would take." Maggie shook her head, laughed and said, "I can't shake this image of Tekla running around the hood, building rafts and playing drums in a garage band!"

"Yep. Moonwalker's just like her mama, strong and sassy!" Blanche put the lid on her invention and seemed lost in thought for a few beats. Her dark brown eyes were moist as she looked up, smiled and said, "No Maggie, that one will be running the hood, leading the band and patenting her rafts."

Clyde stuck his head in the kitchen and said, "Time to get started. Everyone's freaked about driving home in this mess, so we need to get going and finish early."

Willie was sitting at the titular second-head of the table, with an empty side chair waiting for Sam. Without the usual jousting for position, muscle flexing and name-calling among Clyde, Sam and Willie, the room felt listless. The Eights had been meeting two years now and the men always started these meetings with locker-room banter. Blanche once joked she knew the meeting was ready to start when she heard Clyde call Sam a dickhead.

Although the furnace was running non-stop, Webster's old collie Marmalade was pressed against the only heating vent in the dining room, and damp, cold air from the Michigan basement was working its way through the floorboards. Clyde, at the official head of the table, cleared his throat and waded through a short list of actions by the NAACP and Southern Christian Leadership Conference before moving into deeper waters.

"Some of you may have heard that The Wilmington Ten, in North Carolina—a civil rights group like The Eights—have been charged for inciting a riot and the death of two people early last month. No details yet, but we need to be all over that junkyard dog. On February twenty-fifth, Nixon finally met with members of the Congressional Black Caucus and appointed a White House Panel to study their recommendations. As you know, these kinds of studies can take longer than a Ph.D. so let me know if you get wind of anything. And, if you haven't read *The Detroit Weekly* today, do it. The STRESS Unit got some positive press when the *Weekly* reported both blacks and fellow cops call the dick with the most notches on his belt, Mr. Stress. This creep gets his rocks off shooting unarmed blacks. If we stroke his ego by calling him Mr. Stress, we might as well pull the damn trigger. No more. Let's get this out to the streets."

"STRESS Unit my ass—Jim Crow with a shiny new handle keeping us down and dirty in the ghetto," said Willie.

"Got that right, Mr. Johnson," said Robin. "Jim Crow will be rearing his ugly head on the moon if we don't stop shucking and jiving. Time to get organized, register voters, run for office and get out the votes. About time Detroit had a black mayor."

"Amen to that," said Loretta, "a black, woman mayor."

"If pigs could fly," Stella laughed.

"Look at Indira Gandhi," said Blanche.

"Or, Barbara Jordan," said Robin.

"If we dare to dream it," said Clyde. "On another playing field, Leroy Satchel Paige was nominated for the Baseball Hall of Fame. Not only is he the first player from the Negro League to be nominated, he's also the first black pitcher in the American League to be honored." Clyde whistled, shook his head and said, "Gee willakers, Andy! Imagine some darkie smart enough to make that little white sphere dance over home plate.

"Just now, when I said *darkie,* I wasn't being precious. Blanche and I are done saying n-i-g-g-e-r in this house. Free speech and all, we don't help ourselves by thinking it's black jive. Kind of like calling a serial killer Mr. Stress—we're shoveling coal into the burning fire of racism when we call each other n-i-g-g-e-r."

"I hear you. I cringe every time I hear that word. But—and this is a big ass but—I'm not sure it's a bad thing. I think words carry more power when they're forbidden. The first few times I heard the word Gestapo it scared the bejesus out of me. Later, I began to see it was just a word that meant a bunch of psycho-criminals who wanted the world to look like them. When I first said the word fuck, it made me feel like a gangsta. Now it's nothing. So, here's the rub, your boys are going to hear the word nigger on the streets. Maybe it won't hurt so bad if they've had the chance to say it, put it under a microscope and see it for what it is," said Loretta.

"Loretta's got a good point. I'm not sure banning words makes us smarter or kinder. Kids are better off if they learn how to deal with ignorance and racism. Not to say they don't need to learn how to be kind and respectful, but it helps to know the contrast between crude and kind," said Stella.

Willie looked around the room, shook his head and said, "What the fuck? You think you can deep-six the word nigger and pretend it'll change the petrified minds of Jim Crow and the silent majority? Your boys got to hear the word from you and know they can talk to you about anything. I was five when some peckerwoods threw stones at me and called me nigger. I was scared shitless. My mama was twelve when a redneck drifter, peddling vegetable seeds, talked her into meeting him in the neighbor's barn one night to show her his world globe. Every time I look in a mirror and see my sorry-ass blue eyes, I want to kill him. I had no dad. So, you listen up. The word nigger is not some fucking impolite, bad word. The word nigger enslaved entire nations and turned black men, women and children into cargo—packed on slave ships, like boxes of nails, and sold to the highest bidder. If they got sick or died, they were tossed over the side of the ship and written off as lost goods. The word nigger is a lightning rod, but when we wipe the floor with it, it loses its shine, little by little, it loses its shine."

Everyone's eyes were fixed on Willie. As long as they'd known one another, no one had asked him about his blue eyes or his family. Maggie thought it was because so many blacks had ancestors who were impregnated by white slave owners, bosses and landlords, that it was a given. The horror of that 'given' had not shred her heart the way it did tonight—through Willie's blue eyes, broken heart and the absolute terror his twelve-year-old mother endured.

Clyde put his hands together as if he was going to pray and said, "Thank you for kicking down my door with the unbearable pain and razor-sharp edges of truth. The last thing Blanche and I want to do is polish that truth. Don't let me go to sleep again. Okay,

Maggie, what's the buzz in Livonia these days? Are they ready for a little color?"

After Maggie's tale about the Woman's League at the Feminist Conference, the energy and chatter at Clyde's dining room table jumped an octave and Loretta did her fist-pumping dance. Maggie knew Loretta was one of Violet Johnson's biggest fans. A black woman with a doctorate was one thing; a black feminist revolutionary was far beyond any adjective's reach.

When Loretta sat down, Maggie said, "The bad news is someone pitched a rock through our kitchen window when I was on my way to bed last night. I barricaded myself in the bedroom until Sam showed up and scared the crap out of me by trying to force the door open. The note on the rock said 'n-i-g-g-e-r lovers go home.'"

Sleet began to pummel the dining room windows like a machine gun, and the room grew colder.

"Damn, Maggie. Sorry you had to go through that. Too much to ask anyone, and it's not your fight. You got to do what you got to do. I know, because Kenny's been ostracized and harassed by most of his so-called-friends and the guys at the shop because he dates me. I have no idea why he stays. No one would blame you for checking out."

"Oh, Stella, the last thing I want is to sit on my lily-white ass and watch the world go by. What would that say about me? I want to stop the craziness of people who try to catalog and separate us by color, gender, religion and income as if we're part of some human Dewey Decimal System."

"Listen up and listen up good. First of all, and I told you this before, you've got the blackest ass I've ever seen on a white girl. That's a compliment. Second, if you and Sam ever, and I mean ever, feel the least bit threatened by what's going on, you get your selves and Moonwalker in your car and head this way. You can stay with me, move in if you want," said Loretta.

"Same with us," said Robin.

"And, if Sam needs help from the dicks or the dons, you tell that sorry husband of yours to call me," said Willie.

Surrounded by friends who had her back, Maggie began to shake off the weight of doom. Clyde smiled and nodded his head as if he understood the quick shiver of her torso. One smile, one nod from someone she'd always loved and trusted, and Maggie knew intuition counted when nothing else made sense.

While Maggie was at the door hugging goodnights, Blanche moved upstairs to the converted attic, now bedroom/playroom, to wrangle the wrecking crew into pajamas and Clyde left for the kitchen to catch the phone.

Maggie was shutting the door against an arctic blast when Clyde walked in. His expression held her like a vise. "Maija's on the phone. Tekla's fine, but Sam was in an accident on his way home from work. She isn't sure of the details but thinks he slid off the road into a ravine. An ambulance took him to St. Mary's. When the cops didn't find you at home, they called Maija. She said she's okay to wait until after you see Sam. Do you want to talk to her now or after we get to the hospital?"

During the three-breath pause, Clyde lost himself in pantomime as Maggie mentally scrolled through the message, lengthened her spine, and strode into the kitchen. From the living room, Clyde heard Maggie say, "I know, I know. That's good, he's conscious. I'm sure he'll be okay. We don't want to scare Tekla. If she hears you crying, she'll worry. Yes, we can be strong together, you and me and Tekla. I know. Sam's a tough Finn, a true *Suomalainen*. We're good. We can do this if we don't get scared. I know. We've got all the courage we need. Yes, *sisu!* Clyde said he'd take me to the hospital. Yep. We'll be careful. Sure. I'll call you after I see Sam. Try to get some sleep while you can. I know. Love you, too."

Clyde refused to let Maggie follow him to Livonia in her car. The roads were covered in black ice and visibility was next to nothing. Blanche pulled out some warm scarves, mittens and blankets; filled two thermoses with black coffee; and packed a small lunchbox with crackers, PB&J, bandages and a small flashlight just in case. And, Clyde put two large sandbags, a small shovel and heavy work gloves on top of a pair of snow chains in the trunk in case they got stuck—survival skills they learned in Jack & Jill Clubs because blacks were banned from joining the Scouts. With dry weather, it was an easy twenty-minute drive. Tonight they faced a blizzard; anything could happen. Frantic with worry, Maggie knew she had way too much at stake to indulge in fear. Right now, she had to stay focused and strong—put on her sneakers and get ready for the next lap.

11

The Blizzard

I felt a cleaving in my mind, as if my brain had split; I tried to match it, seam by seam, but could not make them fit.

—Emily Dickinson

MARCH 12, 1971, NIGHT—Maggie pulled her navy wool pea coat tight and wrapped one of the blankets over her lap. The heater in Clyde's old Chevy was working overtime, but the cold was holding its own. With the sleet, snow, and starless night—the near-empty roads framed a post-apocalypse scene through the windshield fog.

"Hey, Maggie, you okay? Warm enough?"

"I've got a bad feeling about this. Sam's a good driver. I don't believe this was an accident."

"Come on, Ms. Maggie, take a look. Good drivers or not, these cars are yeehawing down toboggan slides. Flying off the road in this mess would be normal."

"Not after last night. The rock through our window wasn't normal. No doubt I freaked out some women at the conference, not to mention the mayor's wife. Think about it. After my wild-ass monologue on sundown towns, and forty-five minutes of eye scolding in the car, she drops me off. A few hours later someone throws a rock through our window. I file a report. Now, Sam careens off the road and ends up in the hospital. You tell me why your antenna isn't up."

"Talk to me, Maggie. What's going on? You and Sam wanted to see me after the meeting. What was that about?"

"Last night, before the rock, I went through the notes we had on Aunt Jo's interview because something kept nagging me and I didn't know what. Turned out to be two different things. The first had to do with how you wrote up the notes. The second had to do with Aunt Jo's answers and . . ."

The car began to skid out of control as it reached the top of an overpass. Vehicles were spinning and sliding in some grotesque display of centrifugal force run-amok. Clyde's profile tensed as he pumped the brakes and kept the steering wheel from turning. Maggie stifled a scream before she downshifted into a chasm of ice-cold clarity—her lifelong adaptation to threats. Seconds seemed like minutes seemed like quarter-hours as they whizzed in slow motion past panicked drivers and bobsledded through the pile-up of rubber and steel. When they reached the other side of the overpass, Maggie let go of her captive breath and said, "Holy mother of god. I thought we were dead."

Clyde looked across the front seat and saw the whites of Maggie's eyes in the ambient light from the dash. The car was moving at twenty miles per hour when he loosened his grip on the wheel. "Cheated death again, Ms. Maggie. You okay?"

"I think so. Do you want me to tell you what I found?"

"I do. But, right now, I need to focus on the road. We'll talk later. I promise."

Maggie looked at Clyde's shadow. He had Sam's same habit of clenching and jutting his jaw when he took charge as if pointing the way, or signaling other homo sapiens to stay the hell out of his way.

Although St. Mary's Hospital sign was poorly lit, it was a welcome beacon after their near-crash experience. When Clyde drove up to the ER, Maggie was brought back to the night Tekla was born and Neil Armstrong made his giant leap for mankind. Then, the ER was practically empty because everyone was trying to catch the moon shot from the nearest TV. Tonight, the ER was lit with fluorescent lights and bustling sound. Weather warriors—broken, wounded and bleeding—filled the corridors. Clyde was stopped at the entrance by a guard who asked to see his ID. Maggie got in line at the reception desk.

"May I help you?"

"Yes, please. My husband, Sam Tervo, was brought in by ambulance this evening."

The volunteer candy striper said, "I think you just missed him." Running her pink polished index finger down the blue-lined paper log, she said, "Yes, here he is. Samuel Tervo. He was transferred to Detroit General, the old Detroit Receiving, about ten minutes ago."

"Transferred? What's wrong? Why did you transfer him?"

"Oh, it wasn't us. Two police officers showed up with paperwork to transfer him to Detroit because we don't have a prison ward here."

Maggie looked around and felt a tremble start in her knees. The noise in the ER faded, lights dimmed and her voice echoed in the void. "No. You must be confused. Sam, his name is Sam Tervo. His car slid off the road. It was an accident. He wasn't committing a crime. Did I say Sam? Try Samuel. Samuel Tervo."

Keeping her eyes on Maggie, the clerk backed her chair away from the reception desk. "I'm sorry, Mrs. Tervo. I remember your husband's platinum hair when he was brought in—it matched his Finnish name. After my supervisor signed off on the transfer,

I opened the door for the gurney and watched the police help load him into an ambulance."

"What police? Where were they from? Did you check their credentials?" Maggie demanded.

"I'm sorry. What do you mean?"

"Were the police from Livonia, Detroit, Farmington? Where? Did you check their ID? Was there a name on the ambulance?"

"Mrs. Tervo, there's no need to raise your voice. You're scaring the patients. Let me find the supervisor. Please take a seat."

When Maggie sat down, she looked around. Clyde wasn't in the waiting room. The guard at the door was gone.

"Mrs. Tervo? I'm Sister Mary Margaret. The clerk says you're upset. What seems to be the problem?"

"The problem?" Maggie looked into the tired, blue, bloodshot eyes of a woman encased in a penguin outfit—all black with a starched white wimple and coif helmet under yards and yards of draped black serge. Maggie's own frame seemed weighted down by the habit. She wanted to sink to her knees, kiss the nun's hem and ask for mercy. Instead, she said, "My husband, Samuel Tervo was in a car accident and the police called my mother-in-law to tell her Sam was being transported to St. Mary's. My friend and I spent an hour on icy roads driving from Detroit to get here. The clerk just told me Sam was transferred to Detroit General. I'm exhausted, worried, and yes, upset. The *problem* is my husband is no longer here. The *problem* is he was on his way home from work and not committing a crime. I don't understand. I want to know what happened."

"Mrs. Tervo, we don't ask questions. When there's a police order, we release the patient if he's safe to travel. One of our doctors stitched his wounds. When he left, he was sedated and resting quietly. His x-rays didn't reveal any broken ribs or fluid in his lungs. Except for the cuts and abrasions on his neck and face, there were no other obvious injuries. Detroit General will take over his care."

"Will you at least tell me who picked him up?"

"I understand you're worried, but your husband is no longer our patient. I suggest you give Detroit General an hour to make sure he's checked in before you call." Sister Mary Margaret turned her back on Maggie, then turned back, bent down and whispered, "You didn't hear this from me, but if I were a betting person, I'd say the gumshoes were from Livonia and the warrant had to do with illegal drugs. He's going to need an attorney." When she saw the surprise on Maggie's face, she winked and said, "Luck of the draw. I'm an Agatha Christie devotee. May God shine a light on your unchartered detour." Then, resuming her scowl, Sister Mary Margaret took Maggie's hand, gave her a hard, holy look in the eye and with the kindest, smallest voice said, "Mrs. Tervo, something tells me you'll get where you're going and kick a little ass along the way." Stunned, Maggie had never before noticed the person inside a habit. The bloodshot blue eyes had somehow pierced Maggie's hidden self, under the many layers of her fabricated self.

Sam, she thought, *we've got to find Sam.* Maggie headed toward the exit to look for Clyde. According to the clock over the reception desk, it was ten-thirty; she needed to call Maija before it got too late. But first things first, Maggie needed transportation to get to Detroit General and she needed support. *Where was Clyde? Did the guard send him away?* She pushed through the sweating glass door and was hit by bitter cold. Clyde and the guard were pushing cars stuck in the icy slush in front of the ER. When Clyde saw her, he waved and she burst into tears. Clyde rushed up to hug her. "Maggie, oh Maggie, what's wrong? Did you see Sam?"

Maggie shook her head and tried to speak.

"What? You didn't see Sam? Is he here?"

Maggie shook her head no, then wiped her nose with the back of her coat sleeve and said, "No. He's not here. They took him away."

"What do you mean he's not here? Who took him where?"

"The candy striper said two cops loaded him into an ambulance and took him to Detroit General. Based on a tip from a nun, he might have been arrested for taking drugs. I don't know."

"Maggie. I'm sure Sam's fine. They wouldn't have transported him if he wasn't fine. Did you call Maija?"

"No. I wanted to find you. I saw the guard checking your driver's license and thought you were arrested for being black in Livonia."

Clyde flattened his lips and squinted his eyes in what Maggie called his 'you-know-me-too-well' smirk. "Close," Clyde said. "I got the third degree until I offered to help push cars stuck in the ER drop-off lane. Why don't you give Maija a call and let her know Sam's okay? Tell her it might be morning before we have details. She doesn't have to know he was transferred. Not now. Tomorrow we'll know more. And, if you would, call Blanche and let her know it's going to be a long night. I'll get the car and warm the engine. When you're done, come out the ER door and look straight ahead. I'll park as close as I can without getting stuck. When I see you, I'll blink my lights."

By the time they passed Five Points the roads were clear. On overtime, Detroit road crews were out in force, plowing and salting, opening routes for weekend and Canadian tourist traffic. Compared to the ride out of Detroit, the ride in was quiet, voiceless, almost transcendental.

Clyde dropped Maggie off at the ER entrance before he parked the car. When Maggie resisted, he said, "No way in hell am I going to risk walking next to a white woman after dark in Detroit. And, Maggie, when you get to the waiting room don't let your guard down. This place is stacked with petty thieves and con artists. Hang on to your purse, and do not, under any circumstances, stare at anyone. Cardinal rule. You stare at someone, you're asking for trouble. *Capisce?*"

"*Capisco*."

Detroit General's ER was a war zone, with two cops for every inmate being triaged. Inmates, gangbangers, victims of violent crimes—along with the poor who waited too long to get healthcare—were lined up on gurneys next to one another. Some wigged out on drugs or alcohol. Cops with guns stood watch in the clinical areas; hospital guards—mostly cops who moonlighted—manned the doors and checked for weapons, drugs and other prohibited items. Ordinary citizens cowered in fractious waiting areas with rival gang members, warring neighbors, and stealthy vagrants claiming squatter's rights.

After emptying her pockets and having her purse searched, Maggie headed to the reception desk where she was given a numbered plastic fob on a metal shower hook. Twenty minutes later, Clyde walked in and sat on the edge of her chair.

"No word?

"None," she said.

"How long?"

"Three more numbers."

Conversation was impossible and the activity was too compelling to ignore. When her number was called, Maggie left her coat with Clyde and walked through the crowded waiting room to the reception area and handed her plastic fob to the receptionist.

"Patient's name?"

"Samuel Tervo. T-e-r-v-o." Maggie watched as the clerk opened the index card file to "T" and looked through the cards twice.

"I don't see a Tervo. Let's check the S file. Samuel can be a last name. Hold on."

Maggie was holding her breath and tapping her fingers on the counter. She didn't think she could handle five more minutes of not knowing if Sam was okay.

"Here it is. Someone wrote Tervo Samuel. Sorry about that. He's on the guard floor, room three ten. The only approved visitor is his wife. Is that you?"

Maggie exhaled and said, "Yes."

"When you get to the third floor, you'll check your purse, coat and any other items at the front desk. They'll give you a receipt. But keep your driver's license. The guard assigned to room three ten won't let you bring anything in and will hold your driver's license until you leave. If the guard thinks you're carrying any contraband, you'll have to agree to be frisked by one of the female matrons before he lets you enter. You have one hour. Any questions?"

"None, not now. I'm so glad you found his name."

"I hope all goes well, Mrs. Tervo."

Maggie waved Clyde into the hallway so they could hear each other.

"Me only. I'm sorry, you must be exhausted."

"Maggie, I don't want to be anywhere else. I'm fine. Sam's room might be bugged. If you talk, do it under his sheets in soft whispers and in code to the extent you can. Tell him not to talk to anyone without a lawyer. We'll get him one as soon as we can. If he's not conscious, insist on seeing his doctor to find out what's wrong."

"He doesn't have his own doctor. His doctor is whoever is on the floor today."

"Even better. He'll have to pull files. Ask for copies. And, Maggie, use your charm and wit to pump the guard for information. He might not know the details, but I'm sure he has the gist of the case and will want to impress you. Then, ask him what lawyer he'd hire for the alleged offense. Use the word 'alleged' when you ask. Got it?"

"Got it. Clyde, I'm exhausted. I hate the idea of taking time to eat when Sam's here, but I'm not sure I'll make it through the next phone call with Maija unless I have something to eat."

"We'll eat as soon as we can. How long do you have with Sam?"

"An hour."

After waiting ten minutes for an elevator, Maggie squeezed into the front just before the doors slid closed. The smell of wet wool and cheap perfume on an empty stomach might have put her over the edge, but the guy behind her was grunting into her ear and talking about getting a little white meat. When the elevator reached the third floor, Maggie bolted. No way was she going to let revenge against this creep steal a minute of her time with Sam. The front desk visitor-check-in sign was sitting on the counter of a nursing station. Maggie pulled her license out of her wallet and handed her purse and jacket to a guy who looked like he'd been around a few blocks. His nametag read Henry Walker, Attendant. In return, Henry gave her a wristband with the number of the hanger as a receipt.

"I'm here to see my husband, Samuel Tervo in room three ten," said Maggie.

"Hah! Would've guessed you were with the white guy. I've been matching up visitors to jailbirds since I got out of juvie in fifty-six. Makes the day go faster. Your husband's guard is a whack job, loves to hear the sound of his own voice. Ask him anything about himself and let him talk. You'll be reeling him in before he realizes he took the bait. Ask him a question about the arrest, and you'll piss him off. To your right, all the way to the end of the hall."

"How'd you know I wanted to ask him questions?"

"Who else you going to ask?"

Maggie smiled, nodded her head and gave him the peace sign. He raised his right arm and made a proud, black knuckled fist. For some reason, Maggie was struck by the idea that longing for peace and power, might itself, be an addictive, mind-altering fantasy.

On her way to three ten, Maggie felt the eyes of cops who sat half-asleep on folding chairs outside the rooms of street hoodlums and syndicate bosses; inmates hospitalized for a host of miseries, from gonorrhea to gunshot wounds. Although intimidating as hell for the uninitiated, Maggie realized this was the perfect symbiotic relationship. Cops who'd rather sit than pound a beat all day, protecting crooks, pimps and murderers who would have been shark chum in any other setting.

Sam's guard held his eyes on her from the moment she stepped into the hallway. Maggie guessed he was in his forties, no wedding band on his left hand, no home-cooked love handle around his waist. All muscle, sinew and flex, with dark hair, dark eyes and perfect teeth. Magazine good looks that women fall for. But, when he smiled at Maggie, she felt assaulted and exposed. There was no warmth, no one inside. His badge read Gary Linz.

"Let me guess. Mrs. Samuel Tervo?"

Maggie tried to keep her face relaxed, handed him her driver's license and said, "Yes. Thank you. I'm here to see my husband."

He looked up at her then back at the driver's license and said, "I need you to turn around slowly to make sure you aren't carrying contraband."

Maggie made what she thought was a slow turn, aware of his eyes on her.

"I need you to do that again. This time with your hands over your head."

Maggie put the palms of her hands on top of her head and moved as slowly as she could. She knew he was trying to intimidate her and he was. Maggie pictured Tekla at Maija's house and Sam behind door number three ten—both waiting for her to show up.

"Let's do this one more time without the sweater. Hard to see what you're hiding under all that bulk."

Maggie bit her bottom lip and considered her options. Without a word, she pulled off her navy-blue cable knit sweater. Charged by static electricity, her blue cotton blouse clung to her breasts. She could feel the cold shrinking and hardening her nipples. This time, Maggie put her hands on her head without being asked and turned as slowly and seductively as she could. *Get a good look you désolé bâtard,* she thought, *good enough to open door three ten.*

With a long, exaggerated look up and down her body, Officer Linz said, "Looks like you're hiding some goodies, but no contraband. You can put your sweater back on."

Maggie kept her eyes on him as she drew her sweater over her head, and let it catch on her breasts before she pulled it down. She'd never used her body to overtly entice a stranger. Now, she was willing to do whatever it took to help Sam.

The guard was standing and smiling—more like leering—when he opened Sam's door and said, "One hour."

12

One Hour

We're gonna cause talk and suspicion, we're gonna give an exhibition, we gonna find out what it is all about. After midnight, we gonna let it all hang down.

—Eric Clapton, Lyrics from *After Midnight*

MARCH 12, 1971, MIDNIGHT—Sound asleep under caged fluorescent light, Sam's face was bruised and sallow. Two angry, sutured cuts along his left jawline formed a crescent moon. Despite ice forming on the inside of the chicken-wired window, Sam's hair was matted by sweat. Maggie combed his bangs away from his face with her fingers and said, "Samuelsan, I'm here. Do you hear me?"

Sam's lids flew open and he recoiled from her touch.

"It's okay, babe. It's me, Maggie."

Maggie held her finger to her lips as she climbed into bed with him and pulled the scratchy sheet and flimsy, over-bleached flannel blanket over their heads.

Whispering, Maggie said, "Sam, there's a guard outside your door. Clyde thinks the room might be bugged. We're going to keep our voices low and talk under this blanket. Are you in pain?"

"Oh, god, Maggie. You have to leave. It's not safe."

Sam's face held both tenderness and panic; she felt off-balance. "Shh, Sam, listen, we only have an hour. I need your help. You can't spend this time asking me to disappear. I won't. *Sisu*, Sam. Tekla and I are counting on you."

"Tekla? Is she okay?"

"Tekla's fine. She's with your mom in Farmington. Tell me, are you in pain?"

Sam tried to turn his body to face her and winced. "Pain? Some. My head feels like a cotton ball, and I'm sore all over; everything else seems to work."

"Do you remember what happened?"

"Let me think. We finished the layoff plan and I think Ben opened the bar. We all had a drink or two. No more. I felt a little woozy, not drunk. The next thing I knew, I was in St. Mary's with two cops at my side. They said I was in deep shit and on my way to the prison ward at Detroit General. I think someone gave me a shot to help me relax. I don't remember. Must have knocked me out. Next thing, I was in this bed hooked to an IV."

"When you felt woozy, did it feel like you'd been drugged?"

"Mag, I don't know. I'm so tired. I have to sleep."

"No, Sam. You have to stay awake. Please, stay awake for just a few more minutes. Did anyone read you your rights, or tell you why you were being arrested?"

"They said . . . something . . . like I was in deep shit and on my way to the prison ward at Detroit General."

"Okay, that's good. We covered that. What next? Did they tell you why you were in deep shit?"

"I am in deep shit because . . ." Sam's eyes closed.

Maggie put her mouth next to his ear and in a louder voice whispered, "Come on, babe, just a few more questions. Stay with me. You are in deep shit because why?"

Sam started crying and said, "Oh, Maggie, I'm so sorry and so tired. I'm in deep shit because I took LSD. They said I took LSD."

"Sam, who said you took LSD?"

"The cops. They said I took LSD."

"Did they say anything else?"

"I can't tell you."

"Yes, you can. Help me here. Do you mean you can't tell me or you don't know?"

"I can't tell you. If I tell you, they'll hurt you."

"Sam, what do you mean? Who will hurt me?"

"The cops will hurt you if I don't keep my mouth shut."

"Sam, it's me, Maggie. You can tell me anything. We'll fight it. We'll hire the best lawyer. Let them take us to court."

"Maggie, Maggie. This isn't about courts or law or justice or lemonade. These are the big boys, the powerbrokers. In this world, the Mafioso is pabulum."

"Sam, stop! What are you talking about? You can't just walk away from your life, me, Moonwalker. Come on. Help me."

Sam kissed Maggie and held his finger to her mouth and in the smallest voice whispered, "Call Jacques today. We need money and time. Ask him to get someone to turn our house into a fortress. He can make it happen. And, have him hire a lawyer. You can't. People are watching you, Clyde, The Eights. Mag, I don't want to walk away, but our only chance to escape this madness is to have Jacques on our side. That's all I can tell you. Straight up, Mag, you can't second-guess me. This time, don't question Jacques, rewrite the script, or edit—just let 'er rip."

"Okay, Samuelsan. I'll let 'er rip." Sam closed his eyes as Maggie drew her finger around the quarter-moon on his face. They slept.

A loud knock on the door and a five-minute warning from the guard woke them both. It was almost one. They held each other for four minutes. Then, Maggie got up, straightened the covers over Sam, gave him a kiss, and headed to the door.

"Hey, Mag, give Moonwalker a big hug and kiss and tell Ma not to worry."

Maggie nodded her head and said, "Soon. I'll be back soon."

Officer Linz was pacing at the end of the hall. "So, Marguerite Tervo. How was your little visit?"

"Too short. It sounds like we're in a world of hurt, and I have no idea where to begin."

"Yep. You got that right. I've met a lot of turds in my life. He takes the cake."

"This is hard for me," said Maggie, as the bitter taste of bile lashed at her tongue.

"Don't take this wrong, you're hot. Why on earth would he be paying for it if he had you at home? I guess some dudes just like chocolate."

"They arrested the wrong guy," said Maggie, with more wrath than she intended.

"Yep. Maybe they did. But I'm here to tell ya, that didn't happen. Albino hair is super rare—like a neon sign in any lineup. No way in hell do they have the wrong guy. He'll need the pope as an eye witness to get outta this."

Without looking up, Maggie whispered, "Sounds like there's not a lawyer in Detroit who'd take this on."

"One, maybe. Bruce Shelton. Makes a killing working the small stuff for the mob; sometimes takes on a case no one else will touch. He might be game."

Maggie knew she was being had, big time. Officer Linz was singing like a well-rehearsed chorus of canaries. No way did this pass the sniff test. The cops get a good bootie show, and in return, Henry gets tips or favors, and some third-rate lawyer gets a client. Everyone has an angle. As for Sam, had he been drugged then videotaped with another call girl? Or, she thought, *was I completely had? Who knows if that dickhead guard has any of it right. Maybe this is all some perverted intramural game of Clue.*

When Maggie reached the check-in counter to check out, she was pissed. Henry was still charming. Maggie decided to play their game.

"Thanks for your help, Henry. I hope you'll take care of Sam while he's here."

"Mrs. Tervo, you can count on it. Did you get the information you wanted?"

"I did! That and more, thanks for the advice."

By the time she got downstairs, Clyde was asleep in the waiting room. Maggie touched his shoulder and said, "Hey, Clyde."

"Hey, Maggie. How was it? Sam okay?"

"Lots to talk about after we get some sleep. My hunger passed. If it's okay with you, I'll crash the rest of the night on your couch."

"Sure, Maggie. Give me fifteen, twenty minutes to get the car. I'll be up front."

13

The Thaw

As for these deserters, malcontents, radicals, incendiaries, the civil and the uncivil disobedients among our youth . . . Yippies, Hippies, Yahoos, Black Panthers, Lions and Tigers alike—I would swap the whole damn zoo for a single platoon of the kind of young Americans I saw in Vietnam."

—Spiro Agnew, Vice President

MARCH 13, 1971—*Rivulets of light through upturned venetian blinds sluiced the ceiling with promise,* thought Maggie, as she pulled the Superman quilt up to her chin and edited that thought with, *Ugh! Who on this side of heaven talks like that?* Good or bad, she never knew what to do with these bursts of poetry. Writing it down seemed to dampen the wonder and not writing it down meant any salvageable phrases were lost on the cutting room floor. When Maggie first read Hafez, his call to 'leave something in the marketplace' seemed inspirational. Now it was beginning to piss her off.

"Hey, Maggie, you up? It's almost noon," said Clyde.

"Oh, god! Are you serious? What about Sam? Where are Blanche and the boys?"

"Blanche dropped the boys off at her mom's and is kicking off a pre-school conference at Wayne State. As for Sam, I asked Willie to do some sleuthing to see why they're holding him. He's meeting us at Big Boys at one. Maggie, he doesn't know anything about anything—just that Sam was in an accident and somehow ended up in the prison ward. I also called Maija and told her you were sacked out on our couch and that Sam's doing fine. I told her he was transferred to Detroit General; she didn't ask why, and I didn't tell her. And Tekla's fine. Maija said they're planning a hats and gloves tea party at Claridge's in London. I told her you'd call after we saw Sam today."

"Poor Sam. He's in the hospital with a lunatic guard and I'm under a Superman quilt composing terrible poems and thinking about a double-decker Big Boy."

"Poems?"

"Nothing, never mind. I need to find a few rolls of quarters and make some calls. I'll meet you at Big Boys as close to one as I can."

"Maggie, if you're thinking of calling someone to get Sam out, you might want to hear what Willie has to say before you call."

"I can do both. The people I'm calling aren't easy to reach and I don't want to lose more time."

"Think on it. More information might be more efficient. The bathroom's all yours. I'll broom the slush off your car and make sure it starts."

"You know, sometimes you can be scary sweet."

Clyde's toothy smile was like sunlight. "Seriously, Maggie? Are you trying to charm a charmer? Grab a cup of joe and get the lead out."

Two rolls of quarters weighed heavy in Maggie's empty pockets when she decided to reverse the charges. *Is this some weird test of loyalty?* She almost hung up when the operator asked Jacques if he was willing to accept long-distance charges for Marguerite Tervo, calling from Detroit, Michigan in the United States of America. The merging of unknowns, personal agendas, geography, voices, connections and the transfer of calls between telephone operators in two countries was dizzying. Maggie knew the precipice and implication of this one act held danger far beyond her reckless imagination.

"*Bonjour, mon cheri* Marguerite! How are you?"

Without warning, tears flooded Maggie's eyes and backed down her throat. She began to cough.

"Maggie, you okay?"

Maggie tried to say *no*, but the word stuck in her voice box.

"Take a deep breath, take your time. I'm here."

Across the long-distance lines, Jacques heard Maggie's sorrow escape through forced breaths and swallowed air, as she tried to unharness the impossible tension between fear and courage.

"Oh, Jacques, I'm sorry I called collect. I have two rolls of quarters in my pockets."

"My dear Maggie, I would have been hurt if you didn't call collect. That was our agreement. Talk to me."

"Sam's in trouble and he asked me to call. I'm not sure I trust you, or anyone for that matter, but Sam trusts you and we need help. Sam told me to 'let 'er rip.' So, I'm here to let 'er rip."

"Good. I'm glad you called. Go ahead and let 'er rip. I'm listening."

After Maggie described the events of the last several months, and more particularly, the last few days, she said, "Whatever The Puzzle is, we can't put it together if we don't have a picture. If you think I'm psycho, say so. If not, we need you on our side."

When the phone line went silent, Maggie said, "Jacques, are you still there?"

"I'm here, Maggie. You're not psycho. And, no doubt, Sam's been targeted. I won't go into details right now, but you're smart enough to know there have always been powerbrokers determined to tip the balance of wealth and influence; conspiracy theorists who trade in fear mongering; and lost souls with placards threatening the end of the world. It's not written in the stars but carried in our collective memories. When we're afraid, we tend to give up our power—that's what the brokers are counting on."

Maggie grabbed on to this line and shook it, "You mean like Nixon, and his toady Agnew, hiding behind their attacks on a crooked press and giving life to some bogus silent majority to make us think we're the misfits?"

"Good bet," said Jacques. "History is cluttered with the rise and fall of monarchies, dictatorships and banana republics that traded in fear and xenophobia. On a small scale, it starts with comments like 'keep your women barefoot and pregnant.' On an empire scale, it's about munitions and military force strong enough to demonize other countries, entire races or genders."

"Wait, I know you wanted to keep this short. But, do you mean . . ."

"Maggie, I do get carried away; we'll talk more later. Right now, we need to tackle some immediate problems. First a safe place for you, Sam and Tekla. We'll get Pepe on an early flight to Detroit tomorrow. He'll do what he can to secure the house. Until then, he'll live with you. Don't let that freak you out. Pepe's honed the art of invisibility. He'll curl up in some remote corner and you'll forget he's there. As you know, nothing is one hundred percent. It still takes you and Sam being hyper alert. In the meantime, I'll get Sam a lawyer and handle the costs. For now, you take care of yourself and Tekla. I'm a phone call or plane flight away."

"Pepe? The last thing he told me was he'd come to Detroit when he had an 'insane urge to outrun bullets.'"

"That's Pepe. What did you call him once, 'a serial curmudgeon?' He's that, and he's also one of the smartest, most inventive men I know. He doesn't suffer fools or crooks lightly."

"I'm good with Pepe. And, relieved and grateful to have you on our side, whatever side this is. Speaking of fools, the cop guarding Sam gave me the name of a lawyer. For what it's worth, he said Bruce Shelton does work for the mob, but also takes cases no one else will touch."

"What's the cop's name?"

"Linz, Officer Gary Linz."

"Huh. Well, as luck would have it, Bruce Shelton is my attorney, the guy I'm about to call. This might be a total fluke or a glimpse of how deep this goes. For now, we'll use the information as an advantage. As for Bruce, he's on our side. He'll let you know if you can trust Linz or anyone else you meet between now and the date they dismiss the charges."

"Dismiss the charges? How can you be so sure?"

"Trust me, dear Maggie. None of the players want Sam behind bars. Give me about three hours and call me back. And, please, use a pay phone and reverse the charges. I don't want you fishing for quarters and feeding the meter. I'll put you in touch with Bruce and he'll guide you and Sam. Bruce will also pick up Pepe and deliver him to you. For now, Bruce is your primary contact in Detroit. He'll help you explain Pepe in your life and set him up with a new name and identity."

"How much can I tell Sam, Clyde, Aunt Jo, others?"

"Nothing until you talk to Bruce. And, Maggie, I mean nothing. As far as we're concerned, this conversation did not happen."

Clyde and Willie were on their second Coke when Maggie walked into Big Boys. By the time she sat down, the scent of food had sent her salivary glands into a frenzied jitterbug. When the waitress showed up, Maggie added two side salads to her double-decker burger. When Clyde rolled his eyes, Maggie exaggerated her eye roll and said, "To ward off scurvy, Clyde."

Clyde laughed. "You get your calls made?"

"Some. I haven't called Maija or talked to Tekla. I'm pathetic as a mother."

"Give yourself a break, Maggie; you've got a full plate."

"You talk to Sam today?" Willie asked.

"Not yet. No way to contact him by phone and visiting hours are four to six."

Willie began to straighten his napkin and utensils, then looked up and said, "Maggie, I did some checking around, and gotta ask, does Sam drop acid?"

"No way. Sam doesn't do drugs. Before he left work on Friday, he was with a bunch of yahoos celebrating a layoff. Seriously, celebrating a plan to lay off workers. So, who knows? Any one of them could have laced his drink."

"Looks like the charge is 'Possession and Use of a Schedule 1 Drug.' Big time, Maggie. If Sam was a brother, he'd be cooling his jets in DeHoCo for three to five. If he's got connections, he might get a hand slap. You never know. There's only one lawyer I'd recommend. He's pricey, but he's the William Kunstler of Detroit. No one wants to dick with him. Charges get dropped before he opens his mouth." In response to Maggie's wide eyes, Willie said, "Mafia influence. He represents some scary-ass dagos. Name's Bruce Shelton."

"You know him?" Maggie asked.

"Talked to him a few times. He's a big Red Wing's fan. Likes to hang out after the game and watch me clean ice. Calls it his

'Meditation on Ice'—you know, a spin on the book *Soul on Ice*. Dude wouldn't know my name or recognize me off the Zamboni."

"Okay, but how do you know he gets charges dropped?"

"Maggie, that's what I do. I spend half my life in court keeping my own records on arrests, sentences and quote, the effectiveness of representation, unquote. You name it. My mission is to nail the cops and justice system to the wall with their own statistics. Any question that racism is alive and well? Stop by criminal court. Everyone knows Bruce Shelton is the majordomo. More like Attila the Hun! Doesn't give a shit if his client is innocent or guilty, and sure as hell doesn't care if the judge likes him. There's no way he'd stroke some judge's hairy legs to get a verdict. He wields law like an Uzi. When he shows up as counsel, the old men in robes piss their pants. Now that I think of it, we might be doing this civil rights thing bass ackwards. Could be the threat of mafia is the key to ending racism. Whadda think?"

Lost in thought, Maggie nodded her head. "Whatever it takes, Willie. I'll accept help from anyone, mafia or not."

"Hey, Maggie," said Clyde, "how about dessert?"

Maggie looked at her three empty plates and two friends. "I don't know what I'd do without you guys to lean on and feed me. But, right now, I'm going to get three chocolate malts to go and head to Maija's. I need some women kin vibes and Moonwalker hugs before visiting hours. All this testosterone is turning me into a guy."

Maggie took the long way to Maija's so she could stop by the house and pick up some clothes and diapers for Tekla, a few changes of clothes for herself and check on the cardboard window patch. As she pulled into the driveway, she sensed a chill, lifelessness, as if the house had been abandoned and the family who lived there scattered across the countryside. *Holy crap*, she thought, *maybe it's time to give up poetry and write noir screenplays.*

The knob on the outside door to the utility room seemed loose; when Maggie turned the key, she didn't hear it click. Yet, when she pushed the door, it opened. Shaking her head, Maggie wondered if today's cloak and dagger plans had inspired her inner gun moll. *Enough*, she thought, *I'm awfulizing*—a word she coined to describe Aunt Minnie when she imagined catastrophes to freak herself out. The water dripping down the three steps from the kitchen into the utility room was not her imagination. "Please no," Maggie whispered, as she opened the kitchen door to find the cardboard patch floating in two inches of water. The furnace was pumping like it struck oil.

Backtracking, Maggie grabbed the rag mop and pail she kept behind the washing machine and set to work. The linoleum was soaked through and Maggie was sure it would buckle. Although the cold air from the window wasn't bitter, there was no way she could leave it uncovered. Pulling out the silverware drawer, Maggie removed the wooden flatware tray and a few utensils. Then, she held the bottom of the drawer against the broken window. Not a perfect fit, but close. After lifting the broken bottom window sash up, the drawer made a tighter fit against the empty frame and blocked the chill air. Now she needed a way to cinch the drawer to the upper sash and hit on an idea, *Sam's leather belts*. Maggie caught her reflection in the kitchen mirror, held up her right forefinger, smiled and said, "Okay, I got this!"

When Maggie stepped into the dining room, her confidence cracked. The bottom drawer of the blond-veneer buffet cabinet was pulled out and water-stained papers were spilled across the floor. She froze then stepped backward. Her heart pounding in her ears, Maggie knocked over the pail of water and slipped on the kitchen floor. Getting her footing, she grabbed her purse, scrambled through the utility room door, raced to the car, jumped in and locked the doors.

Her hand was shaking so hard it took three tries to fit the key into the ignition. *Oh, god, please start.* Pounding the gas pedal like a mad woman, she took a breath and looked around. No one in sight, but thought, *someone could be looking through a window.* The car flooded. *Wait, wait, wait,* she thought, but didn't believe she could. She took a deep breath and remembered the advice of a car jockey she once dated. With the gas pedal fully depressed, she turned the ignition for twenty seconds. The car started. Then, as if someone snatched her body, she threw the car into drive and drove across the lawn, pin-wheeled back through two large trees, stood on the gas pedal when she hit the gravel shoulder and skidded onto Six Mile.

Five miles later, Maggie slowed to the speed limit and decided to stop at K-Mart for diapers, a few outfits for Tekla, and at least one change of clothes for herself. She was inhaling her second chocolate malt and trying to keep her legs from shaking.

14

The Tears

My Lai, March 16, 1968: US Troops raped, tortured and killed hundreds of Vietnamese villagers—unarmed men, women and children. Stop. Stop. Stop. A baby crawling out of a ditch was thrown back and shot in mid-air. Stop. Stop. Stop.

—M. S. Tervo, Unfinished Poem

MARCH 14, 1971—Twenty-two pounds of weight on her chest and fingers peeling open her lips were punctuated by the cries, "Maggie, up! Wake up! Maggie, Maggie, UP!"

"Hey, pumpkin girl. Is that you?" said Maggie, her eyes closed and hands searching the air.

"Here, Maggie. HERE! Pumpkin girl!" said Tekla, her fingers trying to pry open Maggie's eyes.

"Oh my gosh! Tekla Moonwalker Tervo! Is it really you?"

Tekla giggled and said, "NO! Pumpkin girl!"

"Did your Grandma Tervo tell you to wake me up?"

"Wake up! Wake UP! Pancakes," said Tekla as she slipped out of Maggie's grasp and slid to the floor.

"Okay, I'm getting up. Tell Grandma Tervo I'll be there in a flash."

Silver nitrate's alchemy with moisture and neglect left the antique mirror in the guest room mottled in black, stripping it of almost all its reflective power. *Like tears*, Maggie thought, as she took a deeper look in the mirror. She was still there, the same Maggie. But nothing was the same. Yesterday, she dropped off two boxes of pampers, an orange corduroy romper and one, very tired, chocolate malt, before changing into a pair of cheap black polyester slacks and a black tweed fur blend. Tekla's raucous hugs and wriggling during her short visit might have been traced to too much sugar, or too little mothering. The fact was, Maggie had too few minutes. Sam, Jacques, and now Bruce Shelton, were depending on her to pull the chord.

Yesterday, Maggie talked to Jacques from a phone booth on her way to see Sam. The call was short and to the point.

"So, Maggie, how goes it?" Jacques asked.

"Frantic for help. On the way to Maija's I stopped by the house. Someone broke in. For all I know, they're still there. The drawer with notes from The Puzzle was pulled out and papers were strewn all over. That was enough. I got out of there so fast the willow trees are still billowing."

"Glad you haven't lost your keen sense of tropology and humor."

"Tropology? Are you serious? That's my favorite, all-time secret word that no one ever knows. Where did that come from?"

"Little known fact, I was once asked to help grade final thesis papers for a twelfth-grade rhetoric class at the Amadeus School for Girls. The instructor had an appendicitis attack, and apparently, they were desperate. When I came across a paper by Marguerite Soulier, I of course knew it was yours and made every effort not to be biased. Then, when I came across the word tropology in your thesis, I was almost giddy. Word snob that I am, your paper sent me to the dictionary and I've used the word tropology every chance I get."

"I remember Monsieur Dubois's appendicitis attack, but not the paper. I had the worst crush on him and found out later he was gay.

"Today my tropology about willows billowing is more about fear and hysteria. I blame it on the weather, lack of sun and my life behind enemy lines. I know it's fear. I want to be brave, but now that I have Tekla, I'm scared out of my mind."

"I get that. The threats are no longer just about you. Yet, our sense of fear, and our fight or flight instinct to survive, are essential. Courage is responding to our instincts with focus. My sense is you do that well."

"No focus this time. I went totally batshit, ballistic into flight. I couldn't get out of there fast enough."

"Listen, Maggie, you were whacked with a medicine ball to the gut and you acted on instinct, and I would venture, with freeze-dried focus. I wish we had more time, but my day's crashing in on me and Bruce is waiting to hear from you. Any chance you can call him now? He'll bring you up to date."

"Sure, I can do that."

After Jacques gave her Bruce's number, Maggie hung up the sticky phone and wiped her hands on her new slacks. Unable to find a tissue, Maggie stood up and spit on the back of the receiver, used the elbow of her jacket to rub it off, lifted it off the hook, dropped in a quarter, dialed, then flipped her moleskin notebook to a clean page.

"Bruce Shelton here."

"Mr. Shelton, this is Maggie Tervo. Jacques Ruivivar gave me . . ."

"Maggie, call me Bruce. We'll be spending a lot of time together over the next few weeks. I'm going to put Carol on the line so she can take down the information we need for Sam's bail request and get that going."

Carol collected Sam's address and phone number, Jingo's address and phone number, and the phone numbers of two friends or relatives. Maggie's first instinct was Clyde, but she chose Maija and Issie—reasoning a black man was far more vulnerable to guilt by association than a white woman.

Before Maggie had a chance to thank Carol, Bruce jumped back on the line. "Okay, Maggie, we've got lots of work to accomplish in a very short time. I know you have questions about Sam, but right now we're going to set up your new reality. Starting with Pepe, your Uncle Pete, who happens to be fluent in French. We're trading out his sailor cap for a beret. Pete has full authority and funds to secure your house the best we can. It's no doubt bugged and there's going to be some tearing apart before he cleans it up. You can help or get out of the way. No other choice. You cool with that?"

"Is Pepe French?"

"There is no Pepe. You cool with helping or getting out of Uncle Pete's way?"

"Got it."

"Nice. For the first week, you don't talk to me, Jacques, Sam or anyone else about the arrest, charges—or what you call The Puzzle—without getting clearance from Pete. He'll make sure you have a clean line or safe space. He'll also set up some rules to live by. The big rule is no routines. No favorite restaurants, grocery stores, drug stores; no regular walks or meetings. He and Sam will find new ways to get him to and from work. You can both count on your cars being bugged. *Capisce?*"

"*Capisco*," said Maggie.

"Nice. When you see Sam today, keep the conversation light. Tell him his attorney will be coming by later tonight. No more. Don't mention my name. If he asks, shake your head no and hold your finger to your lips. Do that for any questions he has about me, or the charges against him. When I see him, I'll give him written details about the bail hearing on Tuesday. In the meantime, I'll make sure Sam stays put. The hospital's safer than jail.

"Monday morning I'll pick Pete up at eight thirty. Call my office at eight forty-five from a pay phone. Carol will tell you where to meet us. When we get together, you'll have a chance to ask questions. Tonight and tomorrow night you and Tekla will stay with Sam's mother. We'll have someone watching her house and yours. Keep the faith, little sister. We've got your back."

"Did you know someone broke in?"

"Not surprised. We'll make sure it's secured."

"Another question. Is there an end to this?"

"An end to what? There are many endings and beginnings."

After breakfast, Maggie shooed Maija and Tekla out of the kitchen to watch one of Billy Graham's Crusades. The Rev. Graham had finally captured Maija's attention; she thought he was handsome and sexy. And, because of Tekla's intense attraction to TV, Sam had dubbed her 'a born-again anthropologist'—studying people who lived in a box, waiting for them to step out.

When the phone rang, Maggie grabbed it, "Hello?"

"Hey, Maggie, that you? Long time no speak! I've tried you a dozen times! You're never home."

"Hey, Issie. It's been nuts. Good to hear your voice, I've missed you."

"What's up?"

Maggie closed the swinging door between the kitchen and the rest of the house and felt the gathering tears. "Oh, god, I can't go into it all. Sam's in the hospital and Maija's been keeping Tekla so I can run the traps. Everything is *up*. I'm not sure about the landings."

"What? Sam's in the hospital and you didn't call? What happened?"

"A car crash Friday night, he's going to be fine. I don't want Tekla to hear this. We can talk later."

"No later, Maggie! I'm heading there. Eddie and the kids are going to the matinee to see *A Boy Named Charlie Brown*. Can we meet for lunch?"

"If it's during Tekla's nap. I've had so little time with her, and Maija's been through second molar meltdowns for three days. She's wiped out. How about Mama Mia's? I don't think I can eat another hamburger. One o'clock?"

"You're on. I've missed you."

"Me too, Issie. I've missed you."

Maija knocked on the swinging door and stuck her head in. "Okay to enter?"

Maggie nodded her head and began to cry.

Maija put her arms around Maggie and said, "Oh, my. What is it? Is Sam okay?"

"That was Issie. She wants to meet me for lunch. I feel so torn."

"What's tearing you up? You worried about leaving Tekla with me again?"

Maggie nodded.

"Listen to me. I haven't been this happy in a long time. I love having Tekla to keep me company. Right now, we're good for each other. Besides, there are some things you can say to a sister that you can't say to anyone, including your husband. Go. Don't fret. You've got real things to worry about. Don't be making up stuff about me."

Maggie stepped back and looked at Maija. And, maybe for the first time, saw her as an intelligent, kind, complex woman, rather than the bearer of the too-often maligned bit part on the world stage, mother-in-law. Then, the storm; Maggie burst out crying. Maija stepped into the space and gave Maggie another hug. Not to miss out on the action, Tekla raced in the kitchen and hugged them both around their legs, jumped up and down and said, "Me, too! Me, too!"

Maggie headed out after a morning of block building and three readings of *The Little Engine That Could*—more for her sake than Tekla's. Outside, Maggie checked the cars in the neighborhood to see if she could pick out some guy keeping watch. No one looked the least bit suspicious. Maggie laughed, shook her head and thought, *ditz. The whole point is to be unnoticed.* Two doors down, a woman with a blond chignon, sitting in a candy apple red 1968 Chevy Impala, noticed and recorded the time of Maggie's departure.

Spaghetti and salad with French dressing was a feast. Maggie was sure she'd lost any remaining post-baby weight over the last few days, in spite of the two chocolate malts she'd inhaled. That, or the multiple-day wearing had stretched her few outfits a full size.

"You look tired," said Issie. "What's going on?"

"I can only give you the bare bones. You okay with that?"

"Maggie, whatever. I'm here to support you, not stress you out. The secrecy thing is a little unnerving because I worry about you, us, getting Raymond's crazy gene. You know, he was a raging conspiracy theorist. I get that he and Anna knew things that triggered dark thoughts. He couldn't handle it, she could."

"What kinds of things triggered his thoughts? Do you remember?"

"No. But, if I did, I wouldn't talk about it right now. Tell me. What happened to Sam?"

"Friday night on his way home from work he skidded off the road and ended up at St. Mary's with cuts and abrasions on his face."

"No shit? Really? Maggie, there were hundreds of car crashes on Friday night. The roads were sheets of ice."

"I know, but I can't tell you about the other things he dealt with before this happened. And then, he got arrested because they said he was under the influence of LSD. Issie, Sam doesn't do drugs. No way did he take LSD, unless someone laced his drink."

"What rock have you been living under? Numbnuts are spiking drinks all the time; it's become an American pastime. That said, I hope to hell you get him a good lawyer."

"Issie. Don't make me crazier. Sam's in the prison ward at Detroit General. He's been arrested for drugs, and I'm trying to keep it all together with Tekla, Maija, the house. Which, by the way, has been targeted more than once by white racists."

"Oh my god, Maggie. Get a hold of yourself! You moved to Livonia and you think everyone there is racist. Maybe that's not true. Maybe you've just got too much time on your hands and you're dreaming this up? Possible?"

The last thing Maggie wanted to do was cry again, but the floodgates were still open. She started bawling so hard she could barely talk. "Fuck you, Issie!" Maggie gasped. Drawing in deep breaths, Maggie's heart was beating so loud, the sound of pizza tins, thick white porcelain plates, silverware, ice against glass, and the low rumble of blended conversations seemed to disappear. "You don't know what you're talking about. I can't tell you anything. I thought you'd understand, my mistake. You don't. And now . . . now you want to lay Raymond's crazy gene on me?" Maggie couldn't catch a breath as tears streamed down her face. Issie's pupils kept sliding toward the exit door.

"Oh, Maggie. There I go again, hitting you with my stupid fears. I'm sorry. I want to be here for you, but I'm scared and worried and . . . I don't know how."

Just then, the waiter came by to check on the meal. He said, "Is everything all right?" Maggie and Issie looked at each other, broke into hysterical laughter, and scared him off.

Leaning forward, Issie said, "Maggie, please accept my apology. I promise to help you through this . . . this rough patch. You don't owe me anything—no explanations, no rational behavior, no stiff upper lip—fuck you very much dear Aunt Minnie. And, baby girl, if I act like an asshole again, you can tell me to fuck off."

Maggie looked at her with such sweet sincerity that Issie braced herself for an onslaught of tenderness. Instead, Maggie nodded her head, smiled and said, "My pleasure."

Issie burst out laughing, licked her right finger, swept the air down and said, "Point Maggie."

"I'll take it. Okay, Issie, your turn. What's going on in the Austin household?"

"Oh my god. Are you ready for Eddie's most recent venture? Fast food breakfast! No joke. He wants to buy a small travel trailer, paint it like a fried egg and call it Egg On the Run, kinda like the song, 'Man On the Run.' So, I've been wracking my brain to come up with a name for this year's madcap venture. But here's the shocker; this year I actually like his idea! The problem is Eddie's still on the union's shit list for blowing the whistle on that druggie three years ago. And, it spooks him big time. He's afraid to give up his job and fall on his ass. Eddie used to be the happy one and I was the grouch. No more. Now I'm the happy one, which is a joke no one thinks is funny."

Maggie started to laugh before she caught Issie's expression. Issie was dead serious. "Oh, Issie, I laughed because I could have said those same words about me and Sam. He used to be the happy one, the one to cheer me up, bring me food, take care of me. Now, he's depending on me to keep things going. What's that about?"

Issie shook her head and said, "No way am I going down that murky philosophical path. Let's boogie shoo before we get in too deep!"

In the parking lot, they hugged. Issie said, "I want you to know we Soulier girls are a gang of two. I don't do philosophy, but I can make a mean casserole and three dozen Toll House cookies without a hitch."

Maggie smiled and shot her power-to-the-people right fist in the air. Somehow, they'd survived militant, activist parents and coming of age during a time when radical hope was censored by corruption, bigotry, endless wars and assassinations. Maggie liked what Bruce said about endings. Nothing stays the same as we begin, end, and begin again.

Before finishing that thought, Maggie's mind flipped to Maslow's Hierarchy of Need's bottom rung—food and shelter—and decided she'd better learn to cook or they'd all end up with scurvy.

Sunday night at Detroit General was quiet compared to the last two nights, only a few street people in the almost empty waiting room. Maggie wondered if it was because of too few dupes in the city or roast beef, mashed potatoes and gravy with the family.

When Maggie's number was called, she felt the confidence of having been through this routine twice. At the reception desk she said, "Mrs. Tervo to see Sam Tervo."

Without checking her files, the receptionist said, "I'm sorry, Mrs. Tervo, your husband's attorney is here and we only allow one visitor at a time. You'll have to wait until he leaves or come back later."

"Did he say how long he would be?"

"Two hours is the limit for visitors, attorneys have more leeway. Other than that, we don't ask. Sorry."

Maggie looked for the best catbird seat in the waiting room to keep her eye on the elevators. Two hours passed; no man in a suit with a briefcase exited the elevators. There was no way she could see or talk to Sam tonight. Tomorrow, she'd rip Bruce a new one. Where does he get off seeing Sam during her only visiting hours? This time, Maggie checked her rambunctious tears, threw her shoulders back, and walked like someone who knew who she was, where she was going and where she'd been. Her practice at looking like a badass might be working. *Or,* she thought, *maybe Issie was right. Maybe Raymond's crazy gene is waiting in the wings, ready to make its entrance with a few shuffle-step, ball changes.*

15

Pretextual

And that's the terrible myth of organized society. That everything that's done through the established system is legal. Six million people in Europe during the Third Reich, legal . . . hundreds of rape trials throughout the south where black men were condemned to death all legal, Jesus legal, Socrates legal . . . because all tyrants learn that it is far better to do this thing through some semblance of legality than to do it without that pretext.

—William Moses Kunstler

MARCH 15, 1971 ANTI MERIDIEN—When Maggie stopped at a phone booth to call Bruce's office at eight forty-five, she was ready with a small travel bottle filled with Windex and a clean rag. After wiping off the receiver, Maggie had her pen and moleskin ready as she inserted the quarter and dialed the number.

"Hello, Shelton Law Office, this is Carol. May I help you?"

"Hi, Carol, this is Maggie Tervo. Bruce asked me to call."

"Sure thing, Maggie. Do you have a pen handy?"

"I do. Go ahead."

An easy drive, West Bloomfield was one of the newer, ritzier white-flight burbs northwest of Detroit, about ten miles north of Farmington. According to Carol, Bruce's house was off Orchard Lake Road on a winding, unpaved street in a new development; the address painted on a small board near the driveway. Because the doorbells weren't hooked up, Carol told Maggie to enter the front door and give a shout. Bruce would be there before nine thirty and the meeting was planned to last through lunch. Adding, "Bring your appetite because Bruce loves smorgasbords—think Eastern Market revisited!"

After making a few wrong turns, it was nine forty-five before Maggie finally found the address on a tipped-over board in a drainage ditch. The house looked like it belonged in another galaxy. Curved steel and windowed walls, with narrow-cut sandstone for the siding and winding garden fences, the house appeared to be floating, gravity-free.

Intimidated by the mammoth steel, walnut and frosted glass front door, Maggie's shoulder was poised to push it open. But when she pulled down the brushed steel handle, the door swung into a foyer large enough to hold the string section of the New York Philharmonic. White oak flooring, with an asymmetrical design of inlaid flagstone, was picked up in random-lengths of three-inch thick white oak shelves that looked as if they'd grown through hand-rubbed, off-white painted walls. Each shelf held one piece of pottery that looked Native American or First Nation Canadian. Each exotic. With its collection of museum quality art—the form, color and light of this remarkable space was mind-blowing. Only once before, at the Sistine Chapel, had Maggie found the combination of striking beauty and arresting mystery almost more than she could bear. Like ecstasy, the tension was too great to hold.

"Maggie?" came the voice of a man standing under one of the three foyer archways. Perhaps the most remarkable-looking man Maggie had ever encountered. Well-groomed, his salt and pepper hair was pulled back in a neat ponytail, but his acne-pocked face, deep-set dark eyes, wiry body, threadbare jeans, black tee and bare feet gave him a wild, visceral look. A man who looked more like a wolf than a human—more like a bodyguard than a lawyer.

"Bruce?"

"Glad you found us! Pete's on a call with Jacques, but we're set up to meet in the kitchen. Lots of coffee and food."

"Your house is incredible! Did you and your wife have it designed?"

"No wife. But, yes, I had it designed. Started planning it when I was a grasshopper. My nine-year-old ideas grew and grew and grew, like a beanstalk. I decided I couldn't afford to dream about it anymore. So here I am in West-Blooming-Nowhereville, in a house that belongs on the moon. My tight-ass, early-American, missionary neighbors are outraged," Bruce laughed. "Come on in. We'll get some coffee and talk about Sam's charge before we pick up a few Puzzle pieces with Pete."

Maggie was good with words, but there were no words to fully describe the kitchen. The cupboards were white oak, with engraved waves, that opened with the slight touch of the hand on the edge of the door. All the kitchen drawers were housed in an island shaped like a dolphin and topped with black soapstone. Small and super-small drawers and cubbies edged dozens of wider, shallow drawers that must have held any and all kitchen items looking for space. "They're so shallow," Maggie remarked.

"I know. I often wish they were more enlightened," laughed Bruce. "Here's the deal, when drawers are deep, you waste two to four inches of depth times length times width. Or, you end up stacking items then can't find a damn thing. I've always had this obsession about order and decided to design drawers for everything.

And, I pretty much have that. The problem is now I need a goddamn key-map to find anything!"

"Our kitchen would probably fit on top of this island. I'm dazzled; totally bedazzled!" said Maggie.

"Do I hear a familiar voice? *Bonjour*, Marguerite!"

"*Bonjour, Oncle* Pete!" Maggie said, with an emphasis on the *oncle*. She barely recognized Pepe. He seemed taller, thinner and younger. But, it was definitely Pepe, now Uncle Pete. She gave him a big hug. "Have you lost weight?"

"A bit." Stepping back and holding her arms, Pete said, "And you, Ms. Maggie, look beautiful. Marriage, a child, and getting slammed around by unknown forces must be good for you."

"Look closer, Pepe . . . I mean, Uncle Pete. I'm a mess."

"We'll fix that. Sam first. I'll sit in if it's okay."

"Absolutely," said Bruce.

"First off, Maggie, when I tell you not to call Pete by any other name, I'm dead serious. The Puzzle, as you like to call it, is not a goddamn game. You'll put yourself and lots of other people at risk if you can't make this turn in your thinking. You're not stupid. I expect you to pay attention and get this right. If you can't, Jacques will call Pete back to Canada. Your choice, make it now."

Maggie's eyes were dry, her mind clear. To think her talk with Aunt Jo had been a dive into *Dante's Inferno* was a joke. Compared to this moment, it was a candle flame. Here, now, Maggie knew she was in the company of men who played high-stake's poker and she still didn't know the difference between a straight and a royal flush. Here, in this otherworldly kitchen, Maggie felt like the proverbial biblical lamb. Clearing her throat, she said, "I'm not stupid. I can make this turn."

"Nice. We've got a lot to accomplish, and we're going to eat while we talk," said Bruce as he waved his arm for Maggie and Pete to sit down.

U-shaped chrome legs supported an old, planked barn door—finely sanded, painted dove gray and finished with a thin coat of polyurethane. Surrounded by six Marcel Breuer cane and chrome chairs, there was plenty of room to stretch out with paper, pens, coffee—and an all-day breakfast and lunch buffet that Bruce insisted he'd set up on the island without help. Maggie watched Bruce pull stainless steel serving plates of sausage, cheese, tuna salad, chicken salad, deviled eggs, sliced prime rib, grapes, lemon meringue pie and condiments from the built-in refrigerator; and crackers, French bread, bagels and chocolate candies from the pantry. He then placed them with authority and care on the dolphin-shaped island. White dishes, white bowls, walnut-handled modern flatware, orange linen napkins, and a walnut pepper grinder and salt shaker were set up on the dolphin's fin. A pot of minestrone was put over a low flame on the built-in stovetop.

"That does it! Lots to eat, so help yourself when you're ready. I've got juice, pop and Perrier in the fridge and fresh coffee on the table," said Bruce.

Maggie leaned across the table and picked up one of the orange and white striped mugs and filled it with coffee. When she drew her hand back, it was shaking. Bruce caught her eye and she had no doubt he'd seen how unwrapped she was. Maggie knew men like Bruce didn't suffer fools or dumb broads. She'd have to prove herself if she wanted to be heard. And, it sure as hell wouldn't happen if she followed her maternal instinct to offer to pour the coffee and serve the food. *Focus*, she thought, *they don't need a mommy.*

"To be clear," said Bruce, "this is not a banquet, not about the food. The food is only scaffolding to keep us working through lunch. We're all self-sufficient, so no offers to bring food to each other, no sharing a piece of pie, or commenting on flavor. I want a seamless, focused meeting. We've got a lot of territory to cover. *Capisce?*"

"*Capisco,*" said Maggie, with a smug sense of satisfaction that she knew what Bruce wanted before he said it.

"Nice. First Sam. The bail hearing is tomorrow, and I expect the judge will grant us bail. Sam's got a clean record and an employer who wants him back at work. According to Jingo's in-house counsel, his work record will not be affected by his arrest; however, they will deduct pay or apply vacation time for his incarceration today and for any time missed as a result of this arrest. A no-brainer.

"Where I need your help, Maggie, is to assess the threat, if any, of more serious claims by women who Sam says his ex-employer—and possibly Ben Kabul at Jingo—have knowledge of. He told me about the two instances when Louie Zito, his manager at Sheer Juice, accused him of raping or molesting two different women. Sam said you're aware of these claims and it was okay for me to talk to you about this."

"I know what he said he remembers about these claims; he doesn't know what happened and he's never seen the photos or film they said they have. We all, including Clyde, thought this was a set up. If Zito had proof, why not show Sam? So, we think it didn't happen and there is no proof. But we don't know for sure. The frustration is we have no idea why they're doing this. It's not like they've tried to bribe him or extort money from us. What do they want from Sam? He's got no money, no connections."

Maggie looked at Bruce, then Pete. Both were looking at her with an intensity that spoke of disbelief or interest. She couldn't tell which.

Bruce got up, grabbed a salt bagel, sat back down and refilled his cup of coffee. Then Pete got up and fixed a plate of sausage, cheese, crackers and grapes and sat back down. No one spoke.

Finally, Maggie got up and loaded her plate with deviled eggs, prime rib with horseradish sauce on French bread, and grapes. Although tempted to speak, to fill the empty air, Maggie bit into a deviled egg and almost swooned. She couldn't recall the last time her taste buds were captivated by a new flavor, a time when she wasn't inhaling her food just to settle an empty stomach. *Holy mother of god,* she thought, *how many moments have I missed in my escape to an uncertain future?* When she looked up, Bruce was watching her. The rule against talking about food made the experience of eating almost erotic. *Forbidden fruit and mastication,* thought Maggie, *like some strange form of foreplay.* Each pleasured by one another's arousal, without touching, without speaking.

"Earth to Maggie, are you there?" Bruce asked.

Maggie smiled and said, "Yes, I'm here. I'm serious about my question. Why would anyone target Sam? We've got mortgages, car payments and a hamburger budget."

"That might be a subject for Jacques and Pete. But, right now, my job is to get Sam free of these charges and back to work. Who else knows about Zito's attempt to frame Sam?"

"As I said, our friend Clyde Webster. Clyde, Sam and I formed a triad—even called it The Triad—to figure out The Puzzle. We didn't get very far."

"Anyone else?"

"Oh, I forgot, Aunt Jo. Jo Landry, my mother's sister. She said something to Sam the night of the moon landing, right before Tekla was born. For some reason, she was concerned about Jacques coming to the States. I'm not sure who said what, but Sam must have said something about his experiences because Aunt Jo told him it sounded like he was already in 'The Soup,' which Sam said was her sobriquet for The Puzzle.

"Last fall, I think September, Aunt Jo wanted to stop by to see Tekla and me. I called Sam and told him I was going to ask her about The Puzzle. That set things in motion. A few weeks later, Clyde, Sam and I met with Aunt Jo to gather as much information as we could. We kept our Puzzle notes, including the meeting with Aunt Jo, in the bottom drawer of our dining room buffet. The last time I was home, the drawer was pulled out of the buffet and files were scattered all over the dining room floor."

"Maggie, this is important. Did the notes from your meeting with Jo include any references to Sam's experiences? Anything at all about the women, the names of any people who were involved, the alleged photos or film, alleged drugging, alleged gaslighting, anything?"

"I don't think so, but I'm not certain. Clyde asked the questions and taped the interview. After Clyde transcribed the tape into handwritten notes, he gave them to Sam and me for safekeeping. I reread the transcript several times, but I wasn't thinking about what Clyde or Sam said, just what Aunt Jo said."

"Why so many times?"

"Because something wasn't hitting me right, and I couldn't figure out what it was."

"Did you figure it out?"

Again, the intensity of Bruce's look caught Maggie off balance. Was he simply interested in what she found, or was he incredulous because it took her several reads? If Sam said she could trust Jacques, and Jacques said she could trust Bruce, could she?

Taking a sip of coffee, Maggie formed words in her mind before she said them. "No, I didn't figure anything out. But, I came up with three open questions. The first was where did Clyde learn how to transcribe notes? The words he captured, and the style, looked like he had training or experience in interrogations or transcription.

"The second two questions went to Aunt Jo. In one of her answers, Aunt Jo said she met Jacques before my mother, Anna, met him. My sister and I always thought Anna knew him first. I'm sure this sounds insignificant, but it was a bombshell for me because I lived with Aunt Jo for five years and it never came up. The last question might sound like I've read too many Nancy Drew mysteries, but you'd have to know Aunt Jo to understand how big this is. When Clyde asked Aunt Jo about the trip my parents made when they went missing in 1950—the last time anyone had seen them alive—Aunt Jo said she wasn't paying attention because she was young and in love. Here's the rub, Aunt Jo has worn thin her reason for living a solitary life. Everyone who knows Aunt Jo knows the love of her life died in World War II, before 1945. A framed photo of Phillip Xavier is the only photograph on her bedside table and the only framed photograph in her house. Why would Aunt Jo lie about something like this?"

"Nothing more about Sam's alleged crimes against women, or someone spiking his drinks, or gaslighting?"

"None that I remember. Clyde was focused on Aunt Jo and what she knew."

"Okay, we've started the shift from Sam to The Puzzle. Before we go any farther, we're going to get down and dirty. You know I don't mince words. Takes too much time and we don't have time. If I sound heavy-handed, it's because this is a matter of life or death, perhaps our very survival. Starting today, no more Triad. You, Sam and Clyde have no fucking idea what you're dealing with. You've unwittingly risked the lives of people you know and love, and those you've never met and may never meet. This is no game and there's no room to bargain. Starting today, you'll close your eyes and trust us to walk you across what will seem like an endless hemp-rope bridge. One hundred feet below this wobbly stretch is a narrow crevasse filled with diamondback rattlers and the skeletons of travelers who stopped trusting."

Maggie shook her head. Damn bees again. *Who the hell does Bruce Shelton think he is? And, where does he get off treating me like an idiot?*

"Maggie, I can only imagine how farfetched this sounds, but I meant for it to hit you in the solar plexus. What's going on?" Bruce asked.

"Oh, I just remembered. When I started to tell Aunt Jo about Sam being afraid someone was after him, she held her fingers to her lips to quiet me. She thought our house might be bugged. Then, she laughed and talked about how new fathers worry, then pointed me out the door. We talked out in the yard, on the picnic table. She warned me not to talk in the house, garage or car. So, no, I'm sure we didn't talk about Sam's problems in places where we might be heard."

"That's good, Maggie. Now tell me why you're pissed off."

Maggie looked at the two men sitting at the table, sharing food and conversation. Just moments ago, it felt dreamy, almost surreal. Now Maggie felt like she was on the hemp-rope bridge, off-balance, alone, afraid. The word *trust* felt like a bad joke, but what options did she, Sam and Tekla have? If they couldn't trust Bruce or Pete or Jacques, who could they trust?

"I'm pissed because I don't trust you or Pete or Jacques or anyone else. Somehow, Sam and I backed ourselves into this corner and now we have to rely on you. That's why I'm pissed."

"Oh, and here I was worried that you didn't like me," Bruce said.

Maggie gave him her hard, don't-mess-with-me look then attempted a smile.

"Welcome to Oz Maggie. Oz is our sobriquet for a quiet revolution that began before the Second World War. Oz opposes tyranny, racism, xenophobia, and any actions or laws that impoverish humankind. This includes any attempts to: restrict freedom of speech or expression; dismantle knowledge; or in any way limit collaboration, creativity and invention across borders.

"Six million people slaughtered while the pope and other religious leaders turned their backs. Six million people died while we drove to work, talked about the World Series, and drank green beer on St. Patrick's Day. Six million people dead because Hitler's regime used racism and nativism to generate an enemy and tame the masses. And, who are we as a people when we continue, every day, to turn our backs on those who are denied life and liberty? I hope you're pissed."

16

First Crocus

They tried to bury us; they didn't know we were seeds.
—Dinos Christianopoulos, Poet

MARCH 15, 1971 POST MERIDIEN—"Must be hard to take in what you just heard. But, you might be relieved to know we're not the bad guys," said Pete.

"I'm not sure what I took in. More like entering another dimension. What does any of this have to do with Sam?"

Pete looked at Bruce to pass the question. Bruce said, "Sam either pissed off someone or poses a threat. Probably both. Let's hold off on this conversation until Sam's in the room. Right now, we need to focus on getting him out of jail and nailing down the house on Six Mile.

"And, Maggie, regardless of what you might have read or seen on TV, having the little wife and baby in the courtroom for a bail hearing is bad business. Attorneys have used this ploy from the days of Judge Roy Bean and I'm sure he knew it was a ploy. The gavel-banger we have tomorrow will go schizoid if he sees you and Tekla hobnobbing with the bottom-feeders. Stay home and work with Pete."

"Question," said Maggie. "How do I explain Uncle Pete to Aunt Jo and Issie?"

"Jacques said Raymond talked about a large family, but they never showed up. No one ever met your dad's family. Not Anna, Aunt Jo, Issie or you. Your story is Uncle Pete found you through Jacques, which is true. And, Pete wanted to visit America and offered to help you with work around the house in return for a place to sleep, which is true. You and Sam said, 'come on down,' which is mostly true. For all others, Uncle Pete won't draw questions and there's no reason to explain anything."

Checking out the chocolate candies on the island, Pete turned and said, "Maggie, we'll talk later, but my passport and driver's license identify me as Pierre Soulier from Windsor, Ontario." Sticking his hands deep inside the pockets of his black chino-styled pants, Pete did a quick and striking Charleston dance move with his feet, then said, "My friends call me Pete. I'm a private building contractor in Windsor, but in the States helping my niece remodel her home in Livonia." Pete's easy, toothy grin spread across his face like a rumor.

"Why don't I want to hear how you made this happen?" said Maggie.

"Don't be coy. You know damn well how we made this happen. We're way past the niceties of polite conversation. We're in this together, and there's a lot at stake. You're the barometer. Everyone is going to depend on you to keep it together. *Capisce?*"

Maggie looked at Bruce and saw the fire in his dark eyes. "You're right. Worse than being coy, I chose to slip into neediness.

Shrinking into fear is one of those weirdly comforting habitual practices I love to loathe. It won't happen again. You can count on me."

Morning turned into afternoon and it looked as if the food platters would last for days. Bruce and Pete had pumped Maggie for the finest details of her and Sam's lives—their family, friends, co-workers, acquaintances and possible enemies. Maggie almost scared herself with her diabolical descriptions of Minnie Fox, Guido, the Women's League of Livonia, Cheryl Cummings, the Livonia Police Department, the night-stalker neighbor, and the window crasher. Then, Maggie retold Sam's story about Carla, a co-worker of Sam's at Sheer Juice, and the first woman he was accused of raping. The night Tekla was born, Carla left a note under the windshield wipers of Sam's car in the hospital parking lot. The note warned Sam to "stop being so predictable" and "bore them to death." Other than Tony Zito, his boss at Sheer Juice, Sam told her he had no idea who Carla meant by 'them.'

By two in the afternoon, Maggie was flat-out exhausted when Bruce put down his Cross pen and said, "Enough. I've got to get ready for a bail hearing tomorrow morning. Once Sam's out, we'll call."

"Does that mean I don't see him tonight?" Maggie asked.

"I'll see him. You and Pete need to get the house ready for tomorrow."

"Will you give Sam my love?"

"Seriously, Maggie? You think I can carry off that kind of message? How 'bout I say Maggie told us to kick ass and take names?"

Maggie smiled and said, "Okay, that works!"

"Time to get the lead out! I've got people to see and arms to twist."

While Bruce filled three grocery bags with leftovers and beverages to stock the refrigerator on Six Mile, Maggie called Maija to see if she'd keep Tekla one more day. There was a different quality about their call; the absence of anxiety and the presence of love seemed . . . well, Maggie thought, ordinary.

Pete was waiting at the car with the keys in his hand, and said, "Help me get the lay of the land. I'll drive, you point out street names, important landmarks and shopping areas. I want to be self-sufficient." Bruce backed his car out of the garage and stopped so Pete could transfer two large army-green duffels and a brown rifle bag from the oversized Lincoln and load them in the compact Corvair. The three grocery bags were packed in the pocket-sized front trunk; the duffle and rifle bags crammed in the miniature backseat. Their bucket seats were pulled as far forward as they could go and Maggie was sure she heard the car groan when Pete put his foot on the gas pedal.

Eyeing the rifle, Maggie said, "Do you remember when you said you'd come to Detroit when you had an insane desire to outrun bullets? I hope that's not the case this trip."

"Me too, Maggie. We've got a lot to do and miles of territory to cover when Sam gets home. Jacques should be here later this week."

Maggie whispered, "Is it okay to talk in the car?"

"We're good to go!" chuckled Pete. "While you and Bruce were cleaning up the kitchen and packing food, I checked out the car."

"Jacques is coming to Detroit?"

"That's the plan."

"Did he say why?"

"Maggie, Jacques is the front man, the '*Che Guevara*' of this quiet revolution."

"Who are the back men?"

"Men and women, too many to name. Jacques will tell you more. Right now, we need to find a hardware store. Count up the number of exterior doors and windows you have—including attics, garages and outbuildings."

Maggie started to complain about the cramped space in the car and suggest they shop after they unload the car. But, she checked and rebuked herself. *For god sake's, Maggie, you invited the army and now you want to tell them how to do their job?*

By the time they stopped to buy eighteen locks at the corner hardware store, and a six-pack of beer at the market next door, it was after four. Maggie cleaned and organized the refrigerator and stocked Bruce's food. Then, she began collecting the strewn documents on the dining room floor. Most were still damp from the wet shag carpet. The legal-size pad with Clyde's transcription of Aunt Jo's interview was missing, as were notes from The Triad's meetings. Maggie wanted to cry but knew it would just slow her down.

A note taped to the front door from the window repair shop was a bill for travel time with a number to call to set up a new date to repair the window. Pete was already heading back to the hardware store to pick up a small sheet of glass, a glass cutter, wood trim and paint. He said he'd fix it. Plus, he'd look for a large fan to help dry the carpeting. Something they could use as an attic fan in the summer.

Maggie moved to the front room and sat down on the couch. It was dry and the heat from the furnace felt warm. She thought if she stretched out and rested her eyes for a few minutes she'd be fine.

Two hours later, kitchen sounds and the smell of paint woke her from the most bizarre dream. She'd been slow dancing with a zebra to Johnny Mathis singing *Chances Are*. With the zebra's long, elegant front legs at her shoulder and waist, he spun her around then dipped her back. Maggie felt both weightless and secure when she looked down and saw that Pete had covered her with the half-finished black and white striped afghan Maija attempted in her first and only crochet class; the afghan Maggie swore she'd finish one day.

Slipping into her road-salt-and-water-stained black clogs, Maggie found Pete in the kitchen. The window was in place and the entire frame had been repainted. "You better be careful, Uncle Pete, I could get used to this kind of service. The window looks great!"

"Trust me, it's a short-term high. Women have said this all my life but end up marrying some joker who can't find his name in the phone book. The thing is, these kinds of quick fixes rock my boat. What do shrinks call it? Instant gratification?"

Maggie looked around. Pete had also cleaned the counters, table, wiped down the stove and refrigerator, and washed, dried and put away dishes that had been sitting in the sink since last week. "Seriously, Uncle Pete, knock yourself out on the instant gratification thing you've got going!" Maggie laughed.

"Yeah? Well don't push it," growled Pete, his old Pepe-curmudgeon coming out.

"Look, I need to talk to Clyde and my friend Loretta before they disown me. Clyde knows about the accident, arrest, charges and hiring Bruce as his attorney. I'm not sure what Loretta knows. But, I know if I don't call they'll send out the cavalry."

"Ms. Maggie, we've got a lot at stake and the biggest risk is you only hold a scrap of knowledge. If this is something you have to do, go to an outside phone booth and keep it short. Remind them you've talked about me before. We forget more than we remember. Tell them Sam needs to chill, so no visitors for now. You'll call back in a few days. That should hold off the cavalry."

At the end of the driveway, Maggie decided to head to Bates Hamburgers to make her calls and grab a sack of sliders to share with Pete. With the public phone inside, it would be a reminder and excuse to keep things general.

The stool next to the payphone was free. She dialed Loretta, who picked up after two rings.

"Hey, Loretta. I didn't want you to send the gendarmes out looking for me so decided I better call."

"Well shut my mouth! This you, baby girl? Where in hell's half acre have you been? I called all weekend and a half dozen times today. You home?"

"No. I'm here at Bates picking up some sliders for me and Uncle Pete and wanted to call before the night got away from me again."

"Uncle Pete? One of Sam's uncles?"

"No, on my father's side. I think I've talked about him, Raymond's youngest brother? In any event, Jacques called to see if I needed some help remodeling because Pete wanted to come stateside. I told Jacques about the break-in and asked him to tell Uncle Pete to pack his tools and come on down."

"Big as my family is, not one of them knows the right side of a saw. I swear, if I have to reincarnate, I'm going to apply for a family of carpenters, plumbers and electricians. But first, tell me how Sam's doing. Clyde said he was in an accident and a world of hurt with the cops coming down on him. LSD? I thought Clyde was putting me on, but no shit, it sounds like he was arrested. Was Sam dropping acid?"

"Did Clyde say that?"

"He said he was arrested for dropping acid and running his car off the road."

"We're not sure what happened. Sam doesn't remember, but I think someone laced his drink. Issie says it happens all the time now. Sam's lawyer says he'll be out on bail tomorrow."

"Lord almighty, girl. You must be a mess. How're you holding up?"

"Pretty good. Maija's been an angel and is playing house with Tekla in Farmington. I was scared out of my mind after the accident, but with help from The Eights, Jacques, Uncle Pete and the lawyer, we'll get through this."

Maggie looked to see if anyone was listening, then lowered her voice and said, "The craziness is we moved from some badass hood in Detroit . . . to what?"

"Bigotry and hate, or ignorance and stupidity. Take your pick. It's hard to see it or fight it. I should know; I still get blindsided almost every day."

"Do you have any idea how much I miss you? I want to talk more, but there's no privacy. Will you let Stella know what's going on?"

"Not to worry, baby girl. I'll tell Stella and bring Willie and Robin into the loop. You take care of that gorgeous baby and man."

Resisting the growl in her stomach, Maggie dialed Clyde.

"Hey, Clyde, this is your long-lost friend. Sorry I didn't call sooner."

"Oh, Maggie, good to hear your voice. I've tried your house a dozen times and thought your party-line might pick up and give me a rash of . . . um, cow pucky."

"Wrecking crew?" Maggie laughed.

"Yep. Just caught one out of the corner of my eye. Tell me. Blanche and I have been worried. Not to mention Loretta who thinks I'm hiding you in the basement."

"Right now, I'm at a hamburger stand and need to keep it short. Hearing is tomorrow, and we got the guy Willie recommended. He's a trip, but he said to look for a homecoming tomorrow."

"Whew, what a relief! What about you and Tekla?"

"We're fine. Tekla is still into her magpie routine and Maija seems enchanted!"

"And you?"

"Better than yesterday. My Uncle Pete from Windsor heard about the broken window thing and showed up today to fix it and install some new locks."

"I didn't know Jo had a brother."

"She doesn't. Pete's from the other side of the family, my father's brother. I know I've mentioned him before. Small time contractor type, handy with tools."

"Huh? Maybe. I don't recall, but that goes with age and parenting. You know I'm a phone call away?"

"Clyde, I wouldn't have made it through the last few days without you and Blanche. I know you're there. Issie came by one day to take my mind off things for a few hours and I'm good. Tired, but good."

"I know you can't talk, but I don't want you freaking out about the mess you found in the dining room. Blanche and I decided the least we could do is cover your kitchen window with plywood to keep out the rain and critters. I waited until after dark to drive to your house. When I got there the side door of the house, by the garage, was wide open. There were no lights on and no cars in the drive. I was on high alert—worried about you, The Puzzle notes, and decided I couldn't just leave. Once I got inside, I found the drawer pulled out of the buffet and papers all over. I looked for you. Thank god you weren't there. Then, I imagined some cop calling one of those NIL, nigger in Livonia codes, and half the force showing up with guns drawn because they had nothing else to do on a Saturday night—my worst nightmare. My hands were shaking so hard they were almost worthless. When I found the notes, I ran like a bat out of hell! I didn't get the window covered and probably left the side door swinging wide open, so tell your Uncle Pete I'm happy to lend him a hand."

"You're kidding? You have the notes?"

"I have the notes. They look like they're all here."

"Holy mother of god. I walked into that mess after I left you and Willie at Big Boys on Saturday. When I cleaned up the house today, the notes were gone and I freaked. If you were here I'd kiss you!" Maggie laughed, then looked around to see if anyone was listening. Cheryl Cummings, in a pair of pressed camelhair slacks and matching jacket, was sitting at the window counter looking at Maggie.

Lowering her voice, Maggie said, "Hey, Clyde. Need to run. I'll call Tuesday or Wednesday after I've had time to help Sam and Tekla make their re-entry."

As Maggie hung up the phone, Cheryl patted the red vinyl-covered stool next to her and said, "Hi, Maggie. Come sit. I need to talk to you."

Maggie's first thought was to beg off, but this was too off-the-charts-synchronistic to ignore. She knew she looked like a poor waif—hair uncombed, no makeup, beat-up clogs, K-Mart-grade polyester pants, pimples forming on her greasy nose and chin—not to mention wearing a pea coat she used to clean off spit on a filthy phone. The only thing missing was a tin cup.

"Hi, Cheryl. Picking up dinner?"

"I wish. I'm here because I'm haunted by what happened to you and Sam. Please sit."

Not ready to commit, Maggie leaned against the edge of the stool. "How did you know I was here?"

"I didn't. I'm here to inhale three sliders to calm my nerves. Why are you here? Dinner?"

Maggie looked into Cheryl's beautiful green eyes and noticed her mascara was smudged. "I'm not sure what drew me here. Maybe comfort food. Did you order?"

"Not yet. When I saw you on the phone, I decided to wait. See if you'd talk to me."

"Let's order. The smell is sending my taste buds into orbit," said Maggie.

They each ordered three burgers with extra onion and pickles and a vanilla shake. When they sat down facing the traffic along Farmington Road, neither spoke until after they'd finished their second burgers.

"Maggie, in spite of what you might think about me and Livonia, I want you to hear what I've been rehearsing I'd say if we ever ran into each other. Because it's rehearsed it might sound insincere, but it doesn't mean it's untrue. I spend so much time choreographing how I look and what I say that sometimes my truth gets lost in the stage props. The only way I regain it is to practice saying what's true for me. I want you to know the truth. I don't want you to waste time thinking I'm the enemy. I'm not."

With her intuition unmoored, Maggie's head called bullshit and her heart pined for a happy ending. "Go on," said Maggie.

"My guess is you think the stone through your window and Sam's arrest are the result of me complaining to my husband, Doug. Here's the thing, Doug is registered as an independent because he wanted to run for mayor. He knew he couldn't do it on a Democratic ticket and he didn't want to register as a Republican, so he ran as an Independent. He's a good man, socially liberal, fiscally conservative. I've always been apolitical because of my family and their investments. But, I want you to hear me say this—Doug and I are not racist."

"Well, you sure have an unusual way of demonstrating your non-racist ideals."

"You're right. I pulled the race card and played it to get attention and support. I'm ashamed of myself and not sure why I wanted to hurt you. Maybe because you were so brave to speak up, to call us on our crude behavior."

"Talk is cheap. I want to believe I'm working against racism, but . . . what? I'm a total slouch. I spend more time and money at Bates than I do on civil rights. Maybe I make up this whole thing to give myself some purpose. Fair trade for my right to breathe the air, soak up the sun, attend a feminist rally, convince myself I'm making a difference in this screwed up world."

"Listen, Maggie. Someone decided to make you and Sam pay for supporting civil rights. I promise it wasn't Doug or me. My guess is someone from the League, at our table, teed this off. If Doug finds out, he'll make sure they suffer the price. But you can't afford to piss off the police. Call me if you want help or need a friend."

By now, Maggie was squarely on top of the round stool, looking at the person she'd painted into a corner with her beauty, wealth and position. Maggie didn't know if Cheryl was for real. *Time would tell, or not*, she thought. The fickleness of perception and perspective seemed closer to the truth.

"Tonight, I wasn't looking for a friend," said Maggie, "but I needed one. Thanks for introducing me to the other you. I know how hard that can be."

Cheryl nodded her head, laughed and said, "Oh, god, what if there are more me's lurking inside?"

17

Incubation

Look what they've done to my brain, Ma. Look what they've done to my brain. Well they've cooked it like a chicken bone, and I think I'm half insane, Ma. Look what they've done to my song.

—Melanie Safka, Lyrics from *Look What They've Done to My Song, Ma*

MARCH 16, 1971—Maggie checked her face in the bathroom mirror and caught a glimpse of her old self. Shiny hair, light makeup, reasonably rested, but there was an agitation she hadn't noticed or felt before—she could see it in her eyes.

Carol, from Bruce's office, called earlier to say she reserved a private room at the Machus Red Fox in West Bloomfield. Sam and Bruce would be there at noon. A tony restaurant, the Red Fox was well-known for movers and shakers of mixed repute. And, Maggie thought, a curious choice if Bruce wanted to keep a low profile. She shook her head and laughed. *As if I know*, thought Maggie. She was there once for drinks after a concert at Pine Knob. Pulling her faux black-suede coat from a wire hanger in the front closet, she brushed the shoulder dust off with her hand, and let out a "whew!" Her left leg was bouncing up and down. Agitation or excitement? She wasn't sure. Was she getting off on the edginess? Or, was this the edge of terror? What was she willing to give up for a bigger purpose? Her marriage, her family? Was she any different than her mother?

Pete whistled when he saw Maggie in a black mini-dress with long Gatsby-like pearls and black patent-leather go-go boots. "Look at you in a dress! Sam's going to have a hard time keeping his mind on the conversation," winked Pete.

Maggie bit back her impulse to unwrap his sexism. Older guys just didn't get it. Instead, she smiled and said, "You too, Uncle Pete, nice jacket. You clean up pretty doggone good for a guy." Pete's blush was Maggie's reward.

Traffic was light, and they arrived with time to spare. Pete saw Bruce's black Lincoln and parked next to him just as Sam, dressed in a new dark gray suit, opened the passenger door. Sam caught Maggie's wave, and before she made the turn to open her door, he was there to help her out.

"Maggie, Maggie. Oh, god. I wasn't sure I'd see you again," he whispered in her ear. "Please don't leave me."

Maggie pulled him so close it was hard to feel the separation between their two beings. "I won't."

"Come on, you lovebirds," said Bruce, "we've got some business to take care of first."

Sam shook Pete's hand and said, "Thanks for taking care of Maggie. Meant a lot to have you here."

"My pleasure, Sam. She's one helluva girl. You're lucky to have her."

Maggie groaned at the unconscious caveman-talk. Based on their expressions, she was sure they took her groan as an *aw-shucks* and joyfully re-fired their DNA.

The *maître d* asked them to take a seat in the bar while he checked to see if the room was ready. Bruce stopped to talk with three men at a corner table.

"Damn, do you know who those guys are?" Sam whispered.

"What guys?" asked Maggie.

"The three guys Bruce is chatting up."

"Nope, no idea."

"The Giacalone brothers—Vito 'Billy Jack' and 'Tony Jack,' big-time mafia capos in Detroit. The guy with the big nose is Joe Zerilli, *the* majordomo godfather of the Detroit Partnership. Zerilli is the only non-New York boss on the Commission."

"What commission?"

"Like the mafia's national board of directors—a mobster corporation model. That's why it's called organized crime."

After Maggie sat down, she couldn't keep her eyes off Bruce and the riveting, fleshy-faced Sicilians. When Bruce joined them at their table, he winked at Maggie and said, "Yes, Maggie, they're friends and clients. They wanted to know why you were staring at them. Makes them nervous."

Before Maggie had a chance to reply, the *maître d* showed up and guided them to a wine cellar lined with casks. Ambient light from a collection of lit paintings—hunters with horses, dogs and prey—tempered the rustic banquet table and stone walls with an uncanny warmth. The table was set with white linen tablecloths; heavy, white pottery; and dark red napkins. Sitting on the opposite side of the table, facing the door, Jacques and Clyde.

Maggie's knees started to buckle, and Sam pulled her closer. She looked hard at Sam and knew he wasn't surprised. No one was surprised. She was the only outsider in the room. If Bruce wanted her to be pissed, this did it. What kind of pathetic lie had she been living? Whose vile game was this? Maggie wanted to bolt. To find Tekla and head where? How do we escape what we can't see?

Sam helped her sit down next to him, across from Jacques and Clyde. Bruce and Pete took chairs at each end of the table.

Maggie glared at Jacques and he returned her look with kindness and a nod of his head. Clyde looked both calm and unsettled. Maggie wouldn't look at Sam. She backed her chair up as far as she could and said, "I don't know what the hell is going on, but I'm about to leave. If anyone tries to stop me, and I mean anyone, I'm going to go totally ballistic."

Jacques leaned forward across the table toward Maggie and in his softest voice said, "Maggie, no one is keeping you here. At this point, you can go, hide, disappear. No one at this table will try to track you down. You're free to leave."

Maggie looked at everyone except Sam. They each nodded their head in agreement.

Bruce said, "Maggie, we won't track you down, others will. Remember my story about the endless hemp-rope bridge? There's always the risk of falling into that crevasse. You're making assumptions because you learned about Oz after we did. We didn't choose to withhold information from you because we didn't trust you, we chose to withhold information because we didn't want you to take on the risk."

"When did Sam . . . take on . . . the risk?" Maggie asked. She knew her voice sounded sharp, mean, sarcastic; she didn't care.

Sam turned his chair to Maggie and said, "I found out about Oz a few months after Tekla was born. Jacques was planning to see you and Tekla, but we put him off because you, Clyde and I decided to keep our distance. Part of our cold war charm approach when we didn't know who to trust. Clyde knew about Oz, but he didn't want me to take on the risk until I had to. After Aunt Jo called to warn me about her soup, our Puzzle, I wanted to find a way to protect you and Tekla. I got in touch with Carla, the woman who left the note on my windshield at the hospital. She told me the mafia was involved and maybe the CIA. She didn't know why they were interested in me, but thought it had to do with something in Canada. I called Jacques. He said he'd see me when he came to Detroit. I've known about Oz for over a year."

Maggie thought she was going to throw up. She felt off-balance, dizzy, unsure of her own presence. Sam's voice sounded like it was coming through a tunnel. There was no one there. Just his voice. Then she heard someone keening and heaving. The vibrations were coming through her, a part of her separated from the rest. *Who was making that hideous noise?*

Clyde circled the table and knelt down next to her. "Maggie, it's me, Clyde. Come on, Maggie girl. I know you're hurt and scared out of your mind. You're strong my kickass, radical friend. You can do this. I promise. Blanche will help. She knows. You're not alone. We're all here because we know this is an irrational leap of faith to ask you to take. I promise you'll make it. And, the days when you didn't know about Oz will be sweet, innocent memories. Hear me say this, you will never, ever want to return to that innocence. You will think you do, but you don't and you won't."

Maggie didn't know how long Clyde was on his knees next to her or when Sam put his head on her lap. She thought she heard Bruce, Jacques and Pete talking, but the tempo was like listening to a seventy-eight RPM record on thirty-three RPM speed.

When Bruce tapped his heavy water goblet with a spoon, Maggie looked up. "Maggie, that's all the time you have right now to indulge in self-pity or dream up revenge scenarios. You told me you weren't going to shrink into fear again. I'm depending on it. Our work relies on it. In ten minutes the waiter's going to serve us veal *scaloppini a la Française* and he's going to find a group of friends enjoying caesar salad and talking about the Tiger's spring training in Lakeland, Florida. *Capisce?*"

With the room in focus, Maggie looked again. Each person at that table was important to her. They were people she trusted or wanted to trust. Now, what? She didn't know; either choice was a risk. She needed time to think. Bruce was waiting for a response. She said, "I'm royally pissed and I'm here until I decide I don't want to be here."

Bruce broke out in laughter and Maggie could hear everyone taking a deep breath. Bruce lifted his water glass in a toast, "To Maggie, who's royally pissed yet willing to give us a shot. Welcome to Oz!"

For some reason, this toast filled her with a sense of family, of being part of something bigger than she'd ever known. She reached for Sam's hand and squeezed it. He squeezed back and whispered, "This is good, we're okay. I promise."

When the waiter served *scaloppini*, the guys were talking about the Tigers. Maggie thought there was a Tennessee William's stage-play quality to the conversation and found herself thinking about Liz Taylor's role as Maggie in *Cat on a Hot Tin Roof*—manic because Paul Newman, her husband Brick, had lost his sex drive.

"Earth to Maggie. Are you there?" said Jacques.

"Sorry?"

"I asked if you had a favorite Tiger."

"Not really. Well, maybe. The catcher Bill Freehan."

"I would have guessed you for a Kaline fan. Why Freehan?"

Maggie felt her face blush when she said, "Nice smile and cute butt. All those squats behind the batter obviously work."

Everyone laughed, including Maggie, who felt as if she was watching herself laugh from the other side of the room. Then, she flashed back to Issie's story about their dad, Raymond, flipping over the patio table and calling Anna a cunt because she made the mistake of putting cherries on his banana split. *Maybe Raymond wasn't crazy. Maybe he was just coping with the insanity of his world.*

"What do you think, Maggie?" Bruce asked.

"Sorry, my mind keeps drifting."

"Okay. Stay with me. I just explained Sam's options. If he returns to Jingo Motors and maintains positive employment with them for one year, the court will drop all charges. If Jingo Motors refuses to keep him on, he has one month to find other gainful employment; however, the terms are the same. He'll need to maintain positive employment with them for one year.

"Sam's second option is to accept a reduced charge of 'driving while under the influence of an illegal substance' and serve six months in the Detroit House of Corrections—better known as DeHoCo—with one year of probation upon release."

Maggie looked at Sam, then turned to Bruce. "That sounds like a no-brainer. Why would Sam even consider going to jail and living with a record?"

Sam held up his index finger and said, "Let me do this. Maggie, Oz wants someone at Jingo Motors. They, I mean we, think Jingo is laundering money. Where and for what reason is less clear. But Oz thinks they're part of a global consortium that incites protests, riots and coups—to spread fear and influence elections."

"Fear?" Maggie asked.

"To gain control over the masses," said Jacques. "The consortium's ultimate interest is the world's richest, natural resources—especially nickel." Seeing Maggie's reaction, Jacque continued. "Nickel, dear Marguerite, is the war metal. Chronic shortages have plagued industrial and military production since the early fifties.

"In the northern hemisphere, Russia, Canada and Cuba hold the largest reserves. When Castro nationalized American nickel mines after the revolution in fifty-nine, the U.S. had to rely on the Sudbury Basin in Canada. A little-known fact, Canada has produced 99.9% of all nickel five-cent coins since 1922. Forget uranium deposits or plutonium ore; nickel is the gold standard for winning wars. The 1969 Sudbury Basin strikes crippled military production for the war in Vietnam."

Maggie forced herself to feel gravity and wrapped her hands under the seat of her chair. The last thing she wanted was another out-of-body experience. Taking a deep breath, she said, "Jacques,

I have no idea why you're giving me this kind of detail or what it means. What I want to know, to understand, is why Clyde, Sam and I are in this room, at this table, talking about wars."

"Fair enough. We'll use a talking stick like the Maasai people in Kenya, except it will be a soup spoon. I'll take no more than two minutes to tell you why I'm here and we'll pass the talking stick around the room. When it gets to you, Maggie, you'll tell us why you think you're at the table. If you don't know, or don't want to talk, you can pass the stick to Sam, and we'll continue clockwise around the table twice. Only the person holding the spoon may talk. After everyone has had two chances to speak, you may ask each person one question. Then, we're done for today."

Maggie watched Jacques pick up the soup spoon and clear his throat. After his lecture about the economics of war, she was stunned by the mockery of this childish, schoolgirl's game. *Holy mother of god,* she thought, *maybe we're all crazy.*

"I'm at this table because the force for good needs more than prayers. To fight greed, corruption and violence, we need a systemic plan to protect life, liberty and knowledge. That means we develop effective interventions to remove or destroy threats to these freedoms. To do that, we need more than Amnesty International; we need an international underground army—an invisible brain trust and network."

Accepting the talking spoon, Bruce said, "I'm here because nothing else makes sense. Even the law gets flipped on its ass. Liberty doesn't exist without knowledge, and knowledge doesn't exist without liberty. I'm here to make sure Oz has an advocate when we're up against dirty cops, dirty judges or dirty politicians."

Maggie accepted the spoon from Bruce and passed it to Sam. Sam said, "I'm here because my life was becoming a living hell. I knew I was being targeted and it threatened not only me, but you, Maggie, and Tekla. I don't know of another safe place. I don't know how else to be in this world right now. There are times when

I wonder if Oz is nothing more than a super cult. But, Clyde has been my best friend for years and Jacques is someone I've gotten to know and respect. There's never been any pressure to join or stay. I'm here because it makes sense. Oz is . . . well . . . a place where I know who I am and what I stand for."

Pete took the spoon and said, "I'm going to make this short. Jacques saved me and dozens of other Cubans who would have spent most of their lives in prison or labor camps. Before the revolution, I was a metallurgist and oversaw the nickel reserves. Today, I'm fluent in English, Italian, Spanish and French. I've learned to be a chameleon and I'm good at it. That's why I'm still here. No one has forced me to do anything."

Clyde accepted the spoon from Pete. "Maggie girl, I know it hit you hard when you saw me sitting at this table. Me, of all people. You are my friend. You'll find out soon enough why I didn't expose myself to you earlier. You'll learn the same discretion. We are part of an underground, global effort to end discrimination, racism, sexism—you name the 'ism.' It takes more than a village. It takes a tangled web of resources and people willing to work through the kinks, misunderstandings, religious dogma and tedious bureaucracies we carry in our backpacks. I spent three years interrogating and torturing Vietnamese POWs. By the time I got back to the States, I was sure I'd lost my soul. I deserted and found my way to Toronto. Jacques found me in a shelter. Bruce ran the traps and got me a medical discharge. The work of Oz is my work. That's why I'm here today."

Maggie was fighting back tears when Jacques took the spoon and passed. Then Bruce spun the spoon through his fingers, smiled and looked at Maggie. "I'm still here because these edge walkers are my best friends. I don't have to prove myself anymore. They know I have their backs. For what it's worth, I think you've found a home."

When Maggie took the spinning spoon from Bruce, she held it in a fist and looked around the table. "I'm tired. I'm here today because I was hijacked by men I thought were my friends. I don't know if you're friends. Part of me is curious and excited to know there are men like you in the world who've bet their futures against the most oppressive odds. If I were going to pick friends, I'd want friends like you. But I'm still pissed. Still angry that you kept me out of the loop for so long. I want to replay every conversation I've had with each of you and find the lies and beat you with them. Bruce said no more time for revenge thinking, but that battle will take time. Now, I want to pick up Tekla and go home and pretend for a few hours that I'm living an ordinary life. As my sister Issie would say, fuck you very much."

18

Larva

We must be free not because we claim freedom, but because we practice it.

—William Faulkner

MARCH 31, 1971—Maggie felt like a monarch caterpillar on a small leaf. Not that she knew where she wanted to go, or what to do, but her restlessness over the past two weeks felt as if she was preparing for hibernation or flight. One or the other. No doubt her refusal to talk about anything more complicated than the weather was falling like acid rain on everyone's leaves, including hers.

Uncle Pete had finally installed the window and door locks, plus three security cameras—one at each entrance—front, side, and back. Every inch of the house and garage had been checked for hidden cameras, microphones and recorders. Short of building a moat or hiring twenty-four-seven armed-guards, both Sam and Pete said the lock and camera set up—plus a German Shepard—would provide the best security. Maggie nixed the dog because each bark would resonate like another rock through the kitchen window. And, if they were being targeted because of their civil rights work, some hyped-up Jim Crow might poison the dog out of sheer stupidity or meanness.

For the past two weeks, Sam had slept on the floor in Tekla's bedroom and Pete slept in his 'cabin,' more commonly known as the unattached garage. Although they all shared the bathroom, Pete insisted on showering at the YMCA in Detroit or the local sauna on Five Mile Road, noting, "Unlike antiseptic Americans, most of the world doesn't feel the need to waste fifteen minutes and thirty gallons of water every twenty-four hours to stay clean."

The day after the Red Fox lunch—or, as Maggie called it, her 'shock treatment'—Sam and Pete had rented a U-Haul trailer to pick up building supplies, a twin-size mattress, a space heater, bar refrigerator, hotplate, percolator and floor lamp. Bruce had convinced Sam to take two weeks off work to recover and recalibrate. Sam didn't argue. Except for the stitched crescent moon on the left edge of his jaw, he looked fine. But inside, Sam was like a punch card that got stuck in the computer then tossed out. Sam had always taken his center of gravity and internal compass for granted. No more.

After they unloaded the trailer and checked in with Maggie, they headed to Maija's to rescue a multi-colored, rolled-and-tied, eight-by-ten rag rug that had languished for twenty years in the basement. Maija held onto this old rug in the event she ever wanted to rip up her carpeting and go back to wood floors. No way was that going to happen! Maija finally realized the only people with wood floors these days were farmers who couldn't afford carpeting; the Grosse Pointe and Birmingham folks who had maids to wax and un-wax floors every six months; or women who had some masochistic/narcissistic need to get on their hands and knees and see their reflection in a wood floor. When the guys showed up at Maija's, Sam was surprised to see her in full makeup with no gray showing through her blond hair. She'd lost some weight chasing Tekla around and looked slim in her black cords and a snug, pink fur-blend cardigan with the top three buttons undone. As a teenager, Sam was always uncomfortable with his mother's striking figure and comments about her resemblance to Marilyn Monroe. Now, Sam felt tenderness and appreciation for a woman whose kindness and courage led to a full life. When Maija started dating, Sam felt protective, and he was surprised to discover, a little jealous. After he married Maggie, he began to see his mother through a less child-like lens. Maija was the real deal. Her self-confidence, looks and brash charm were off the charts. Pete was putty.

Sam got out of the car and gave Maija a hug. "Hey, Ma, this is Pete Soulier, Maggie's uncle from Windsor."

"Pete Soulier, nice to meet you," said Maija, smiling as she tucked a wisp of her hair behind her ear and caught his eyes.

"Pleasure is mine," said Pete. Sam shook his head when he saw Pete blush through his olive-toned skin.

"I've got some coffee on and fresh *rieska*, right out of the oven, if you've got time for a break."

"Thanks, Ma, but as Maggie says, we've got miles to go before we sleep."

"No hurry at all," Pete interrupted. "What's v-es-ka?"

Maija laughed, put her hand on Pete's muscled shoulder and said, "I know it sounds like a 'v,' but the spelling is r-i-e-s-k-a and the pronunciation is pure Finnish-Yooper. *Rieska* is a flatbread that tastes like dessert. With real butter and Aunt Jo's rhubarb preserves . . . well, I have to warn you, you'll be hooked."

"Sounds like a risk I want to take," said Pete as he placed his hand at the small of Maija's back and admired her tulips pulling sun into the cold earth.

The next day, Sam and Pete crafted a simple attic floor in the garage by placing a four-by-six-foot sheet of plywood across the two-by-four support beams at the ceiling's edge—at the back, left side of the garage. Then, they moved all the miscellaneous garage items and storage boxes into this small attic space.

With the aid of a pressed-shirt-cardboard pattern, Pete drilled holes in the four corners of two other four-by-six-foot sheets of plywood. One sheet of plywood was placed across the two-by-four support beams at the ceiling's edge—at the back, right side of the garage. Using metal shackles and Halyard Hitch knots, Pete secured the ends of four ten-foot lengths of heavy-duty hemp rope to the beams, then threaded the rope through the new attic floor. Pulling one rope end at a time, Pete threaded each of the four corners of the third sheet of plywood and secured the rope with more knots and shackles on its underside. Now, hanging three feet off the concrete floor, Sam and Pete lifted the twin mattress onto this platform, fitting it neatly between the four lengths of rope.

Maggie and Tekla walked into the garage at the exact moment Pete was testing the velocity of the swinging bed. To say Tekla's eyes popped out of her head would not be an exaggeration. When she began to shake, jump and squeal with hysterical giddiness, Sam thought the stress of the last few weeks had been too much for her tender spirit. But Pete caught her vibe, jumped off the bed and lifted Tekla up in the air. "My dear Miss Tekla, when you graduate from the crib, I promise," Pete cleared his throat, then sang, "to come over the river—or through the tunnel—to Tekla's house I'll go—and build you a bed, your own swinging bed, and off to sleep you'll go!"

Tekla's giggles felt like a benediction. *Maybe,* Maggie thought, *we don't choose our family, our family chooses us.* Maggie looked at Sam and found him looking at her. Tears were glistening in his eyes. How fine this line between sadness and joy.

The third day after Maggie's shock treatment, Pete asked her to take on the interior decorations for the cabin. With a budget of two one-hundred-dollar bills to buy pillows, linens, a light quilt, towels, and a "big, manly coffee mug," Maggie and Tekla spent the morning trolling the Livonia Mall and K-Mart, pulling together a palate of navy, khaki and burnt orange linens, plus a wicker storage basket that might serve double-duty as a bedside table. When they returned, a note on the kitchen counter said:

Dear Womenfolk,

Taking care of poor car and getting lunch. See you later.

Love, Sam

While Tekla napped, Maggie lost herself in decorating the garage, like she used to do when she was turning an old shed into a playhouse or designing floor plans in the snow.

Late that afternoon, when she heard Sam and Pete pull into the driveway, she ran outside and held up her hand for them to stop. Then, Maggie opened the heavy metal vehicle door to expose the full-size diorama and waved Sam and Pete forward. Pete stepped out of the car and whistled. "Ms. Maggie, you've turned this sad little garage into a cabin worthy of honorable mention by *Outdoor Life* magazine."

Sam's smile slid across his face as he crossed his arms and nodded his head. Maggie knew Sam wanted to hug her, and there were moments like this when she longed to lose herself in his arms. Yet, her need for revenge loomed large. And, as all revenge-players discover, bitterness rebounds like a missed free throw.

That night, Pete deep-fried beer-battered lake perch and fries. Maggie shredded cabbage for coleslaw and sent Sam to the corner store for Miracle Whip. Anyone looking in would have seen three friends and a toddler sitting around the dining room table, laughing at Pete's stories about his time in Cuba—spliced with questions and comments about Maija; then, the four of them singing rounds of *Row, Row, Row Your Boat* to the beat of Tekla's spoon on her Melmac plate.

After Sam read *Good Night, Moon* to Tekla for the third time, he tucked her in bed and joined Maggie on the sofa. He watched as Maggie began knitting a small afghan for Tekla's swinging bed. Ten minutes passed before Maggie put her yarn and knitting needles on her lap, looked at Sam and said, "What is it?"

"Maggie, I know I hurt you. And, I understand why you want to hurt me. In so many ways, I deserve it. But, it's hard to be next to you, to see you and not touch you. How long do you plan to seek revenge?"

"Maybe a year. How does that sound? Let's see. How long did you play your charade? Eighteen months? That might work. Let's plan on eighteen months."

"Is that what you want? Do you want to take the next eighteen months of our lives and play out this game or do you want to build a life with each other?"

"Seriously, Sam? Build a life with what, Tinker Toys? You and Clyde let me run in circles pretending we were The Triad, that we were responsible for managing this diabolical attack on our lives. Are you kidding me? Now you want me to believe you're the adult in the family? Capable of intimacy? Give me a break."

"Maggie, I want to give you a break. I want to do whatever I can to make this better. I know I've been handled. And, I know you don't like being handled any more than I do. At the least, let me tell you why I thought it was safer for you not to know. It might help you deal with anything new that comes up."

"Are you handling me right now?"

"I don't know, Mag. Is that what you think? What I know is I love you. I was scared out of my mind that you and Tekla would be hurt. I didn't know the players and I sure as hell didn't know the magnitude. You heard Jacques and Bruce. Oz is the opposite of organized crime. An organization committed to the imperfect, messy evolution of a new kind of world—not based on greed, wealth, possession, money. There's no perfect name or explanation. In Hebrew, the name Oz means strength, power and courage. For most of us, Oz is a magical place where each person can be and do whatever they believe they can. You said you'd want men like us as friends. How about husbands, Maggie? I want you on my side. No, that's not what I mean. What I mean is I want to be on the same side . . . with you. Tekla needs both of us." When Maggie didn't respond, Sam said, "Okay, Maggie, I'm here. I'm not going anywhere. You can try to force me to stop loving you, but I won't. And, my beautiful, badass wife, I won't leave unless you tell me that's what you want." Sam picked up the *Detroit Free Press* from the coffee table, walked the few feet into the dining room, sat at the table with his back to Maggie, and pulled down the extendable, flying-saucer-shaped ceiling lamp.

Maggie lifted the clumsy knitting needles and the eighteen-inch-by-one-inch strip of apple green yarn, in a simple *knit two, purl one, yarn over, purl two together* pattern, and dropped it in a small basket next to the sofa. A practice-patch. A diversion from writing poetry, fixing relationships or advancing civil rights.

Taking a few steps to their old secretary, the desk Sam's dad used when he brought his work home, Maggie pulled out the top drawer. Her moleskin notebook and favorite pen were undisturbed. *Quiet,* Maggie thought, *freakishly quiet.* When she lifted her notebook, she was surprised by how strange it felt in her hands. How long had it been? The first few poems were written before Tekla was born. Then, the *Ode to Baby Tervo*, her last completed poem. Blank pages had always taunted her. It was part of the process. Like a blank canvas daring the painter to make her first stroke. But tonight, the blank page looked listless, almost apathetic.

Maggie held the pen as if it was a stone cutter and carved words on the paper.

> If the moon had willow trees, it would look like this winter scene: stark white, without horizons, shadows of shadows, infinite in its longing for definition.
>
> In the after-school dim—dressed in my red snowsuit, white mittens, black boots—green eyes peering over Aunt Minnie's scratchy gray babushka—I tromp out a floor plan in the snow. Careful to leave doors, a living room here, a bedroom there; I mark spaces for sofas, tables, chairs—retrace lines, perfect my design.
>
> Working against the darkening, icy stillness, I push a heavy snowball into the living room to form a chair; patting it, I give it shape and strength.
>
> Sighing, content with my creation, I sit down, smile and say, "Hello Daddy."

Sophomoric, she thought, *a fourteen-year-old's romance with language.* Maggie gripped the pen as if she could force its untapped murky ink into words. Instead, she curved a diagonal line across the poem. The image of a torn-rag on the tail of someone else's kite skittered through her mind. *Was that it? Was she slipstreaming the power of others—Sam, Clyde, Jacques, even Tekla with her remarkable life force?*

Then, as if struck dumb by her own stupidity, Maggie began clicking through the frames of her life, as if she was looking through a View-Master. The pattern was easy to pick out. As long as she had a crisis to keep her attention, a mystery to solve, a man to seduce or rescue, or a job to do, Maggie was sated. But during breaks in the action, when she had time to face the truth about her empty self, Maggie could no longer ignore the void. Who was she when she wasn't a stage prop or bit player in someone else's drama? A little girl building snowhouses and watching them melt?

19

Pupa

It's far beyond a star—it's near beyond the moon. I know beyond a doubt—my heart will lead me there soon.
—*Beyond the Sea* lyrics by Jack Lawrence

MORNING, APRIL 3, 1971—With temperatures nuzzling sixty, April sprung like a Frank Sinatra song. Maggie imagined lilacs swelling with buds, willows flirting with the sun, caterpillars spinning into chrysalis chandeliers. Too soon for Detroit, but somewhere. Early Spring, like first love, croons with so much optimism it's easy to believe in beauty. No more war, famine, racism, broken hearts or battered bodies. But Maggie knew where this ballad led. Snow would fall before the first lawnmower was revved up. And, the returning Spring, chastised for her impetuous start, would slip in unnoticed.

Yesterday, Maija stopped by to drop off two new wood jigsaw puzzles for Tekla: a red and black dump truck and an orange cat. Next to singing and dancing with Uncle Pete, Tekla's favorite play, obsession, was putting together puzzles. Maggie was sure these last two rounded out the entire portfolio of wood puzzles for toddlers.

As for Maija, she looked sassy in a short, pencil-thin black tweed skirt, a form-fitting gold and black striped blouse, and a black cardigan tossed across her shoulders.

Maggie did a double take. Was Maija coloring her hair and wearing makeup again?

"Hey, Maija, looking good! Are you in love?"

"Who's not? Must be the hint of Spring. Everyone acts like they're in love. How about you, Maggie? You guys recovered from Sam's accident . . . and, um . . . all that craziness?"

"Crazy is as crazy does. I'm recovering, and glad Sam took some time off. He heads back to work on Monday."

"Hmm . . . I still don't understand why someone threw a rock through your window." Maija looked around, then whispered, "Anyone can see you're both white."

Maggie snagged her crusader instinct before it found voice. She knew Maija wasn't stupid, so she was hard-pressed to believe she could be that literal or ignorant. Whatever this was about, Maggie didn't have the energy to dig deeper. "Seriously, Maija, you're looking good. Whatever it is, keep it up. How about coffee in the dining room?"

"Huh . . . okay," Maija said as if she was distracted—like someone at a party who chats you up while looking over your shoulder to see if there's anyone more interesting to hang out with. "Where is everyone?"

"Tekla went with the guys to pick up groceries, and I'm sure, a handful of Nutty Squirrels."

"Oh, good! You can tell me about Pete. I don't remember you talking about him."

"I'd be surprised if I didn't, maybe not. Raymond, my very anti-social father, wasn't big on families. Not with his parents, sibs or us. So, Issie and I try to stay in touch with the few Souliers we know."

"When did Pete show up in your life? After your parents went missing?"

Maggie didn't like where this was going. She didn't want to say anything that would blow Pete's cover or back him into a corner he didn't know about. "When I was a kid, Aunt Minnie would send Issie and me upstairs or outside when they had company. It was hard to keep track of who was kin. For sure, most would have been from the Landry side, my mother's family."

"I guess," Maija looked around, sighed then whispered, "Is he married?"

"Maija Tervo, are you thinking of putting the moves on my poor Uncle Pete?" Maggie laughed.

Maija's fair skin flushed pink, "Maggie, it's not like I'm ready to write my damn memoir. I still get the curse."

"Whew! Glad you didn't say your 'monthly visitor.'"

"I might be old, but I've never been square. Coarse, crude and sometimes out-of-touch, but never square," Maija laughed.

"Now that you ask, I have no idea if Pete's married. Just assumed he wasn't because he's never talked about a wife or kids. Who knows? Pete's a part-time curmudgeon who could charm the socks off a scorpion. That's a flashing yellow light."

"Really, Maggie? A flashing yellow light?" Maija smiled and held up her arms as if imploring the heavens and said, "Now, who in this room is square?"

Maggie's eyes shot up to the left—as if she could pierce her collective unconscious to see where the hell that inane comment came from—when they heard the guys coming in through the utility room. Tekla was asleep in Sam's arms as he nodded hello to Maija on his way to put Tekla down for the rest of her nap.

Pete was putting grocery bags on the kitchen counter. When he turned, his brown, gold-flecked eyes lit up when he saw Maija. Maggie could almost hear the 'dum-da-dum-dum' warning from the old Dragnet show. She thought, *Look out, Maija!* Then, shaking her head, Maggie edited herself and re-thought *Run, Pete, run!*

With the French doors to the screened porch cracked open, the chill fresh air and random evening sounds seemed to energize the conversation. Maija and Pete had joined forces to make Finnish pasties without the crust—a finely chopped stew of potatoes, carrots, beef and rutabaga, baked in the oven and served with catsup. Maggie found herself scraping the bottom of the Corning Ware server to catch every last morsel.

"Ma, how's that raggedy-ass brother of mine? I haven't seen him in months."

Maija looked as if she had something caught in her throat and then began to cry. Sam was getting out of his chair, but Maija held up her hand and said, "It's okay, I'm fine."

"What's going on, Ma?"

Maija looked around the table and paused before she said, "I didn't want to say anything because you and Maggie have had more than your share of close calls, but Kenny got beat up pretty bad. He didn't tell me until he got out of the hospital. He'll be off work for about six weeks—broken nose, two cracked ribs and a ruptured spleen. God knows what that means. He either doesn't know or isn't telling me."

"Jesus, Ma. You need to tell me these things. We're family."

"That's why I didn't tell you. You had enough on your plate and Stella and I were there for him."

"Ma, come on, tell me . . . what happened?"

"Kenny and Stella went out to dinner and were heading back to their car when these guys pulled up to the curb and asked Kenny where he got his n-i-g-g-e-r w-h-o-r-e. According to Stella, Kenny had gotten good at walking away. But that night they were celebrating Stella's new promotion, and Kenny had a few drinks and lost it. The three guys got out of their car and started swinging. Stella said she ran to the drugstore to call the cops, but it was twenty minutes before they got there. By then, Kenny was unconscious; the guys were long gone.

"Was Stella able to give the cops a description?" Maggie asked.

"When the cops saw that she was black and Kenny was white, they started to grill her, you know—why she was out in that part of town, how did she know Kenny. Stella said she backed off on giving descriptions and told them it happened too fast because she didn't want to end up in jail. God almighty, it doesn't pay to fall in love with someone who's a different color. I wish it were different, but it isn't, and those two just keep asking for trouble. Bad enough that we have trouble without asking for it."

"Oh, Maija, I had no idea you were that stretched when I kept asking you to take care of Tekla. I'm sorry. I wish you'd said something."

"Maggie Tervo, you and I had our talk. Tekla gives me joy, a place to put my love. That's not being stretched; it's being blessed."

In the silence, Sam, Maggie and Pete looked at Maija, as if trying to figure out how that wisdom applied to them.

Tekla said, "Puzzle."

"That it is, little one. That it is," said Pete.

Maggie and Sam began clearing the table so Maija and Pete could swoon over Tekla's talent to dump, sort, and put her puzzles together, again and again. And, Maggie realized, that wasn't the only swooning going on. Maija had kicked off her heels and managed to sit on the floor by hiking up her tight skirt. With her legs turned to one side and leaning forward, she looked like a teenager. And, Pete, sitting cross-legged on the floor on the other side of Tekla, seemed far more interested in the curve of Maija's legs than the shape of the next puzzle piece.

A dish towel in hand, Maggie waited for the next washed plate and was reminded of the sweetness she used to feel when she and Sam did chores together. That, and how the gentle hollow at his throat used to make her weak in the knees. Maggie couldn't remember the last time she wanted to rip Sam's clothes off and make love to him, but the temptation was rumbling and ruminating.

"Hey, Maggie, are you on strike or wandering around in your mind?"

"Doing some wandering around and thinking about how nice it is to do ordinary things with you."

"Like washing dishes?"

"Yes. And, sundry other things."

"Hmm. I think I like the idea of sundry. Opens up all kinds of thoughts," Sam said with the fullness of his *sotto voce*, eyes, and smile.

Maggie gave him the look, then a smile so tender and loving that the lines in her face seemed to relax and her voice softened when she said, "I think we need to explore those thoughts—*later after*." Words Tekla stumbled upon after Sam told her she had to stop saying the word 'no' because it was lame, and way overused by the toddler set.

When Maija was tucking Tekla in bed, Pete stuck his head in the kitchen and said, "Looks like I better take the car and follow Maija home. Sounds like her carburetor's giving her trouble."

Maggie worked hard to subdue her widening eyes, but Sam kept his game face and said, "Sure, Pete. Wouldn't want her to have trouble with her carburetor."

Before Maija and Pete backed out of the driveway, Maggie and Sam were doubled over in laughter. And, they couldn't stop. It was as if they'd held back as long as they could. Now, it all rushed out—the pent-up stress and thrill of letting go. Finally, Sam took Maggie's hand and pulled her into the living room. Stretching out on the copper-colored shag carpet, they began to tentatively, almost shyly, touch one another. For Maggie, the slowness of it all was excruciating; her rumblings grew louder. Before they reached skin on skin, Maggie climaxed and cried, "holy mother of god," which sent Sam over the moon and back. Then tears—fierce and unbidden—overcame them like a sleet storm that promised a quick but perilous thaw.

On her way to the bathroom, Maggie checked on Tekla. Dressed in panda bear blanket pajamas, with knees akimbo and starlight sliding through the half-closed venetian blinds, Tekla looked as if she was floating in the cosmos. Leaning over to kiss her forehead, Maggie said, "Travel well, sweet Moonwalker."

After slipping on her black robe and closing the French doors, Maggie found Sam in the kitchen heating up milk for cocoa. In the way of tribal practices, the Tervo family wisely chose chocolate to talk about the big things—like kindergarten, manners, puberty, sex, drinking, driving and college.

"Talk time?" asked Maggie.

Sam looked at her with a question in his eyes, and said, "No choice, we have to talk. We're in this together and Tekla's depending on us. Mag, you and I don't always agree, but we're a team. We need to find a way to act like one."

This was one of those times when Sam stood tall in her mind—a strong, intelligent, loving man. Experiencing the weight of the moment, Maggie knew she'd long remember tonight—Sam in white skivvies, an inside-out tee shirt and bare feet, making hot chocolate. With all their missteps, disappointments and brokenness, Maggie understood, could almost see, a radical beauty in the axis between love and fear, strength and vulnerability. And, she wondered why people don't get that you can't attack fear and vulnerability as weaknesses without castrating the power of love and strength. Is it even possible to love without fear, or show strength without vulnerability?

Maggie whispered, "Why you, Sam? That's my biggest question. Why you? Why us?"

Keeping his voice low, Sam said, "Tomorrow we'll have hours to talk about Oz. Tonight it's about why us. And, I hope you'll get why Oz is a better choice than doing Aunt Jo's limbo dance the rest of our lives—desperate to stay under some theoretical, imaginary radar."

Sam poured the hot milk into two large mugs and added two heaping tablespoons of cocoa in each cup. Then, he winked and said in a normal voice, "Let's turn the radio on and sit at the kitchen table." On the back of a coupon for Cheerios, he scribbled: *just in case!*

Keeping her voice low and her agitation in check, Maggie said, "I'm listening," as the radio played . . . *speaking words of wisdom, let it be, let it be* . . . When Sam started to grin, Maggie shook her head and said, "Don't even think it."

Shaking off his smile, Sam looked at Maggie. In times of crisis, he relied on her wild emotion or rigid strength to guide him; she was his barometer. What he was about to say demanded gravity and tenderness.

"Maggie, Jacques told me your parents were actively involved in organizing and leading the Oz Revolution, or O.R., as it was called in the early forties. At the time, the organizers thought the word 'OR,' on its own, might convey that people had a choice, until they hit the wall with the loyalty pledge—the 'being for or against us'—demanded by dictators. That's when the word Oz found its wings and took flight.

"*L'Empereur Est Nu*, your parent's paper, was one of many newsletters set up in several countries to message and find others who would join and support Oz. None were as successful as *L'Empereur*, so your parents were recruited to set up distribution points in the free world and smuggle copies into nations battling tyranny. Although your parents, and other activists, expected resistance from the targeted governments, they never imagined the number of activists and terrorists who wanted to join Oz, or work with Oz—including the PLO and the *Front de Libération du Quebec*." Sam stumbled over the pronunciation and shook his head. Maggie nudged his hand and said, "go on."

"So . . . very soon, Anna and Raymond found themselves in the very difficult and dangerous position of trying to screen industrialists, cartels, human rights activists, terrorists and counter-intelligence agents around the world who offered money, information, weaponry, allegiance. Here's where it gets dicey. Based on global legend, Anna and Raymond discovered and documented actions by many of these industrial giants, government officials and mobsters, who tried to use Oz to promote violence, coups and other civil unrest to gain power and wealth. According to Jacques, these documents would implicate counter-intelligence agencies in the States, Canada and England."

Maggie hit the palm of her hand on the table and whispered, "Holy shit! Are you serious?"

"True or not, it stoked the underground. Oz's reputation as a global force mushroomed—way before Oz had the means to manage its own growth or wield its power. Jacques said Anna and Raymond disappeared along with any records they might have kept. What this means, Maggie, is you're now the target. I assume Issie, your Aunt Jo and Aunt Minnie might factor into the equation. But right now, Oz thinks some heavy hitters are going through me to get to you."

"Wait! Did Jacques say he doesn't know where Anna and Raymond are? Did he say, 'the records they might have kept?' Jacques was in charge. How can he say, 'records they might have kept'—he must have known about the records."

"That's what he said."

"Did he say he didn't know?"

"Mag, I'm not sure where you're going with this. I heard Jacques say Anna and Raymond disappeared and no one knows if there are records. If that's the case, he doesn't know."

"Could it be he knew there were records, and just didn't know where they were kept? Why wouldn't he know? I don't get it."

"Mag, I'm telling you what he said. I might have gotten it wrong, but I don't think so. Jacques acted like he didn't know if records were kept.'"

"That doesn't sound right. But why me?"

"Maggie, like hunters who flush foxes from their den with dogs, they think they can flush your parents out by using you as bait. They want your parents to come out of hiding. And, they want whatever documents are hidden away. Most of all, these hunters don't want to worry about being dragged out of bed in the middle of the night and hauled off to prison or fitted with concrete shoes for a midnight swim in the Detroit River."

"Assuming this is true, how would my parents know I was being threatened?"

"That, I don't know. My guess is the hunters think your parents might be hiding in plain sight, using aliases."

Maggie looked at Sam with the same kind of softness he saw earlier, but there was also a spark. "Screw this," said Maggie. "You're right, I don't like this at all, and I don't have any idea if it makes sense. What I do know is these assholes are not going to rip my family away from me again. I wasn't looking forward to tomorrow. In fact, I was seriously thinking about signing up for a cooking class and buying an apron. Not now. No one is going to mess with me or you or Tekla. No one!"

Sam wasn't sure if Maggie knew her fist was raised, or whether she realized her right breast was peeking out of her robe. He couldn't curb the smile on his face. Somehow it made perfect sense. Later, when his Saint Marguerite was not marching off to war, he'd bring up this moment and they'd share a laugh. For now, he imagined her as Lady Liberty on the Hudson. A strong, smart, loving and very sexy woman.

"Hey Mag, time to get out of bed and get moving! It's after ten, and Bruce expects us at noon. Do you want me to drop Tekla off at Ma's while you get ready?

"Coffee, I need coffeeeeee," Maggie said with her hands crooked like a monster's, as Tekla dove on the bed and said, "Later after, Maggie! Get up! Time to get UP!"

"Later after, Moonwalker," Maggie groaned, as she crawled to the other side of the bed, grabbed Tekla and began to growl. Tekla moved into high giggles—the screeching, ear-splitting kind.

"Okay, I'm going to be the grown up here and make some decisions. Maggie, I'll drop Tekla off, so you'll have time for coffee. And, Tekla, we're going to blow this pop stand and see what Grandma Tervo is hiding in her cookie jar."

Maggie sat up on the edge of the bed and said, "Where's Pete?"

"Gone. Bruce sent someone by to pick him up. I assume to help prepare for the meeting."

"Sam, in spite of last night, don't get your hopes up about this meeting. I've got a lot of revenge going for me, and I sure as hell won't stand in line for a membership card."

"No pressure, Mag. Just listen, see what you think. The last time you were blindsided. Today, you might see things differently."

When Maggie heard the car pull out of the driveway, she checked the locks on the doors and poured herself a coffee. She'd shower and wash her hair, but not dress up. Today it would be bell-bottom jeans and an old sweatshirt, *ala* Bruce. Today she wanted to look like she didn't give a rip. But she did.

As if no time had passed, Sam was pulling up the driveway as she slid into her black flats. Their bedroom was a mass of clothes ripped off hangers and tossed from unclosed drawers. Maggie finally decided on her jewel-toned paisley on red brocade—the A-line dress she last wore in the early months of her pregnancy when she thought Sam was having an affair. When Sam got home from work one night, Maggie was wearing this mini-dress with high heels and makeup. She'd even curled her hair. Using a very French name and accent, Maggie introduced herself and began to seduce Sam as the 'other woman.' But Sam, her sometimes radically wise and loving husband, walked her into the living room and sat her down on the sofa. He kindly explained, although she was very attractive, no one could compare to his wife. Sam looked the make-believe 'other woman' in the eyes and gave her all the reasons he loved his wife, Maggie. Sam said no one else existed for him. Maggie believed him then; she didn't know if she would ever believe him again.

20

Taking Flight

Faith is taking the first step even when you don't see the whole staircase.

—Dr. Martin Luther King, Jr.

AFTERNOON, APRIL 3, 1971—People were being ushered out of their cars by one of three drivers dressed in black pants and black turtlenecks for offsite valet parking.

"Protocol," said Sam.

"Whose?" asked Maggie.

"Oz. All cars are checked for bugs or traps at a garage and parked inside a cyclone fence, topped with razor-sharp barbed wire."

"Traps? As in?"

"Booby traps that might make the car inoperable and cause an accident. Traps like the one they found on my car after the crash."

"You're just now telling me this?"

Dropping his voice, Sam said, "Look, doll, we ain't jawed much since I got outta the slammer." When Sam saw Maggie's reaction, he realized he picked the wrong tone, time and place. "So, Mag, we've got miles to go to catch up. For our sake, and Tekla's, we've got to keep talking, my beauty in a red dress. What inspired you to get dolled up?"

"Don't ask. I have no idea."

"I'm glad you did. You look dazzling, on fire," Sam winked and wrapped her black faux suede coat over her shoulders as they headed up the sidewalk. The temperature was already dipping below forty. Another cold snap.

In the foyer, Maggie heard familiar kitchen noises to the right, but the sound of people gathering was coming through arched double doors to the left. An area of the house closed off on her first visit. Sam led the way to an amphitheater with twenty-foot high walls topped by a dome-shaped, windowed-ceiling. The asymmetrical placement of six-foot-high by twelve-inch-wide glass block windows on curved walls warped the sun's rays and intimated warmth. But, the lighting didn't need much help. The dome windows brought the outside in, like a clearing in the forest. And, thin tubes of artificial light framed every window, producing incandescence without the glare. Maggie thought it was like being in church without the gloom.

Bruce was testing the microphone at the top end of a U-shaped seating arrangement. There were two upholstered Danish-modern swivel chairs for every table. Maggie did a quick count. Eighteen seats around the horseshoe and three chairs with a desktop lectern at the front. There was no check-in table, no name tags, no workbooks, no notepaper, no pencils or pens. Table set-ups included one pitcher of water, two tumblers, a bowl of mixed nuts, and a small tray of nonpareil chocolate mints.

"Testing, testing," Bruce said over the mic. "No need to sit just yet. I want to make a few brief announcements before we begin.

First of all, welcome! We have some new people today and we'll be doing introductions after lunch. Right now, I'd like to introduce you to my partner in crime and anti-crime, Carol. Carol, raise your hand. You'll need to check your coat—plus purses, briefcases, anything you carried in—with Carol in the foyer. We'll take good care of them. As per usual, no note taking or recording. Then, you're invited to pick up a tray in the kitchen and help yourself to the smorgasbord. We've got a lengthy agenda so don't be shy, no getting up for seconds. And, no leaving during the presentation period. If you're here for the first time, there are two small bathrooms in the dome area. Carol will be seated at the entrance with a first aid kit, Bayer Aspirin and Rolaids. Dishes will be bussed during our first stretch break. Bruce looked at Jacques and said, "Anything you want to add?"

Jacques stood up and said, "Bonjour! So nice to see everyone again. I look forward to our day and encourage you to fill your stomachs and keep an open mind. We have lots of ground to cover, and as always, expect some lively conversations."

Other than Jacques and Bruce, Maggie didn't see anyone she recognized. She was keeping an eye out for Clyde and Blanche when she queued up to drop off her coat and purse.

"Hi, Carol, I'm Maggie Tervo. Nice to meet you in person."

"You too, Maggie. This isn't the best place to get to know each other, but now that we've broken the ice, we'll be like old friends the next time we meet." Carol appeared to be in her late forties, early fifties, with gray streaking her short-cropped black hair. Stocky, and well-muscled, Maggie thought she looked like someone who might have taught gym or coached a girls' tennis team when she was younger.

"I like the way you put that—but hope it's not because Sam gets arrested again."

"Oh, god. We don't want that!"

When Maggie returned to the dome area with her lunch, there were paper-tent name cards at each seat. Sam was sitting alone at his table. Maggie's name card was directly across the room from Sam. Her tablemate, a pretty woman with short auburn hair and perfect teeth, was dressed in bell-bottom jeans, a long-sleeve black tee and a form-fitting tan suede vest. Maggie skimmed the room and realized she was the only one dressed for a semi-formal high school dance.

"Hi, I'm Maggie Tervo."

"Hi, Maggie. I'm Sylvia. We don't use last names here. When you introduce yourself, keep to your first name only. Kind of like AA meetings." When she sensed Maggie's confusion, Sylvia said, "AA stands for Alcoholics Anonymous. Obviously, not your thing."

"Sure. I should have known but didn't make the connection here. Thanks for the tip." A *bit creepy,* thought Maggie, *this sounds more like a cult at every turn.* Lunch was just as casual, elegant and delicious as before. But, still scorched from her surprise party at the Red Fox, Maggie ate with less enthusiasm. Deep down, she knew this Oz thing was an either-or proposition. Tyrannical. No real choice. She'd made up her mind to be graceful, enthusiastic and supportive, but part of her wanted to pitch a fit, to make a statement no one would forget. Maybe, even, make a total fool out of herself, to see if they still cared enough to offer her the secret handshake. Maggie wondered if her demands that Sam prove and reprove his love for her was reaching a tipping point. What was the price of betrayal? The cost?

Just then, Bruce stopped by and leaned over her side of the table.

"Good to see you, little sister." His lips were inches from her own and she could feel his breath.

"Hi, Bruce. Good to see you."

Bruce looked at her as if he didn't hear right, "Really?"

Maggie whispered, "Yes, why wouldn't I be?" Sam was watching from the other side of the room.

Bruce turned his head, almost touching her ear with his lips and said, "Like the dress, Mrs. Tervo, shows off your legs. Can't help but wonder if you're wearing panties."

Who the hell does he think he is? thought Maggie. She felt trapped, tongue-tied. Anything she said would sound pathetic. She pulled back.

Bruce slapped his hand on the table, leaned in and said, "No meltdowns. None. Bite your tongue if you have to, but do not fall apart."

Maggie's eyes were molten magma, her legs bouncing up and down with nowhere to go. Bruce knew she was seething.

"Nice. Keep biting that comely tongue," he whispered in her ear as he stood up.

Before lunch was over, Maggie saw Clyde and Blanche take seats at a table on the bottom side of the U. Blanche smiled and waved, and Maggie was relieved to have another place to keep her attention. When she looked across the room, she saw Bruce take the empty chair at Sam's table. At the front of the room, Jacques was adjusting the mic when two women walked in and took a seat on either side of his. The first was Catherine Caron, his executive assistant from Toronto. The second was Loretta Hood. Maggie thought she was going to lose it. When she turned toward Sam, Bruce was watching her. His face fierce, wolf-like, as if he was daring her to react. Maggie choked back tears. It was hard enough to live with Sam, Clyde and Blanche keeping her in the dark. But, Loretta—her closest friend, soulmate, on-call-psychotherapist—knew and never said word one. And, Catherine, her 'maybe mother'—what a joke that was! What had Sam learned about Catherine over the past two years? Maggie realized her whole life was a sham. Always looking inside from the outside, she was the last girl to be asked to the homecoming dance; the third-string right-fielder who warmed the bench; the poor, pitiful orphan girl who had no one to introduce on Parent's Day—no mother to tell her about sanitary napkins and no father to teach her fly-fishing. *Sob, sob, sob,* she thought, *who gives a rip?*

Maggie could feel Bruce's breath, hear his warning, his vulgarity. Still next to Sam, looking her way, Maggie smiled and nodded her head at Bruce and thought, *let them both think I'm making the turn, signing up for this freak show.* Somehow, she'd get through the day and begin planning her escape with Tekla. Maggie knew she kept secrets better than anyone. An illusionist, her secrets were buried so deep that she didn't know what she knew or didn't know.

After the dishes were cleared, Jacques encouraged everyone to touch their toes, then reach for the ceiling before they sat down. Maggie's mini-dress made both unseemly, and she headed for the bathroom. Touching up her *Red-Hot* lipstick with a tube slipped into the side pocket of her dress, Maggie saw an attractive woman in a red paisley dress—thick dark hair, olive skin and green eyes. Sometimes it startled Maggie to see her reflection, to see an actual person looking back, to know she wasn't invisible. Why did she continue to act like she was? Maggie took a deep breath and shook her arms and legs to get the blood flowing. Then, she looked in the mirror again and said, "Okay, Marguerite, I've got your back."

When Jacques walked up to the lectern, Maggie felt her steely resolve click in. She was prepared to be a quiet, calm, mature observer. No skin in this game. *My god,* she thought, *he is one fine looking man. No wonder I wanted him to be my father.* Jacques took in the room and held it with his gentle smile and a few nods of his head.

"Before we get to the business of the day, let's look at the headlines. By now, most of you know that Charles Manson was sentenced to death on March 29th. He's a sick, pathetic, brutal murderer and he needs to be incarcerated, but not murdered. Most first world, civilized nations have outlawed capital punishment. Here, in the States in 1971, they still murder the murderer and call it law.

"In some bizarre, sad synchronicity, the day after Manson's verdict, Lieutenant William Calley was found guilty of the premeditated murder of South Vietnamese civilians at My Lai three years ago. Although there are differing accounts, we think the total number of villagers killed was more than five hundred. None were combatants. They were old men, women, children and babies. Between the killings, the troops stopped to eat lunch. Women and girls were gang-raped. An infant who crawled out of a ditch was tossed back into the ditch like a football and shot. Like Manson and his cult, Calley and his men are sick, pathetic, brutal murderers.

"My hope is both of these killer squads live long, incarcerated lives, to remind us how violence begets violence begets violence. That Hugh Thompson, the US Helicopter Pilot, who inserted his crew between the surviving villagers and Calley's Troop—willing to shoot other Americans if they raised a gun—will long be remembered and honored for his moral courage. And, that this tiny village of My Lai will forever remind war-happy superpowers of our shared humanity."

Jacques stopped talking and the silence seemed like détente. A time to heal.

"Moving from the harsh realities of death and destruction, I'm honored to pass the mic to Oz members who've demonstrated the kind of passion and commitment we need to create change. Like so many, Loretta has risked or forfeited love, friendship and wealth to support our work. Uniquely her story, but allegorically a story of Oz and our fight for human rights and social justice."

Loretta accepted the mic, bowed her head then looked at the group of people waiting to hear her speak. She was wearing a blue denim, bell-bottom jumpsuit, with a red handkerchief scarf and red, high-heel boots.

"I'm standing here today, right here—instead of a jail cell—because someone believed in me and taught me to believe in myself. Which, if you knew me then, you'd know it would be a long damn stretch!" Loretta smiled, shook her head and said, "I was one of those badass tenement bitches who mocked everything and everybody like it was all one, big fucking joke. In the privacy of my room, I whipped myself into self-pity and self-loathing—frizzy hair, black skin, big feet. I was so lost in my rage that my world shrunk to the size of three square blocks and hope looked like powdered sugar and a straw on a filthy kitchen table. Enter Clyde, my nemesis and muse. He looked at me and SAW ME. No kidding. I was so pissed off; it made me crazy. I played him for a fool and he played me like a Stradivarius violin. And, he wouldn't stop. When I wanted to quit, he played an ode. When I threw a tantrum, he played a lullaby. When I wanted to give up on the world, he played New Orleans Jazz. I ran out of games, but he never ran out of patience. Now, with Oz, I make my own music."

Before the applause began to peak, Steve, a forty-something man with thin, dishwater blond hair, sitting next to Blanche, called out "Bullshit!"

"Okay," said Jacques.

"Who knows what we risk or gain through our work? You said Loretta, *risked or forfeited love, friendship and wealth to support our work.* Based on whose standards?" said Steve.

"Go on," said Jacques.

"If we want to keep score and rate the quality of our lives, then let's sign up to be lab rats."

"Who else?" asked Jacques.

"Steve's right. Everyone in this room makes choices every day. Do the simple kindnesses or bold gestures change the world? How do we know? And, who, by the way, is keeping score? Why would we want to?" said Alice, a birdlike older woman next to Clyde.

"What do you think?" Jacques asked the group.

A large man sitting next to Sylvia stood up. "My name's Henry, and this is my first meeting. I'm not a Machiavellian thinker. I don't think the end always justifies the means. But, when we keep score, we impose our pea-brain methodology on others. For example, is it a lesser gift if people give to the poor because it makes *them* feel good, rather than making the gift because of generosity? I know, I'm rambling. My point is, sometimes we improve the world with selfish intent. Does it matter? Should we inventory intent and keep score?"

"Other thoughts?" said Jacques.

Maggie quit biting her tongue and said, "Strings. If the gift has strings attached to it, it does matter."

"Go on," said Jacques.

"If someone offers food to a third-world country, on the condition they quit educating girls, it matters."

"Anyone?"

Bruce stood up. "Maggie has a point with several prongs. If people are starving, Maslow's hierarchy kicks in. Food and shelter first. Nevertheless, her take supports the proposition that intent carries some weight."

Maggie stood up. "Maslow's hierarchy is theoretical. But that doesn't mean I'd oppose food as a more important short-term fix. That said, I think the intent of the donor should always be considered."

"Maggie, are you saying there are times when we should judge, keep score?" asked Jacques.

Maggie paused and looked around the room. Sam's pride was written in his eyes, the set of his jaw. "I think we have to make conscious decisions, which means we use whatever raw material we have to judge. Judging is not the same as keeping score. I don't think there's any way to keep score—and what difference would that make? But, decisions demand judgment." As Maggie took her seat, she caught Loretta's smile and thumbs up signal.

"Any rebuttal to decisions requiring judgment? Any advocates for keeping score? None? Well, then," said Jacques, "In addition to Henry and Maggie, we have another first-time guest today—Catherine Caron. Her working title is executive assistant. At headquarters in Toronto, we call her empress of the universe. Would you like to say a few words?"

Catherine shook her head as she stood at the lectern. "Seriously," she said, "Jacques thinks he can charm me into working more than seven days a week by calling me empress of the universe. As they say in Texas, that dog won't hunt!

"Jacques also knows I'm not a woman of few words. I tend to ramble and thank Henry for his transparency. We ramblers sometimes get a bad rap.

"Although this is my first meeting with the Michigan Oz, I've met with other Oz groups all over the world. At one time, my job was to write, print, bundle and deliver newspapers to fiefdoms—places I'd never heard about, names impossible to pronounce."

Maggie couldn't take her eyes off Catherine. Totally absorbed, she listened for every word, every French inflection, every breath.

". . . but I'm getting too old to bundle and deliver. Now we have faster, more sophisticated printing and delivery systems." Catherine paused and looked at Maggie. At least, Maggie read it as a look. Could have been before or after the pause because Maggie was frozen in time.

"So," Catherine continued, "I'm excited to be part of today's gathering. For too long, I've been sitting in my castle tower—just kidding!" Catherine laughed. "During the break, I hope you'll take a moment to say hello and tell me about yourself."

The room applauded. If Maggie hadn't lost herself in Catherine's presentation, she would have seen Sam, Bruce, Clyde and Blanche watching her instead of Catherine. If she hadn't frozen herself in time, she would have caught Loretta staring at her through tears.

Jacques stood at the lectern and looked around the room. "Merci! I always enjoy our open discussions and appreciated your thoughts about judging and keeping score. Two different things with many shades of individual perception and perspective. We also had the chance to hear from each of our welcomed guests—Henry, Maggie and Catherine—and, of course, the usual suspects."

Jacques' update of Oz's quiet interventions and programs in third-world nations was impressive. "This year, the focus was on the education of children and adults to: eliminate the practice of female genital mutilation; . . . bring western medicine to third-world countries; end wars; . . . topple brutal regimes; . . . and, of course, to continue our core mission to establish and maintain the uncensored distribution of information and knowledge . . ."

Which, to Maggie, seemed ironic, because Maggie couldn't imagine Jacques not screening a report from Oz. Yet, it was easy to grasp the far-reaching, expensive, dangerous and compassionate efforts Oz makes to build and sustain social justice.

Maggie tried to pay attention to Jacques, but her eyes kept slipping over to Catherine or Loretta. After hearing them talk, and feeling their tenderness, Maggie was a dishrag. Without the drama of challenges, demands and apologies, her anger had almost evaporated. What is, is. She wanted the battles to end. Even if Oz was a cult, it seemed like a good cult. Maggie half-smiled to herself. Issie was right; she'd spent most of her life like the baby chick in P.D. Eastman's book, *Are You My Mother?*—hoping someone would say yes.

21

The Harvest

After more than twenty years as Mr. Zamboni, William (Willie) Johnson was fired by the Detroit Red Wings' organization. Although no official announcement was made, inside sources confirm Mr. Johnson was terminated for cause. By noon yesterday, more than fifty of Mr. Zamboni's fans were carrying placards at the entrance to Olympia Stadium to protest his firing.

—The Detroit Weekly

MAY 15,1971—Pouring her first cup of coffee, Maggie was thinking about Aunt Jo's Annual Rhubarb Harvest. Today would be the first-ever All-Women Harvest Day. The guys would keep the kids. Since no one was getting married or having babies, there were no showers. Aunt Jo decided the harvest would be a great way to get the womenfolk together without having to buy Sarah Coventry jewelry or Tupperware containers.

"That dickhead! What the hell?" Sam said.

"Nixon, again?"

"Not Nixon. Willie. Sounds like he self-imploded and got fired."

"About what?"

"No idea. Robin told Blanche she was worried because Willie wasn't sleeping or taking care of himself. After crashing headlong into apathy for too many years, he's been conjuring up a hunger strike or a naked sprint down Woodward Avenue at rush hour—anything to expose the pandemic of locking up or gunning down a generation of black men."

"Did you and Clyde talk to him?"

Sam looked at Maggie and felt every unsaid word. He and Clyde had been so wrapped up in their own stuff, in the big-hero business of changing the world with Oz, they'd ignored a friend's call for help.

Maggie watched Sam take in the unspoken words and wondered how many times she ignored someone who needed her because she preferred the esoteric, abstract—the serpentine poetic nature of the unsaid, untouched, unknown.

Sam wrapped his arms around Maggie and said, "My wise, thoughtful wife."

"You too, Samuelsan, for seeing with your third eye and hearing with your third ear."

"Third ear?"

"Maybe. Why wouldn't we have some divine overdrive for each of our senses?"

Clyde's brazen fifteen-year-old niece, Bessie, had cut a deal for a dollar an hour to watch the wrecking crew, plus twenty-five cents extra per hour for Tekla, pepperoni pizza from Angelo's for lunch, and an extra fifty cents for making sure the toys and games were put back in the toy closet. All of this, plus a cross-the-heart-promise from Clyde that he would not leave her alone with his 'peculiar Webster acorns.' Clyde had shaken his head and laughed, so like Blanche's side of the family to bring up *The Mayflower*.

Thus, the Backyard Confessional, between Clyde, Willie and Sam, was born as the male compendium to the first All-Women Harvest Day. Dressed in jeans and short-sleeved tees, drinking coffee that would dissolve Bondo, the guys knew spring was ready to tip seventy-nine degrees. It'd been a long cold winter.

"Oh, man, I'm so fucking screwed," said Willie.

"Let's hear it, dickhead. The good, the bad and the ugly," said Clyde.

Willie tossed the last swallow of coffee down his throat before he realized it was packed with bitter grounds. "Holy shit, Clyde, you trying to kill me off before I set myself on fire? What do they call it when someone torches his body? Like that monk from Vietnam. Self-immolation?"

"Jesus, Willie, don't go there. Talk to me. What happened?" asked Clyde.

Willie looked at Clyde, then turned to Sam. "Hey, white boy, don't get your honkie ass in a wringer when you hear what I'm about to say. It's not personal, it just fucking is. No soundtracks, this is bile in the stomach. You white boys own it, and if you own it, you got to hear it. Makes no sense for us black boys to field all the balls.

"Three days ago, my supervisor pulls me off the Zamboni and tells me the General Manager wants to see me. 'No fucking way,' I say. What the hell. Why would the G.M. for the Red Wings want to spend two minutes with his Zamboni driver? Not that I'm not proud of what I do, I am. But, for real? The G.M. is up in the counting-house, and I'm down here with the flea-bitten cats, birds and mice who come out at night to do a clean sweep of the stadium while I scrape ice. My supervisor says, 'No choice, Willie boy. Get thee your ass to his office.' So, I go.

"No shit, I'm shaking and jumping up and down, like a six-year-old boy waiting for his fifteen-year-old sister to finish straightening her hair so he can pee. I could almost feel the warm trickle down my leg when I reached the big man's office. Not office, the cracker has a suite. What the hell, I think. Maybe they want to give me a promotion—put me in marketing because of my Mr. Zamboni shtick. Who knows?" Willie took a breath and looked around as if planning his escape. "Screw this," he said. "Nothing makes any difference anyhow. Who are we kidding? The Eights? Do we really think we're going to get anyone's attention, change anyone's mind?

"In America, we're incarcerating or killing off half the black men under the age of thirty for what? Petty-ass drugs, party-store grabs, overdraft checks . . . failure to sign up for the draft? Then, we send the good boys—the sincere, god-fearing, law-abiding rest—to Vietnam to serve as enemy targets in the killing fields. For what? Black gold? Ironic, isn't it? Black men for black gold. Why not?" Willie bent over his lap and let his head hang toward the ground. His single cry sent robins and crows scrambling for cover.

Instead of moving in to talk to Willie, or putting his arm around him, Clyde stretched his legs out and said, "Willie, the day is yours. The week if we need it. This is your story. It's important. We're here to help."

Sam rubbed the worn knees on his Levi's. Clyde was the mediator, peace-keeper, priest in this confessional; yet, he knew, understood, that at some other level his voice and presence was essential. Still a novice in understanding the human physics of shared experience, Sam knew what was said, and what happened in Clyde's backyard, would ripple in some way—leading to a place where other imperfect people would gather to find love and acceptance.

Maggie was waiting for Maija to show up.

Last night, after a bottle of Blue Nun wine, ring bologna and Franco-American spaghetti, Pete announced he'd be moving out tomorrow. Maggie's first thought was, *with dinners like this, who could blame him?* But, no.

". . . Maija offered to rent me her dormer bedroom and bath at a fair price."

Before Sam or Maggie had a chance to raise their eyebrows, Pete said, "We're shacking up. Look, everyone who knows us knows we're involved. Marriage is not in the cards." When Pete saw Maggie's eyes begin to lift, he said, "Stop right there. I'm not married, have never been married, and have no kids I know about. Commitment might be good for some people, not me. Now that we've got security set up, and local connections to Oz, there's no reason for me to hang out in your garage."

"Pete, we're not talking about anyone, we're talking about my ma. I'm not going to ask you what your intentions are. You and Ma are old enough to make that call. But, why move in?"

Pete furrowed his brows, crossed his arms and leaned back as if he was contemplating a complex, theoretical problem. He sat in that pose for so long that Maggie had to resist an impulse to start clearing the table and get on with her evening. Willing herself to sit tight, she looked at Pete and wondered if he forgot where he was or where he was going.

"Here's the lowdown, I've slept on concrete floors, so having a mattress and garage of my own is cool. I'm always on-call and never know when or where my next gig or bed will be. I can live with that. But, I'll be goddamn if I can come up with a single reason to cram four people into a loo the size of a phone booth if we don't have to."

Both Sam and Maggie felt the guilty-pleasure rush of relief and newfound freedom. Three adults and Tekla's potty-training had pushed the limits of their little Zen-like bathroom and need for privacy. Although Pete 'watered' the yard at night, he sometimes showed up in the house when Maggie or Sam were in the throes of lovemaking or hostility. The thin walls communicated every word, cry, footfall, belch, fart, grunt, wheeze, creak of the bed and lift or drop of the toilet seat.

Sam held up his hands in surrender. “No argument here. What’s Ma’s story?”

“Maija’s story?” laughed Pete. She’s telling everyone—shopkeepers, total strangers—that her daughter-in-law’s uncle needed a place and she could use the extra income.” Pete shook his head and dipped back into some memory. “Of course, no one who’s seen us together believes that story, including the shopkeepers. But your ma, she’s got some dusty, old Victorian veil she hangs on to. Like a Cuban boy I used to know. He thought he wanted to be a priest until he prayed with the widow down the road. Decades later, he still clings to the cloth.”

Jaw dropping thought Maggie. She realized this was no hackneyed phrase; her jaw clearly dropped without pretense. “A priest? You?”

“Ms. Maggie, everyone needs a Plan B.”

“The G.M. wanted you to quit?” asked Sam.

“Turns out one of the team’s biggest sponsors has a nephew who wants to drive a Zamboni. The G.M. said the kid is nineteen and clueless. His uncle could afford to buy him a fucking skating rink and Zamboni, but not in this true-life adventure. No. They want me to hang up my keys after almost twenty years and thank them for five grand. Maybe do a few backflips and soft shoe because I’m nigger-rich.”

“Uncle Clyde!” Bessie yelled out the upstairs window. “Clyde Junior says he’s not listening to another word I say. Do you want to come up here and give him the what for, or do you want me to?”

Clyde curled his lips in to hold back his grin, then said, "Bessie, you're the one making the big bucks today. Handle it!"

By the time Maggie and Maija showed up at Aunt Jo's, the party was in full swing. Windows and storm doors open to the warm, dry air. The back screened porch was abuzz.

"There you are, my sweet Maggie! Ready for the harvest?" Aunt Jo was dressed in a pair of rolled up jeans, a tight-fitting navy and orange Detroit Tiger's tee, and navy tennies with rolled down bobby socks. Her platinum white hair, hanging loose.

Maggie walked into her outstretched arms and whispered, "Auntie Jo, you've got to let go of the rolled socks, they're showing your age. They fell out of vogue in the fifties. Time to fold your socks down."

Aunt Jo leaned back from their hug and looked down at her ankles, "No kidding? All these years watching my wrinkles form and skin sag, and all I needed to do was fold down my socks?"

Maggie cracked up. When Aunt Jo was on her game, no one even came close.

Except for a fresh coat of paint in the living room, the house looked the same. So many things to draw you in—color, form, light, books, shells. Nothing matched, yet each was inseparable—a united nations' collage. So much had happened in the eighteen months since Aunt Jo hosted her baby shower and so much had stayed the same. Maggie pictured herself stretched out on the recliner with a Virgin Bloody Mary, pregnant with Tekla, talking about disposable diapers. She barely recognized that earlier self.

"Good genes in our family. Look at you! I don't think you've ever looked so vibrant and beautiful," Aunt Jo said, pulling Maggie out of her reverie. "But, might be time to meet me downtown for a wardrobe check."

Maggie looked at her old black cords. A few formula stains and pulled threads, the inside seam holding its own against Maggie's trademark thunder thighs. She shook her head and laughed, "Oh my god, Aunt Jo, what would I do if I didn't have you to prod me into new clothes every few years? I'm ready when you are."

Loretta walked up and said, "Shopping? Did I hear shopping?"

Maggie spun around, grabbed Loretta around the waist and brought her down to the floor in a heartbeat. The buzzing stopped. Stella, Maija, Issie, Robin and Blanche ran into the living room when they heard Maggie's shriek. Maggie was on top of Loretta, straddling her waist. Loretta held up her hands to keep everyone back.

"It's okay, baby," Loretta said. "I know you're hurt. I'd be hurt too. Now's not the time. We'll talk, but not now. Tonight, tomorrow, whenever you want."

Maggie looked around and wondered how the hell she ended up on the floor on top of Loretta. "Oh, god, Loretta. I don't know what got into me."

"Sure you do, baby. You've been through so much stress with someone throwing a rock through your window, Sam's accident, Tekla's teething, your Uncle Pete moving in. Like being drop kicked a half-dozen times before being buried under a two-hundred-fifty-pound fullback. All that adrenalin has to find its way out." Loretta attempted to sit up.

Maggie stood and offered her hand.

"Go on," said Clyde.

"Go on? You know how this fairy tale ends."

"I want you to tell me."

"My first thought was screw this. He can take his five grand and stick it up his ass. But, I nodded my head like I was thinking about the offer. I could tell the guy was letting down his guard, getting ready to check this off his to-do list. He was sneaking peeks at those little yellow phone messages by moving his eyes and keeping his head straight. Then, he moved some papers on his desk to see what was waiting for him when he was done with me."

Willie leaned forward and scratched the top of his head as if pausing to refresh his memory or deciding whether or not to continue. "I cleared my throat and . . . I don't know . . . said some asshole thing like, 'I love my job and I'm good at it.' Then . . . what? Like someone facing the hangman's noose, I start babbling, saying shit like, 'people hire me for parades . . . which is all good, you know . . . Mr. Zamboni and all that. Good marketing for the team, good for everyone.' Some scared, bug-eyed little boy who couldn't come up with a better word than *good*.

"By this point, I'm back in my ten-year-old body at my uncle's shoe shine stand—smiling, shucking and jiving for a nickel tip. My voice, so small, I sound like Buckwheat when I say, 'How bout I take five grand to give up my Zamboni job and move to the marketing department? Like . . . if the kid gets bored, we don't miss a lick and I'm back on my job. If the kid stays . . . well . . . you've got an experienced guy drumming up new sponsors.'

"He says, 'You're fucking kidding me, right?'

"I say, 'No, sir,' but now sirens are going off in my head and the Klan is outside the fucking door. I move deeper into my shoe-polishing jive; my feet are doing some kind of jambalaya tap dance under the chair, my mouth's so dry my tongue's sticking to my teeth. I say, 'Just trying to think this through . . . you know . . . come up with something that works for you . . . works for the kid . . . works for me. If this doesn't work for you . . . well, then . . . no. No . . . we don't do it.'"

"The guy looks at me like he forgot I was in the room and says, 'No shit, Sherlock. You've got some major balls for a colored boy. I'm going to cut to the chase. You've got two choices—you walk away with five grand or you get fired for insubordination. You need a definition? You might think you'll sue, but we both know how that courtroom door swings. I've got things to do. So, take the money and run, or I'll call someone to throw your sorry ass outta here.' "

Issie grabbed Maggie by the elbow and walked her into the kitchen and said, "Jesus, Maggie. What was that all about? Are you sure this Uncle Pete is a Soulier?"

"He's a Soulier. Issie, you need to drop this right now. Short of putting myself in a straight-jacket, I'm getting it together. I promise. Just . . . just some things I can't talk about." The look on Issie's face reminded her that no way, no how was Issie going to buy this refrain. Maggie leaned into Issie and said, with a fierceness she didn't know she felt, "Back off, Issie, and don't give me that know-it-all look; you know nothing. This is not about Raymond's crazy gene."

Just then, Aunt Jo walked in and said, "Time for the harvest to commence! I've got burlap bags hanging off the fence with small name tags." When she looked at their faces, she backed out of the door and said, ". . . or, maybe not."

"Maybe yes," whispered Maggie as she threaded her arm through Issie's. "Sorry, Iss, we said we wouldn't do this again. I promise, no more throwing my friends down on the floor or getting pissed at you for caring. Let's go get us some rhubarb!"

Everyone was wearing one of Aunt Jo's wonderful full-brimmed hats. Loretta walked up to Maggie, gave her a bear hug, then plopped a purple straw hat on her head. Maija topped Issie's head with a red, white and blue striped canvas beach hat. By the time half the crop of rhubarb was cut, seven burlap bags were packed full and seven women boasted mud-caked tennies and legs, sweat-streaked arms and hat-band heads. Rinsing off with the hose had mixed results. The water was ice-cold, yet somewhere between Maggie's unhinged attack on Loretta and the backyard shower, the gathering of women found warmth—laughter, purpose, play, affection. And, during the ellipses of these moments, Aunt Jo had managed to set up a spectacular feast in the dining room. The centerpiece was one of Robin's off-the-charts creations—a marble cake in the shape of a woven basket, iced with textured brown and white frosting, and holding eight star-shaped brown-sugar cookies covered in silver *dragées*. One for each harvest woman.

Bessie yelled, "Uncle Clyde, little Tekla took off her dirty diaper and is sticking it down the toilet!"

Sam grinned and called, "Hold on, Bessie, I'll help." To Clyde and Willie, he said, "Maggie's inspiration for toilet training. She told Tekla if she didn't use the potty-chair, she'd have to dump and rinse her diapers in the toilet. Tekla thinks it's a riot to plunge her diaper in water; Maggie says give it time." Sam shook his head and said, "Women! I'll be right back."

Clyde looked at Willie who seemed lost in thought. "Hey, man, the guy's a prick. Maybe that lawyer you told Maggie about . . . what's his name . . . Bruce? Maybe he'll take this on, work out a deal."

"No fucking way. In Detroit, you don't mess with the Wings. It'd be like sending the lynch mob an engraved invitation."

"You took the money?"

"Hell no. I told him he could take the check and stick it up his subordinate, ass-kissing dung hole."

Blanche caught Maggie in the kitchen and crooked her right forefinger in a signal to follow. Loretta was waiting for them in the small hallway outside Aunt Jo's bedroom.

Loretta pulled Maggie close and whispered, "We three need to talk. Sam said he'd come by and pick up Maija, so she has a ride back to your house. We'll drive with you or follow you to SistaHood.

The shop's a safe place to talk, but the streets are safer if you're with us."

Maggie smiled, and with hands in the prayer position below her chin, she bowed her head. "Whew!" she whispered, "flipping you on the floor to get your attention was my kamikaze move."

22

Cleaving

Our lives begin to end the day we become silent about things that matter.

—Dr. Martin Luther King, Jr.

MAY 15, 1971—For as long as she'd known Loretta, Maggie had never been to SistaHood. West of downtown, near Bagley and Trumbull, the salon was in Detroit's old Corktown section. Once a colorful, lively community, visages from the sixty-seven riot and white flight told a different story—skeletons of abandoned and burned-out houses, orphaned factories, empty tool and die shops, boarded up stores, and the too-visible slow pace of people with nowhere to go.

Corktown had survived the Civil War, both world wars, the stock market crash and the churning plight of immigrants. Beginning with the Great Irish Potato Famine in 1840, a large settlement of people from County Cork, Ireland found their way to Detroit.

After the Civil War, the Germans, then an influx of Mexicans and Maltese contributed to the growth and prosperity of this tiny boom town. By the 1930s, the great migration of black and white southerners to Detroit to earn five-dollars-per-day building cars was in full swing—infusing Corktown with the richness of a multi-cultural, big city experience with neighborhood charm.

Detroit Central Station, Eastern Market and Tiger Stadium still pumped traffic through this exotic fifty-acre neighborhood, but it wasn't enough to feed the struggling economy and attract new people. Detroit had been vilified for four years following the riot, and the slashed prices on homes and businesses facing foreclosure did little to offset the fear of crossing the invisible, but very real, color line.

SistaHood was the smallest storefront in the short block of retail buildings. The word SistaHood was depicted to look like some black, wrought-iron clothes stand. Painted across the window, the commercial artist hung bright-colored African caftans, hats, scarves and purses from the tall letters. The two o's in the word hood looked out as dark brown eyes with heavy liner, mascara and gold eyeshadow. Loretta and Blanche were outside the door waiting for Maggie to finish parallel parking her Corvair.

Inside, Loretta locked the door and turned on the lights. The walls covered in bold black and white striped vinyl wallpaper, the wood trim painted a high-gloss black. Maggie had never been inside a salon that catered exclusively to black women, and she explored the products as if she was in a foreign apothecary shop. Dixie Peach, hair dressing; Ultra Sheen, hair crème; Nadinola, double-strength skin bleaching cream; Ever-Perm, curl relaxer; Posner's, curl-out. On the wall, there were photos of Cicely Tyson making news with corn rows, Diahann Carroll in a smooth bouffant, and Angela Davis with her signature afro. *Jet, Ebony* and *Essence* magazines shared space with *Redbook*, *Look* and *Life* on a table near the door.

There was one hair-washing sink with a reclining chair, one salon chair facing a gold and black leopard print-framed mirror, and two gold vinyl swivel chairs sat under free-standing hair dryer hoods. The small hallway to the bathroom held a corkboard with photos of customers, postcards and business cards for all kinds of local services.

The *joie de vivre* was the eight-by-ten-foot bathroom. Walls painted with stripes in every shade of pink and orange; it was fitted with a pink sink and pink toilet. A large, round bamboo-framed mirror over the sink was Loretta's most treasured gift from Africa. Painted by one of the Maasai people, the mirror's four-inch-wide frame showed children—of every color, dress-style and faith—holding hands in the circle around the mirror, their mouths open in song. On the far, back wall, a six-foot-long, narrow, black leather bench with chrome legs held a bright orange pillow and pink angora afghan. Centered over the bench, a miniature two-by-four-inch pen and ink drawing of a cat, curled up in sleep, seemed to float under glass in a six-by-twelve-inch zebra-striped frame. Maggie pictured Loretta catnapping on the bench, waiting for her next client to trigger the ring on the front door. "Loretta, I'd give anything if we had a bathroom like this. You could start a martial arts class for women."

"Maybe! Carol's a black belt."

Maggie shook her head and said, "Do I know Carol?"

"Bruce's Carol, she teaches judo."

"For real?"

"Yep. She's been doing the kung fu thing for years. You wouldn't want to try and flip her on your Aunt Jo's living room floor," Loretta laughed

"Oh, god. I don't know what came over me . . ."

"Give it up, Maggie. I know. That's why we're here. You felt royally screwed, but there was no way else to do it."

Loretta pulled the swivel chairs away from the dryers and turned the salon chair around. "Maggie, you're the shortest, take the high chair.

"Before we begin, you need to know that Blanche and I got special dispensation . . . or whatever the pope calls it . . . to meet with you. No Sam, no Clyde, no Jacques. Just us girls. It's okay, baby. I want you to take a deep breath and let it go. We've got as much time as you need. Tekla's with Sam and the wrecking crew are home with Clyde. And, I've got enough coffee to get us through the night. Okay?"

Maggie nodded her head and took a deep breath.

"This is how it works. You ask whatever questions you have and we'll either answer your question, tell you we don't know or tell you we can't answer."

"If you and Stella can't answer, will you please tell me why?"

"Probably not. If we can't tell you, it's because it would put someone at risk. No one at Oz gets to highjack anyone's safety for peace of mind. Besides, peace of mind is fleeting; once we accept this, we find peace of mind. I know this sounds nuts. The point is, we don't have to know everything to make our way in the world. Sometimes . . . most times . . . it makes no difference. About killed me to get this through my thick skull." Loretta shook her head back and forth and folded in her lips as if she was trying to clear her mind of regrets. "I grew up thinking if people would just say what they mean and mean what they say we could get through all the bigotry and hate. Then I discovered, like peace of mind, what we believe becomes our made-up reality . . . mostly fiction . . . and, god forbid, might depend on when we last ate or slept or got laid."

"Loretta, not sure I follow you. Truth is truth."

"Not so. Most of what we take as truth has been twisted by legend, gossip and groupthink. Tales we've passed down for centuries. That's how we trip ourselves up."

As competent as Maggie was in emergencies, and dramatizations, she still lacked control when it came to eye rolling.

"I know this sounds like I'm talking out of both sides of my mouth," said Loretta, "so, let me try again. Truth is truth. The problem is how we get to truth. Before we can get there, we've got to let go of all the claptrap bullshit we've picked up along the way."

Maggie nodded. "Okay, I get it. Before we begin to recognize truth, we have to learn to 'go placidly amid the noise and haste' to work through our made-up world."

"Yes! I taped a copy of Desiderata inside the cupboard door where I keep clean capes—reminds me to stay placid when my next non-stop-talker walks in. You know, we hair stylists, along with bartenders, are the working classes' first line of defense for mental health," said Loretta.

"That does it. Once I'm done being pissed off at you for keeping me in the dark, I'll schedule a haircut. I need all the help I can get. Until then, tell me who you really are and how you both ended up with Oz?"

"I'll go," said Blanche. "Six months after Clyde and I got engaged, he realized our marriage wouldn't last if I didn't join Oz. I thought I loved him enough to do anything for him, but this wasn't one of them. Too many white guys. More Canadians than Americans. I wasn't sold. After I met Jacques and spent more time with Catherine, it was an easy decision."

"Why easy? What hooked you?"

"The kindness and lack of pressure to join. Plus, they put me in touch with a dozen or more immigrants they'd rescued from Cuba, Africa and the Middle East who shared my interest in early childhood education. It's been almost fifteen years and I've never looked back or second-guessed myself. The work is like weaving a cloth. Everyone does what they're best at doing in the ordinary course of their lives. Members often show up in my early education seminars.

It's not like I have to set aside hours of time—more a state of mind, a state of being and working toward peace."

"You heard my story about Clyde seeing me and not giving up on me. He led me to Oz," said Loretta. "For me, it was more about salvation. I didn't know how I was going to live in this godawful world. Religion was never my strong suit; I had too many doubts. I liked that Oz wasn't big on organized religion but fierce about freedom of religion and expression. My trust in Clyde, and what Blanche just said, are important to me. If we can build a more peaceful world where differences matter, where skin color is part of the bouquet, I'm all for it."

"Is Catherine my mother?"

"Say what?" said Loretta.

"You heard me. Is Catherine my mother?"

Blanche and Loretta looked at each other then back at Maggie. Blanche said, "We think she is. When we watched her talk to the group at Bruce's place, it was like the two of you were the only ones in the room. But, Maggie, we don't know. It's just as likely Loretta and I talked ourselves into believing this reality because we wanted it for you."

"What would you do if you were me?"

"Ask her," said Loretta.

Blanche nodded.

"What about Sam? Do you know why he's being targeted and why Oz would recruit him?"

"No one can be sure why Sam's being targeted," said Loretta. "There's so much shit going down right now with the CIA's gaslighting and LSD no-touch torture. Not to mention that lunatic J. Edgar's ongoing battles with peaceniks, civil rights workers, feminists, and the black power movement. All part of the Nixon and Agnew pogrom against free speech and the press." When she saw Maggie's reaction, Loretta said, "Yes, you heard me right, *pogrom*, like the Nazis.

"Sam's connection to you, Anna and Raymond are the obvious reasons for the targeting, but it might be anything. Sam would also be a perfect double agent for or against Oz. We've had some members turned by money and power. We've also planted a few double agents in their backyard."

"My Sam?"

"No one knows who we've planted, except Jacques, Catherine and maybe Bruce," said Loretta.

"Catherine? Oh, god, some feminist I am. I keep putting her in the stereotypical clerical chair," groaned Maggie.

Maggie was waiting for the jibe back; instead, Blanche and Loretta looked at each other in silence.

"Maggie," said Blanche, "Catherine is Oz."

By the time Maggie got home, it was almost ten. Pete had moved in with Maija and Sam had washed Pete's bedding, along with the laundry in the utility room. Maggie found him sitting on the back porch looking at the moon through the willow trees.

"Hey, babe," said Sam, patting his lap for her to sit down, "check out the moon."

"How's our Moonwalker after her day with the wrecking crew?"

"The big news is she pitched her first full-blown temper tantrum."

"No kidding? Over what?"

"Bessie. She wanted to bring Bessie home and I told her Bessie had her own family and home. Then, she totally wigged out. Screaming and yelling, she jumped up and levitated her body like she was at the top of a pole vault, then came crashing down on the grass kicking both legs. Freaked me out because I thought she was having a seizure. I knelt down on the grass and tried to calm her. Didn't work—she'd stop for a second to listen then go batshit again. Finally, Bessie moved me out of the way to lie down next to Tekla.

She whispered something in Tekla's ear and before long they were both giggling."

"Did you ask Bessie what she said?"

"I did."

"And?"

"Bessie said she told Tekla it was okay to cry like a baby, but she had to quit wearing those nasty diapers if she wanted to have her over for a pajama party. Then, Bessie said she told Tekla to look at the waning gibbous moon and say, 'Goodnight moon!' "

"Waning gibbous moon?"

"That's it. Moonwalker's first astronomy lesson. Do you want to talk about your deep dive into Oz?"

"No, I don't want to talk anymore tonight. I just want you to answer two questions."

"If I can, I will."

"Is Catherine my mother?"

"Mag, I honestly don't know. Whenever I see Catherine she either says or does something that reminds me of you, or I'm looking for her to say or do something that reminds me of you. I can't tell which. In fact, I'm the wrong person to ask. I know you want to find your mother, and I want you to have what you want."

Maggie looked at Sam and recalled, once again, why she loved this imperfect, mysterious man. "Okay, last question for tonight." Maggie placed her thumb under Sam's chin, tipped his head back and looked him in the eyes. "If asked, would you agree to be a double agent for Oz?"

"It depends."

"On what?"

"It depends on what's at stake. If you or Tekla were at risk, I'd do it in a flash. I have no idea what being a double agent even means, but for you and Tekla, I'd learn, I'd figure it out."

"What if it wasn't about Tekla and me? What if it was for some greater purpose, would you?"

"Mag, I'm no hero. I can't imagine signing up for something that takes me away from you and Tekla. Is that your worry?"

Maggie moved her thumb away from Sam's chin and curled up in his lap. Listening to the breeze, a memory tugged her heart. She was a little girl, and a man was carrying her in his arms after dark. The air crisp, the moon half hidden behind clouds, she remembered hearing him breathe, feeling the rough texture of his wool coat, and smelling the sweet scent of his cologne. They were in a city, maybe Toronto or Quebec. That kind of a big city with little neighborhoods. He called out someone's name. She got the sense they were arguing. "She's yours, you keep her!" a woman yelled. *Whose voice?* Maggie wondered. Then it clicked. The woman didn't yell "she's yours" in English, she yelled "*elle est à toi.*" She was speaking French. Maggie recalled the inflection; it could have been Anna or Jo. And the man? The cologne? Maggie wondered. Not Raymond. Issie said he was allergic to all scents. Jacques? Someone else?

On the way to bed, they stopped and looked in on Tekla. Stretched out in her crib—bathed in light from the vanishing moon—Tekla seemed content in this small corner of the universe. Maggie took a deep breath and exhaled.

In their own bed, with the windows wide open, and Sam next to her, Maggie felt a sense of freedom she hadn't felt in a long time—a moment of normalcy. Pete was in Farmington with Maija and Maggie would not miss his late-night visits to the loo. Sharing space was one thing, but the imposed intimacy of another man's grunts and groans on the toilet was a grim test of graciousness under fire.

"Mag, you know why Willie was fired?"

"Why?"

"Because some sponsor's nineteen-year-old nephew wants to drive a Zamboni. Willie's the only full-time driver, the only black driver. The G.M. offered him five K to go quietly. When Willie tried to negotiate a transfer, the asshole told Willie he had big balls for a colored boy. He had no idea how big. Willie told him he could stick the money up his ass. What made this worse was, on the way to the guy's office, Willie dared to dream he was being called in because of his Mr. Zamboni fame—maybe a promotion to a marketing position."

Unbidden tears fell before the heaviness in Maggie's chest kicked in. She felt the weight as she pulled herself up on her elbow and looked at Sam. "There's no way we let this happen, not without a fight. Who are we, who is Oz, if we ignore something as unjust and bigoted as this?"

23

Black and Blue

And the end of all our exploring will be to arrive where we started and know the place for the first time.

—T. S. Eliot

MAY 16, 1971—Sunday morning at Big Boys in Farmington was Bruce's weekly dive into unhealthy, greasy-spoon food. Claiming they served the best breakfast outside of New York City, Bruce broke his own rule against routines to splurge on home fries, bacon and eggs. Clyde and Sam met him at the door when he showed up and followed him to his Al Capone booth—facing the front door with easy access to the fire exit in the back.

"No law against firing someone unless the reason for firing is based on animus toward a protected class under the Civil Rights Act. In this case, the G.M. could claim he'd have fired anyone—black, white or purple—to make room for the sponsor's nephew. In private organizations, you can be fired for good cause, bad cause or no cause, as long as you aren't violating the Civil Rights Act. We had one client who owned a small packaging plant who went to an astrologist. The astrologist told him he should avoid Libras. The dude called an all-employee meeting and asked all the Libras in the plant to come to the front of the room. He excused the rest of the employees. No shit, the guy told the Libras to give their ID badges to the personnel guy sitting at a table next to him, then take a seat. Once they were seated, our client told them they were all fired—without notice, severance pay or accrued leave. Fired. The local attorney went batshit and signed up every single fired Libra and filed a class action suit. Guess what? There's no fucking law against firing Libras! Libras are not one of the protected classes."

"So, telling Willie he had big balls for a colored boy is legal? If that's not racist, what is?" asked Sam.

"Being a racist and an asshole isn't enough. It doesn't prove he fired Willie because Willie's black. Fact is, there's no law against being a racist. The law is narrower. It prohibits employers from treating employees differently because of race. That's the key. Willie would have to prove he was fired because he was black. The G.M. would say he was fired because he was the only person occupying the full-time Zamboni driver position and race was not a factor."

Clyde shook his head. "Jesus, Bruce, there must be something we can do to fix this. Public opinion, arm twisting, calling in a favor."

Sam and Clyde watched Bruce chase the yoke from his fried eggs around the plate with a muffin three or four times before he finally looked up and said, "I know the G.M. I don't know Willie, but I've watched him clean the ice after games. He's a proud man. Call Willie and tell him to sit tight and do nothing for the next two days. I mean nothing. He doesn't talk to the press, his fans, his friends about the firing for the next forty-eight hours. If I can't fix it by then, we'll move to Plan B. Call him now and let me know before I pick up the phone."

When Maggie heard a car in the driveway, she thought Sam was back from his breakfast with Bruce and Clyde. She headed out the side door to let him know Tekla just went down for her morning nap without diapers. Bessie's magic seemed to be working. Instead of Sam, Maggie found Cheryl getting out of her car. Not the mayor's big green Dodge van, a small white Triumph convertible with a black canvas top.

"Hey, Maggie!" called Cheryl.

"Hi, Cheryl. I thought Sam was pulling up and wanted to catch him before he woke up Tekla. Just put her down for a nap." Maggie resisted her impulse to brush crumbs off the front of her bleach-stained, once blue, *Make Love Not War* tee shirt, or wipe her sticky hands on her faded jeans. As usual, Cheryl was perfection in a pair of gray worsted bell bottoms and a pink and gray dotted-swiss blouse, with a pink leather belt—so small and narrow—it might have belonged to a ten-year-old girl.

"Sorry to pop in, but found myself on Six Mile, and decided to see if you had a few minutes to talk."

"Sure. Let's walk around the back and sit on the screened porch." As Maggie headed to the back of the house, she was struck by the un-mowed weeds—not grass. Maggie had dreamt about turning the backyard into a botanical garden, but hard to imagine she ever thought about the yard with the old beat up picnic table at the weed-line, the wild-looking lilacs on one side, and the industrial, working-class cyclone fence on the other.

"Wow! Love your enormous willows and the wild look of nature behind your yard. Our neighborhood looks like someone's wet dream about engineering an artificial botanical garden. Everything is so trimmed, clipped, mowed, shaped, fertilized and reshaped.

Trying to perfect nature. Ugh. I want to run through these weeds and enjoy the pleasure of the imperfect and untouched! Let's sit at the picnic table."

It was the first time in Maggie's life when she knew, with certainty, her face was *askew*, a word she'd avoided because it seemed so archaic, foreign, unnatural. "Seriously? You want to sit on that sliver-encrusted beast?"

"Yep!" said Cheryl as she race-walked to the table and slid her one-hundred-dollar slacks across a bed of lead-painted porcupine quills.

Still flinching, Maggie picked up the end of the other bench and gingerly moved it away from the table.

"Maggie, I wanted you to hear from me that the investigation into the stone-throwing incident hit a brick wall. Doug did his own sleuthing as well. He said there was nothing about the note or the stone that gave them any leads. He decided not to ask the investigators to drill the ladies from the Women's League, which might make things worse for you. I'm sorry we didn't find anything."

"Thanks, Cheryl. It was kind of you to stop by and tell me. Seems like years ago."

"How's Sam?"

"Good. Stitches on his face are gone and he's healing well."

"Is there anything I can do for you?"

"Not unless you know the General Manager of the Red Wings."

"I don't know him, but my uncle owns the Red Wings."

"You're kidding, right?"

"No. My uncle owns the franchise."

"Then, yes. I could definitely use your help."

"What the hell, Maggie? You knew both Clyde and I talked to Bruce. Bruce asked us to keep Willie quiet for forty-eight hours to give him time to call the G.M. I hope this doesn't screw things up."

"Sam, are you telling me I should have ignored her offer to help when she told me her uncle owned the Red Wings? Seriously?"

"No. I'd have done the same thing. Let me get Clyde on the line to see how he wants to handle this." Before Sam dialed, he caught Maggie's expression. "Sorry, babe. If Cheryl can make this happen, then nothing else matters and you just kick-started a miracle. Right now, I want to make sure Bruce gets the word before he strong-arms someone."

When Clyde didn't answer the phone, Sam called Bruce.

"Yeah," Bruce answered.

"Bruce, Sam here. We need to talk."

"Shoot."

After Sam gave Bruce Maggie's story, the line went quiet. "Bruce? You there?"

"So, Maggie has a family member of the Wing's owner on the case? Great high-stake's gamble on her part. I haven't made my call. Let's not say anything to Clyde or Willie until we see how this plays out. Once the owner's involved, all other bets are off. I'll need to save my card for another rainy day."

"Does this gamble mean Willie is SOL if it doesn't work?"

"No. It only means we can't work through the organization. We'll have to take our fight to the streets. Issues get dirtier in the public forum, but better there than deep-sixed."

The phone was ringing when Clyde, Blanche and the wrecking crew got home from Blanche's mother's Sunday dinner.

"Hello," said Blanche, ". . . hello, is someone there?" Blanche thought she heard someone try to speak at the other end, but she couldn't catch what they were saying.

"Willie," someone whispered.

"Robin, is this you? I'm sorry, it's hard to hear. Do you want me to call you back?"

"Willie," she heard again, "Oh, Blanche, Willie's gone."

"Gone? Did you say Willie is gone? Where do you think he went?"

"Gone, Blanche. He's gone. Please help."

"Okay, Robin, I'm on my way. Stay there. I'm coming over."

When Blanche hung up, Clyde was waiting. "What's going on?" he asked.

"I don't know. Robin said Willie's gone. I don't think she knows where."

"Blanche, call your mother and see if we can drop off the kids. I'll go with you to make sure everything's okay."

"Do you think she meant he killed himself?"

"He was so broken," Clyde whispered. His heart was beating like a kettledrum when he planted his hands on the kitchen table, leaned over and prayed, "Not now, goddamn you Willie . . . Please, god, not now."

By the time they pulled up to the duplex, it was ten p.m. A few blocks from Olympia Stadium—off Grand River Avenue on Linwood—every window in the downstairs unit was lit. The upstairs unit, completely dark. After the '67 riots, Willie and Robin used all their savings, and a small FHA mortgage, to invest in their future. The plan was to buy a duplex and provide short-term rentals to young black families who needed a leg up. They didn't expect to fall in love with their first tenants—Jasmin Clark, a single mother who worked as a lab technician at Henry Ford Hospital, and her sons, four-year-old Luther and two-year-old Cassidy. A month after they moved in, Willie fenced the backyard, built a sandbox and put together a swing set. After three years of an ex-husband, boyfriends, skinned knees, measles, emergency calls for childcare, and the upkeep of two households, there was no question they were family.

Robin was standing at the open front door. Blanche raced up to hug her and they disappeared into the house. Clyde took a deep breath before heading up the short walkway to the white-pillared porch. Among The Eights, everyone knew Robin had little, if any, interest in material things. So, when she insisted Willie commit to 'dignifying the house' with white pillars before she signed the mortgage papers, he was all in.

Tonight, Robin's dark eyes looked hooded. Clyde wondered if she was trying to limit her vision, screen reality, censor her thoughts. When he hugged her, she felt weightless, as if gravity had lost track of her.

"I've got coffee on. Let's sit in the kitchen in case the phone rings," said Robin in a voice Clyde strained to hear. He wanted to pull her in, help her feel her own weight. But, he was reminded of Vietnam and the soldiers and civilians who escaped the horror of war by 'un-grounding.' A term he used in his Oz workshops when he talked about the need to detach from pain and fear. Not delusional, as most psychoanalysts would claim; Clyde referred to un-grounding as a coping mechanism, one of humankind's more creative safety valves.

The kitchen was Robin's cake-baking studio—taking up floor space from the original kitchen and formal dining room. Door-less cupboards held cake pans of every size—round, square, rectangular—pans for cookies, cupcakes, sponge cakes, flat cakes, layered cakes. In the corner, an old wooden bushel basket held rolling pins—old bottles, with and without necks; wood, with and without handles. The counters, tabletop and stovetops were bare and immaculate. Two large industrial ovens, salvaged from an old hospital, and a three-tiered cafeteria-style stainless-steel cart, took up one wall.

"Talk to me. Tell me what you know," said Clyde.

"This morning Willie said he had a come-to-Jesus meeting with himself—ready to turn the page and get on with his life. He wanted to see if Jasmin and the boys were up for a day at the zoo and a backyard barbeque. He'd do ribs and hamburgers if I'd cook up some beans and grits. When I said yes he ran up the stairs two at a time and knocked on Jasmin's door. She was there with her new boyfriend; the boys were spending the weekend with their dad. I could see the disappointment in Willie's eyes, so I said, 'Let's you and I go to the zoo and eat out; time for us to have some fun!'" Robin looked down at her hands and took a deep breath.

"He said it wouldn't be the same without the boys, and he needed to clean out the back shed, trim the yard, and check Sunday's want ads. Then he got the biggest smile on his face and said, 'No telling what's waiting around the corner.'"

Sam watched Robin lift herself off the chair, pour coffee into her cup and sit back down. "What happened next?" asked Blanche.

Robin stretched her arms across the round, claw-foot table, rested her head on her left arm, and whispered, "After dinner, we smoked a little grass, not much. Willie went into the bedroom and came out dressed in his Mr. Zamboni red shirt, pants and shoes," Robin sat up and looked around the room as if reorienting herself. "I asked him what he was doing. He said he had a gig. I asked what gig. He said he didn't have time to explain. But, he pulled me up from my chair and gave me the longest, sweetest kiss—like the times when he was heading south on a Freedom Ride. I asked him where the hell he was going. He touched his fingers to my lips and said, 'you'll be fine.'"

Clyde touched Robin's elbow and said, "Where do you think he is?"

"My worst fear is he's headed to the Ambassador Bridge. My hope is he's breaking into the Olympia to steal the Zamboni. I don't know where to look and I don't want to leave the phone."

"Blanche can stay here with you while I look for Willie. Don't freak out if you hear the phone. I might call to see if you've heard from him or have any news. Okay?"

Robin shook her head yes and whispered, "Thank you."

The streets were quiet under the incandescent lamplight that outshone another night of the waning gibbous moon. Clyde smiled thinking about Bessie and all the bold, beautiful young black girls who were ready to take the world by storm.

A few blocks away, The Olympia stood like a well-decorated war hero surrounded by troops in fatigues. The dirt, debris and neglect of Detroit were insidious, invasive—as if it was seeking the borderland between the inner and outer cities.

In the shadows, Clyde saw a glint of red. Someone was sitting on a bench at the DSR bus stop. Clyde circled the block and parked on a side street behind the bench sitter.

"Hey, Willie, okay if I sit with you?" said Clyde.

"Knock yourself out."

Clyde sat and looked at Willie who was looking at Olympia's façade—five stories of red brick with brown terracotta and stone trim. A Romanesque Revival style, Olympia boasted twelve three-story arched windows across its broad front—stretching skyward above the plebeian street-level theatre billboard and retail shops. Willie's face caught in the chance light—bright, dry, blue eyes—black and blue skin. Clyde could almost hear Louis Armstrong keening *What Did I Do to Be So Black and Blue?*

"Feel like talking?

Willie looked at his friend, blessed by warm, chocolate-colored skin. Less scary, and intimidating, and said, "Yeah, I do. I've been thinking about the ice, the Zamboni and my reign as Mr. Zamboni. Who knew?" Willie looked down at his red pants, socks, shoes. "Who knew a black guy dressed like a fire hydrant would catch on? I rode it like a silver bullet. It was mine—my energy, my invention, my personality. For the first time in my life, I wasn't invisible. White guys wanted to shake my hand. Little towheads with blue eyes jumped up and down, excited to see me, touch me. Teenagers wanted my autograph. People didn't cross the street to avoid me.

"Now, I'm gone. No one sees me, the real me. I've shrunk back to that little nigger boy offering to sell his self, his soul, for a kind smile and a nickel tip."

The quiet streets became rivers as Willie and Clyde were pulled into childhood memories. Who taught them not to look white people in the eyes, to keep their hands in view, to move out of the way? When did they first learn not to laugh or sing with abandon or draw attention to themselves? How many times were they shushed?

"When did you learn to be invisible?" asked Clyde.

"I was six. My ma took me to the Detroit Zoo and I thought there was nothing more perfect in the world. I was over the moon. When I saw the giraffe, I ran to the fence and accidentally bumped a little girl eating a *Drumstick* cone. She dropped it on her pink dress and started crying. Her father lifted me up by my skinny arm and tossed me away, yelling, 'You little nigger turd, you belong in a cage. Get the hell out of here and stay out!' Ma helped me up. She was crying. As we walked out of the zoo, everyone stood still and watched. Like a picture postcard, no one said a word. Ma was only eighteen. It was her first time at the zoo."

They sat with their thoughts for several minutes before Clyde said, "I was in the fifth grade. Every day after school a bunch of fifth and sixth grade white boys played baseball. I knew I was good, so one day I asked if I could play. Without saying a word, they huddled together talking and laughing. Then, the alpha dog walked up to me and said, 'Ain't no way we're playing baseball with a nigger, nigger. You want to chase foul balls . . . unzip your pants!' The rest of the boys cracked up. I wanted to cry, but I didn't. I almost cared, but I wouldn't, couldn't. For years I thought the iron curtain I built when I was ten years old protected me. The invisible black me couldn't be touched. Now I know the price. When we disappear, we all pay for it. Big time. We brothers can't quit. If not for us, then for the next generation of black boys who want to go to the zoo with their mother and see a giraffe."

Willie's chin dropped to his chest and Clyde could hear his deep breaths, see his shoulders move with each flattened sob. Clyde put his arm around him and tugged on his shoulder. "Let's go learn to be visible so we can teach others. We'll find some seed money, tear down some walls . . .

END

LIVONIA | DETROIT EIGHT SERIES | BOOK TWO

Acknowledgments

Heartfelt thanks to my *Unpaid but Illustrious Editorial Staff*, Sandra Whitener, Kirsten McLean, Frank Cooley and Dianne Wesselhoft, who've hung in there through multiple drafts for the past three years and two novels. Grateful appreciation to friends, colleagues and muses who shared invaluable details about these moments in history—days of hope, determination and conflict. And, a special shout-out to Judith Helburn, who'd meet me for chips and salsa at Las Palomas, when I needed someone to stir the embers and help me see my work in new ways.

Once again, I had the remarkable good fortune to work with Danielle Hartman Acee, copy/content editing, social media consulting and publicity; and Kenneth Benson for interior/cover design and printing/technology support. Both have helped me navigate the technical, emotional, intellectual and artistic pathways to launch three books. Wicked in their expertise, they have been willing teachers and supportive friends. In spite of my routine bullheadedness and occasional meltdowns, I'm forever grateful they stand up to me when I'm wrong-headed.

Like all stories, this one could not have been written without the love and coaching of friends and mentors who taught me about grace, acceptance, equality, oneness and otherness. Black, white, multi-racial friends and relatives, who had the audacity to speak their truth. Without doubt, each of them breathed life into my characters and helped me find my voice.

Then there's this man behind the scenes. The guy I live with. Loren. On-call editor, hugger, dog walker, cat groomer, hunter-gatherer, poet, psychotherapist, humorist, looks past the third-day-pajamas-and-crumbs-to-tell-me-I'm-beautiful kind of guy. He also produced and published a wonderful collection of poems this year, *Topknot Analysis*. Can't imagine life without him. My husband and best friend.

The Author

A native Michigander, Kathleen Hall co-authored the award-winning non-fiction *The Otherness Factor*, before taking the deep dive into historical fiction with Book One of her Detroit Eight Series, *If the Moon Had Willow Trees*. A writer, poet, lawyer, mediator and workplace investigator, Kathleen's lifelong activism has been devoted to championing equal rights and promoting the power of diversity. She lives in Austin, Texas with her husband Loren, Emma Dog and Ms. Ming Cat.

Dear Reader,

Writing is my guilty pleasure. No doubt. Listening to, and working with my characters, is like having a community of invisible friends to hang out with. Don't get me wrong, they taunt and challenge me, piss me off, but I trust them to push me in the right direction. When we get close to launch, I suffer separation anxiety and they're ready to cut and run. You'd think writing a series would give us more wiggle room, but not so. The fact is, it begins to feel like real life. Is there any such thing as closure? How do we know when we solve a mystery? Pick up the last thread? Turn the page?

If you'd like to support my guilty pleasure addiction, please leave a review on Amazon, Goodreads or any other social book-sharing site of your choice.

To join my readers circle and hear about giveaways, promotions, news or free ecopies of books in the Detroit Eight Series—or receive invitations to serve as beta readers prior to publication—email me at co.optionstx@gmail.com.

Peace and Love,

Goodreads Author Page | Kathleen Hall
Facebook Author Page | Kathleen Hall
Twitter | @othernessfactor

CPSIA information can be obtained
at www.ICGtesting.com
Printed in the USA
LVHW09s0356300818
588628LV00001B/278/P

9 780990 390459